The Smallbeef Chronicles
Book One

A Suffolk's Whispering Heart

Stephen Edwards

A Suffolk's Whispering Heart
Copyright: Stephen Edwards 2011

All rights reserved

No part of this publication may be reproduced, stored in a retrieval system, copied in any form or by any means, electrical, mechanical, photocopying, recording or otherwise transmitted without written permission from the author.
You must not circulate this book in any format.

This story is a work of fiction. All characters are fictitious, and any resemblance by name or nature to real persons, living or dead is purely coincidental.

Edwards and Edwards

Cover illustration by Clean Copy

For some reason, Jennie Harborth does not want to be mentioned for her invaluable technical assistance, formatting and how to write more gooder English, but it was her, Jennie Harborth

1

Are you reading this on a bus, on a train, on your sofa? Or perhaps you're in bed. Your surroundings will be familiar wherever you are. You think of them as permanent. They are always there; that tree, that pavement, that bus stop. But have you ever thought about the ether? Very important stuff, ether. It's what separates one world from the next. You can't actually see it but it's definitely there. Just suppose you could peer through it and glimpse the next world along, a world sharing the very same space as yours but never to be ventured into or shared. A world almost identical to yours but with detail differences. The hills and rivers might be in the same place but what if they are inhabited in a different way? What if someone is lying right where you are at this very moment? You might be on your sofa, but they might be on a bed of hay bales in precisely the same spot. You might be staring up at your patterned ceiling whereas they are studying the dust-laden cobwebs hanging from bare rafters, all very homely, but not your home. And what if they're not actually human?

Anyone who knows anything about parallel worlds will tell you that an object from one world should never enter another…it simply would not do. That is why the ether is there, to keep things separate. That is the wonder of our universe, our planet, our world, and no matter what the scientists or anyone else might tell you, anything is possible. The following story proves it.

You might not be able to put a face to Mother Nature, but you know she is all around you. You can't see her personally, but you know she is in the wind, the rain, and the sunshine. When left to her own devices she provides amply for all. She always does her best...but she is not always left to her own devices is she?

A while ago, during a Hampshire summer in southern England, in your world, the weather had taken a turn for the worse. Thick dark clouds gathered from all around. Clouds so heavy they could barely keep off the ground, and they didn't really care if they did or not. Mother Nature wasn't feeling very well. The earlier Sun had given her a migraine which is why she'd summoned the clouds to turn down the bright sunlight, but now she doubted her judgement in having so many in one place at the same time; clouds can be very bullish when they get together.

The rain pummelled the soft earth in the bottom of the square hole which was being dug by a group of archaeologists. They'd been investigating the supposed site of an ancient building in the village of Smallbeef, East Hampshire.

'It's no use,' called Professor 'Digger' Hole, a rotund gentleman in his fifties with a ruddy complexion and a bald head, and of course a grey beard, they all seem to have those. 'The rain is too heavy,' he continued, 'let's call it a day and try again tomorrow.'

With that, he and his two assistants packed their hand tools away and set off for the local inn where they were staying.

While England slept the sky ran riot all night long, firing bolts of lightning into the ground amid raucous rounds of thunder like the volley from a thousand warships. The ether's constitution was being sorely tested.

Mother Nature felt a lot better in the morning, her migraine had gone and so had the mischievous clouds, but this wasn't quite the same world she'd put to bed yesterday. There was an itch just below the surface, but more of that later, now it's time to move on...

***

The sky breathed easy in the early morning freshness of a new day; so clear and so beautiful with just a wisp of cotton wool cloud drifting slowly by. The blackbird, thrush and robin serenaded any who would listen while the dawn sunshine warmed their hardy little bodies. The birds stared out across the Hampshire countryside, but this was not the Hampshire in your world, this was another world, very similar to yours but not yours.

Between fields of yellow and green a country road wound its way south towards the coast. On the road was a bright yellow stagecoach being hauled by a team of four well-built horses and driven by a heron named Jack. He was as tall as a goose, at seven feet, yes that's right, seven feet tall, coloured black, white, and grey, with a long pointed beak upon which were perched a pair of half-spectacles. His passengers in the coach were all mallards, not quite as tall as him at about five feet eight inches, but a good deal plumper. Mothers, various shades of brown, and fathers with splendid greeny-blue heads contrasting with their yellow bills and white collars, and then there were the children, mostly wearing pale fawn fluff soon to be exchanged for the colours of their parents, all as it should be — in their world. They were on their way to the seaside for a day out, chatting among themselves with not a care in the world.

Ahead of the stagecoach a narrow bridge carried the road over a river. Jack Heron slowed the dark brown horses to a walk in readiness. Beyond the bridge the hedgerows gave way to fulsome bushes and trees. From within those bushes two pairs of beautiful eyes watched patiently.

Jack peered over the top of his spectacles, taking great care to keep his bright yellow coach away from the unforgiving stone sides of the bridge. The eyes in the undergrowth followed his progress. Unfortunately, they weren't the only eyes in the forest that day; others were also watching the coach draw closer; eyes as black as tooled coal – round and dull with bad thoughts behind them.

Safely over the bridge, Jack congratulated himself on his driving. 'My, my, what a clever old heron I am.' He was about to give the horses a giddy-up when the beautiful eyes suddenly made their move and jumped out from the bushes.

'Oh, my word!' Jack shrieked and hauled back on the team with utmost force.

The ducks inside the coach lurched from their seats. 'Good heavens! What on Earth is going on?' They hurriedly tidied their ruffled feathers before craning their necks through the side windows to see a large chestnut coloured horse standing squarely in the road with its soft pink lips almost touching those of the lead mare, who seemed rather taken by the muscular stallion with the soft eye.

'Oops,' the rider on the chestnut horse leaned forward and whispered, 'I think we need to adjust our timing a bit, mate.' The voice was that of a juvenile mallard wearing a blue tricorn hat and a mask over his face with holes through which to see. He and the big chestnut horse remained quite still while casting an eye over the ducks and the heron who in turn were casting an eye over them.

Sydney Sinkalot, sitting inside the coach with his wife Sarah and two ducklings, broke the silence. 'This is a very odd thing – a duck on a horse, whatever next?' he said.

The duck on the horse bore the same colours as the father ducks on the coach. He was hoping the strange hat and mask would disguise his appearance, but he was very much mistaken, he was most definitely a mallard. Unimpressed by all this, Jack Heron leaned forward from his seat up top. 'What do you think you're doing?' he shouted, eyeing the stranger up and down. He was very annoyed at the duck on the horse.

Before any of the passengers could have their say, the duck on the horse replied in a youthful but rather stunted monologue. 'Don't nobody move, 'cos vis is a gaw blimey 'old up.'

Taken aback by the strange terminology, the heron retorted, 'I beg your pardon, why don't you talk properly…and you can start by telling me your name. And you can rest assured I shall jolly well report you for this, you see if I don't.'

'My name is Dick Wa—,' the duck on the horse stopped himself in the nick of time before giving away his full identity. 'Erm…I'm Dick the 'ighway Duck. That's all you need to know.'

'What sort of name is that?' said the heron. 'And what about your horse, has he got a name?'

Dick could see no reason to withhold his horse's name, horses were blameless so what harm could it do? 'His name is Punch,' he said.

The horse rolled his eyes and shook his lovely big head in dismay. *Oh thank you very much*, he thought.

'Would that be because he is a Suffolk Punch horse?' asked Jack Heron.

'Yes, that's right,' Dick replied. 'Now as I was saying, vis is a nold up.'

'A nold up? What on Earth is a nold up?' the heron asked in very precise English as was his way. 'Will you please move to one side so that I may go on my way to the seaside with my passengers?'

'But I can't do vat, guv'nor, not 'til you greases me palm wiv some dosh.'

By now the passengers inside the stagecoach were getting quite flustered. Sidney Sinkalot, thinking he might effect a solution to the problem, stretched his neck out of the window as far as he could. 'What seems to be the trouble here?' he asked of Jack.

'Well, as you can see, Mr Sinkalot, there is a duck on a large horse standing in our way. He won't move over to let me pass, and I cannot understand a word he's saying.'

'Let me have a word with him. I'll soon sort this out,' said Sidney, fluffing up his chest like male ducks do. 'What's the matter, my friend, why won't you let us pass?'

Dick raised his shoulders and sighed. 'It's like I told the 'eron. Vis is a nold up.'

'A nold up?' said Sydney. 'What's a nold up?'

Dick replied, 'No, not a nold up – an 'old up.'

Sydney muttered the words quietly to himself with a puzzled look in his eye.

Dick then exclaimed, 'Gaw blimey, guv. Don't you folks know nuffin? An 'old up is like a stick up but spelt diffrunt.'

'Stick up, hold up?' Sydney paused... 'Good heavens, I think this chap is trying to rob us.'

The duck on the horse continued, 'Of course I am, vat's what 'ighway robbers do, ain't it? So if you'd be so bacon rind as to 'andover some dosh, ven I can be on me way before the currant bun gets too high in the pork pie.'

'He's absolutely barmy,' said Jack Heron.

'Wait a minute,' said Sydney, 'I've heard of a town fifty miles to the east of here – called Lundun; I believe that's how they talk there, they call it rhyming slang.'

'Of course,' exclaimed Jack, 'He must be a Lundunner, a Cockerny, or something of the sort.'

'Look, I can't 'ang about 'ere all day,' said Dick the highway duck, 'I gotta see a drake about a dog, so let's be 'aving yer dosh, by way of a toll, like.'

Jack replied sternly, 'Just you listen to me, Dick whatever your name is. We have no intention of paying a toll, so please be so kind as to move aside.'

'But if I do vat, vis won't be a proper blag will it, and ven I won't be a proper 'ighway robber, will I?'

'But robbing is very naughty, so stop being so silly,' said Jack, not taking the duck too seriously anymore. 'And anyway, I don't think you're a real Cockerny at all.'

'Oh really?'

'Yes really. You were getting your words all wrong, bacon rind and pork pie indeed.'

'But I is a Cockerny I tells yer, so get a move on, only I'm in a bit of a Ruby Murray, if yuh know what I mean.'

'I don't think anyone knows what you mean. I don't think even you know what you mean, so take that mask off this instant.'

'You must fink I'm daft. If I takes me mask off you'll give me description to the peelers, an' before I knows it I'll be behind jam jars.'

'But that's ridiculous,' Jack Heron replied. 'Mallards all look the same so what good would a description be?'

The mallards in the coach put their heads further out of the windows and gave Jack a look of disbelief. *All the same indeed! That's rich coming from a heron.*

'Well I still say you're not a proper Cockerny,' Jack Heron repeated.

'I am,' said Dick.

'Are not.'

'Am.'

'Are not.'

The passengers quickly grew impatient with such nonsense and shouted as one. 'If you're a highway duck, show us your pistol.'

The duck on the horse stared through the holes in his mask and slowly raised his wing.

'Here it is,' he said, pointing at them with what seemed to be a pistol with a handkerchief thoughtfully draped over it, so as not to frighten the youngsters.

Just then the trees rustled to announce the arrival of a gentle breeze. The breeze carried with it the sound of a distant hooter. *Honk honk.* All heads turned one way and then the other way, listening keenly.

'There,' shouted Sydney Sinkalot, pointing his bill into the sky.

Everyone followed his aim, and there, high in the blue sky were seven dazzling mallards flying in perfect V formation. The lead mallard wore an officer's cap while the six following him each wore a tall policeman's helmet. The lead mallard also had a pair of binoculars hanging from a gold strap around his neck, and a hooter clenched in his bill which he squeezed momentarily. 'Honk honk, honk,' it went, to ensure their progress was not impeded as they sped through the sky to the scene of the crime.

Sarah Sinkalot, quite taken by such a wonderful sight couldn't contain her relief. 'Oh, how wonderful. It's the Flying Squad!' she cried.

'Hoorah!' shouted the passengers. 'Hoorah, we're saved!'

While the duck on the horse stared skyward along with the others, the breeze lifted the hanky from his grasp and let it flutter to the ground.

'Look, it's a banana,' shouted Jack Heron, 'it's not a pistol at all.'

Frustrated by his own incompetence, Dick tore the mask from his face so that he could see properly, and stuffed it hastily inside his hat. Not for the first time had he failed in his attempt to become a successful highway duck, or a successful anything come to that. Punch the horse winked at the lead mare before turning and disappearing as carefully as he could between the bushes. For their part the bushes closed ranks behind him to leave little or no sign of his escape route.

2

The trees along each side of the road leaned back urgently to make way for the police ducks to land, their wingspan being easily in excess of fifteen feet. The constables quickly lined up with their chests puffed out and their heads upright with their bills all in line, not an inch out of place. The lady ducks were quite overwhelmed at such a sight. 'Oh, what magnificent mallards,' they said as they swooned and slid down into their seats, fanning their faces with their wingtips.

'Oh my, oh my,' they all agreed, 'they're so splendid.'

The police duck in the cap adjusted his hooter and binoculars to be sure they hung quite straight on his fine chest. He then walked slowly along the side of the stagecoach while looking in through the windows. The eyes of the lady ducks followed him as he passed; hardly any of them could keep from sighing and fluttering their eyelashes.

After walking around the coach, the officer stopped next to the driver and looked up.

'Do you mind if I address your passengers, driver?'

'Not at all, officer,' said Jack, dipping his head and peering over the top of his spectacles.

The officer turned and opened the coach door fully. The lady ducks swooned again, after all, it wasn't every day the Flying Squad came to their rescue from out of the sky.

'Good morning, ducks and drakes, I am Inspector Hooter of the Flying Squad. I have reason to believe you have just had a narrow escape from some sort of highway duck, if there is such a thing?'

'So you're not sure if he was a real robber or not,' said Sidney Sinkalot.

'Well, sir, that is what we have to ascertain,' replied the inspector. 'I have never heard of such a thing before, but perhaps a good description would get us started in our pursuit.'

Sarah Sinkalot spoke up eagerly, 'Well, Inspector, he was wearing a mask for most of the time, but he was definitely a mallard, a juvenile probably. Just before you arrived he removed his mask—'

'Aha,' interrupted the inspector, 'did you get a clear view of the suspect?'

'Oh, yes,' Sarah went on, 'I think he was perhaps an inch shorter than you, with the same lovely colours, but not quite as distinguished of course.'

'Of course,' agreed the inspector, 'please go on, madam.'

'Yes, Inspector – he had two eyes, one on each side of his head, and a beak on the front.'

The inspector interrupted again. 'Surely you mean he had a bill, madam. Parrots might have beaks, but I like to think that we ducks have bills, madam, bills.' He proudly stroked his bright yellow bill with his wing.

'Quite so, Inspector, of course, – erm, that's about all I can remember, I'm afraid.'

The inspector paused for a moment while looking at the ground for inspiration, but none came. 'Well, to be honest, that's not quite the description I was hoping for,' he said. 'After all, I can't think of a duck in the world that hasn't got an eye on each side of his head, and a bill stuck on the front of his face. You are quite sure the bill was on the front, madam?'

'Oh yes, definitely on the front.'

The inspector turned to his constables who were still standing in a perfectly straight line. 'Right, there's nothing for it but to scour the area and question every male duck the same colour as us, but only those with an eye on each side and a bill on the front of their face.'

Suddenly, the heron jumped up in his seat and shouted, 'Wait a minute, Inspector, there is one other thing, a rather large thing in fact.'

'Oh yes, sir, and what might that be?'

'The rascal was riding a chesnut coloured horse with a subtle white flash in the middle of his face, and he said his name was Dick, and his horse was called Punch on account of him being a Suffolk Punch, and a very stout one at that.'

'Splendid,' said the inspector, 'now that's what I call a clue. After all, how many ducks do you see riding a horse? Prepare yourselves, Constables – onward and upward. We shall soon have them.'

The seven mallards were soon airborne in perfect formation, heads tilted slightly forward and wings in perfect time with each other. The inspector led the way with his hooter at the ready. 'Honk honk, honk honk,' it sounded, as they disappeared over the treetops.

Unfortunately, things were only just getting started, other eyes were still watching the stagecoach from the cover of the bushes. Eyes as black as coal.

***

The unshod hooves of the chesnut horse trod gently upon the forest floor, the leaf covered peat concealed the sound of each carefully placed foot. Despite being a big heavy horse, he could be very gentle when necessary.

'Nice and steady, boy – mind the tree roots,' whispered Dick.

'We'll soon be clear of the trees, then we can get a move on.'

Fine strands of sunlight filtered through the leafy canopy illuminating the otherwise shady habitat. Copper highlights glistened across the horse's coat whenever a ray of sunlight touched him. As with all Suffolk Punch horses he was chesnut in colour, light chesnut in his case, (chesnut is spelt without the middle 't' in the horse world). A full mane and tail, and a small white flash down the centre of his face completed the work of art. Standing at sixteen hands two, he presented a truly handsome animal of immense musculature. He soon picked up the pace to a steady canter, swaying one way and then the other, weaving his robust body between the trees which obligingly thinned out a little as he progressed.

The oaks and the pines eventually waved farewell when the duo left them for a familiar stretch of open grass. With little input from Dick, Punch extended his gait going as fast as he dared, but still mindful of the chance encounter with a rabbit hole which could so easily bring their escape to a painful end.

The seven mallards of the Flying Squad were quickly closing on their suspects, but the Sun was faster, every passing minute bringing it nearer to the horizon when Mother Nature would finally wash the land in darkness.

They were about a mile from home when Punch slowed from a canter to a trot, and finally to a standstill. Warm air rose from his body while his breath vented loudly from his nostrils.

'Listen,' said Dick. They both stayed quite still while filtering the sounds of the countryside around them. After a few moments the horse's ears pricked up. Dick could hear it too, a faint honk honk, some distance away but certainly getting closer.

'Uh oh, it's the police, they're onto us. Quickly, into the undergrowth until they've gone by.'

Like best mates, the trees and the bushes welcomed the pair

into their gang, spreading their foliage like umbrellas to bar any prying eyes from above.

Sure enough, the Flying Squad was soon overhead. 'Keep your eyes peeled,' called Inspector Hooter. Their wings were clearly audible to the fugitives below; whish, whoosh, whish, whoosh, rhythmically sweeping through the air while their eyes stared down into the oak canopy, beneath which their quarry was hiding.

The horse and the duck remained absolutely still, hoping that the police would soon pass them by. Their efforts to remain unnoticed were rewarded when Inspector Hooter called out to his squad, 'This is useless, the light has gone westward. Follow me, we'll find somewhere comfy to land for the night and resume our search first thing in the morning.'

With heads and helmets tilted slightly forward, and wings beating at the regulation rate, the squad moved into cruise formation and gradually disappeared into the distance.

Dick leaned forward in the saddle. 'I think they've gone, mate.' The horse huffed in reply and poked his head out from the bushes. Happy that the coast was clear, they continued at a steady trot through the forest, taking care not to trip over any fallen branches, or stumble into a ditch in the failing light. Thankfully the going got easier as they progressed, and it wasn't long before the couple turned off the track into a little caravan park – home at last. The caravans, fourteen in all, nestled snugly in what was once a small sand quarry, three of the sides being quite high which provided a natural shelter from the elements.

The sky had turned pink, and the blackbird's evensong filled the air by the time Dick finally slid down from the saddle. He quietly opened the door to the sizeable shed by the side of his home, and Punch made his way in to what was a cosy affair with plenty of bedding.

Fifteen minutes later, after untacking Punch and filling the hay net and water bucket, Dick took his leave. 'We've had a long day, mate. Sleep tight.'

Punch neighed quietly and began chewing on the tasty hay as the duck closed the door behind him. The light from the other caravans fell softly on the ground, allowing Dick to see his way up the path to his own front door. He looked down at his feet and couldn't help wondering. *Why are they webbed like that?*

***

On the banks of a stream about one mile away from Dick's home, the mallards of the Flying Squad were making themselves as comfortable as they could. With their helmets removed and placed next to them, the constables rested their heads between their wings, all at precisely the same angle of course. Inspector Hooter had also settled down for the night. Next to him was his cap, and next to that was his hooter, and next to that were his binoculars, all perfectly straight.

While they rested among their own thoughts, one or two of them looked down at their feet and wondered just as Dick had. *Why are they webbed like that?*

They each took their thoughts with them as they drifted into a comfortable sleep amid the sounds of the night in the lea of the South Downs. An owl hooted, hoping for a reply in the distance. A family of little humans scampered for cover beneath a hedgerow, trying to avoid the fox's appetite. All as it should be.

3

Next morning Dick opened the curtains and looked out across the yard. 'Mmm, another lovely day.' His heart smiled within his softly feathered chest. As with all animals bar one, the chance to live another day was all he needed; nothing was certain and nothing taken for granted.

The Sun peered over the horizon, warming the chilled air with loving hands of gold. Another glorious summer's day was in prospect.

After a good stretch, Dick sat down to breakfast. *That's odd*, he thought, *no dawn chorus?* He returned to the window and peered out into the eerie silence. The air should have been full of birdsong, not to mention the crude whistling of tiny humans in the undergrowth, but there was none of it. *What can have frightened them away? It can't be the police – they wouldn't have found us already, and anyway, why would the birds hide from them?* Nothing moved nor made a sound; not a rabbit or chicken to be seen. Nothing.

Dick's neighbour, Marvin Plimsoll-Line, stepped cautiously from the safety of his caravan; known for his boldness he would soon get to the bottom of things. He tipped his head this way, and that way. He looked up, down and across. *Nothing*, he thought, *nothing*. His wife, Penny, nervously watched from the open doorway with her baby duckling peeping out from behind her. Marvin waddled to the centre of the yard while looking curiously about.

'Please come in now, Marvin,' Penny called, 'I have a bad

feeling about this.'

Marvin didn't have time to reply before a shadow swept across the ground at amazing speed. Something slapped hard against his head, sending him reeling into the dust.

Faster than anyone could see, the shadow disappeared as quickly as it had come.

Penny rushed out to her stricken husband, screaming as she ran. 'Marvin, oh, my dear Marvin, what's happened? Please be all right, please.' She settled next to him and gently slipped her wing beneath his head, whispering, 'Please say something. Are you all right?' Tears ran down her cheeks as she cuddled her husband to her bosom.

Very soon, all the neighbours had gathered round to see what had happened to their fallen neighbour.

'The poor chap,' said Betty Bottoms-up, 'what on Earth was it? Did anyone see?'

Many eyes looked nervously up to the sky, but there was no sign of whatever had struck such a vicious blow.

Marion Waters-Edge jostled her way through the crowd. 'Here you are, my dear,' she said, setting a bucket of water down by Penny's side and handing her a sponge.

'Thank you,' said Penny, taking the sponge to gently wipe her husband's brow.

Marvin slowly regained consciousness, mumbling faintly, 'Oh, where am I?'

'Oh, my dear, you're going to be all right,' said Penny.

John Paddle-Well helped Penny get her husband to his feet.

'Oh, my head,' Marvin groaned, 'what happened?'

'No one knows,' said John. 'It was all over in a flash. One second you were looking about as right as rain, and the next you went crashing into the ground – out cold you were.'

They carefully turned Marvin round, and gave him a few

seconds to get his balance.

'Daddy, daddy.' His son called anxiously from his caravan's door.

'Wait there, darling,' Penny called, but her words went unheeded. The duckling stepped out and began dolly waddling towards his mum and dad. He was barely halfway across the yard when the mysterious shadow returned. Wings thrashed above the crowd; dust rose from the ground and the air thickened into a dense haze, swirling blindingly about their heads.

The air slowly cleared, bringing with it a short-lived silence. The mallards gasped at what stood before them. It was quite simply the ugliest looking creature they had ever seen. It stood over eight feet tall with leathery wings stretched between its arms and legs. At full stretch its wingspan exceeded twenty-five feet. Strangely, halfway along the leading edge of each wing was a hand from which three clawed fingers protruded. The creature lowered its wings, folding them in half with its hands resting on the ground. The remainder of its wings jutted from its hands, rising up behind its head. The ducks winced at what appeared to be a dreadful deformity, but of course, just because something is a bit different to the norm does not mean it isn't right. To the ducks however, it had the appearance of an ungainly mishmash of evolution, no part of it harmonizing with any other. *Ghastly*, they thought, *absolutely ghastly*.

The creature towered over the ducks. Only the majestic swan could come close to this monster in height, but the swan was full of grace and form – this abomination had no such qualities. It stood on bowed legs with muscular thighs. A barrel chest and long neck supported a head measuring a full four feet from the back of the skull to the tip of its beak, the rows of teeth within suggested it was not a vegetarian. All in all it presented a most unpleasant vision with no colour to commend it. Sparse grey hair covered most of its body apart from its legs which had the appearance of those of a gigantic chicken, scaly, but equally grey. Most sinister of all were its eyes, dull black in their entirety and dead looking, with no light reflecting in them. As such it was impossible to tell where they were looking or who they were looking at, but they were most certainly looking at someone.

The stunned onlookers mumbled among themselves.

'It's hideous, it's one of those pterosaurs I've read about in a book,' said one.

'Don't be silly, they don't really exist,' said another.

The creature heard this and turned in the direction of the remark. 'Hideous am I? Let me show you what hideous is really like.' He spied the young duckling standing alone and unprotected. The youngster desperately waved his stumpy wings to scare the monster away. In a second, the pterosaur had turned with an open beak and grabbed the youngster in his mouth. He threw the helpless duckling high into the air. The fluffy bird flapped his stumps instinctively to slow his fall, to little avail; he landed with a hefty thump on his belly, 'Oof,' raising a solitary cloud of dust as he did so.

Keeping his gaze firmly on the young bird, the pterosaur slowly opened his mouth in readiness for a second attack. Marvin rushed at the ugly monster, slamming hard against his bony chest. The pterosaur didn't flinch. Marvin bounced off and fell to the ground. By now the duckling had got to his feet and stood wobbling and dazed. The pterosaur stretched his neck towards him once again. His hard beak touched the soft rounded bill of the youngster, and slowly opened to reveal the rows of saw-like teeth. The adult ducks stood with mouths agog, unable to utter a sound and helpless against such an awesome creature.

A terrifying silence fixed itself in the yard for what seemed like an age.

Silence – silence, until a faint sound could be heard in the distance –'honk, honk, honk.' The sound grew louder, 'honk, honk, honk,' and was soon immediately above them, 'honk, honk, honk.'

All eyes looked up into the sky, except those of the pterosaur, his stare remained nailed to the duckling.

Seven mallards in brilliant kaleidoscope blues and greens appeared in the sky, in perfect formation and with hats and helmets tilted forward at exactly the correct angle.

'Hoorah, it's the Flying Squad, we're saved!' exclaimed one mother.

'Hoorah, hoorah!' shouted all the other ducks with great relief.

The police mallards looked magnificent. They turned in the sky with the Sun glinting like beacons from their helmet badges. Within seconds they had landed in the yard and formed a line between the crowd of ducks and the huge pterosaur. Bravely they stood with their inspector standing out in front with his binoculars and hooter hanging perfectly straight from around his neck.

The pterosaur did nothing to acknowledge their arrival, but stood defiantly with his mouth still open as if about to snap up the duckling at any moment.

'Stop, in the name of the law,' ordered Inspector Hooter, sounding as important as he possibly could.

The pterosaur turned his head and fixed his gaze on the immaculate police duck standing before him. Hooter gulped heavily. The creature's expression changed; his brow creased above the eyes creating a very menacing look indeed. Inspector Hooter was a very brave mallard, but in all his years he had never seen such an awful looking thing in all his life.

The pterosaur looked down, Hooter looked up, and then up some more until their eyes met. In deep gargling tones the creature spoke: 'Did you say something?' it was obvious he didn't really care what the inspector had to say.

'Yes, I did. I am Inspector Hooter of the Flying Squad, and I am ordering you to leave this place now – right now, or I shall place you under arrest for worrying these ducks.'

'Oh, you will, will you?'

'Yes, I will,' Hooter replied, 'so be a good bird and go quietly, if you please.'

The creature sneered in reply. 'Well, I think you should get your facts straight, you funny little police duck.'

The crowd were shocked at such rudeness. *Really!*

'How do you mean, sir?' said Hooter, managing to appear calm on the outside while a thousand tiny ducks ran amok on the inside.

'Let me educate you.' The sneer was still evident as if the conversation could be ended at any time, with dire results for the ducks. 'How many birds do you know with two feet…and two hands?'

'Er, none,' said Hooter, his neck beginning to ache from looking up.

'And how many birds do you know who have hair instead of feathers?'

'Actually, none,' said Hooter, in as bold a voice as he could muster.

'And how many birds do you know with one of these?' The creature raised his long tail, which until now he had kept hidden behind him. The spade-like tip appeared to one side of his head for just long enough to be seen by all, and then it slowly resumed its position out of sight. It was this that had dealt the blow to the unfortunate Marvin Plimsoll-Line.

'Well, I'm waiting, how many birds do you know who are like me?'

'Well, er, none really,' said Hooter, unsure of how he could regain control of the situation.

'That's because I'm not a bird at all.' The creature held the entire audience in anxious silence, 'I am not a bird I am a beast – a flying reptile – a type of pterosaur in fact.'

'I knew I was right,' said the duck in the crowd who had first recognized the creature.

'But I am not just any old pterosaur; I am a special pterosaur. For millions of years my peers adapted and grew – they lost bits and gained bits – but I have all the best bits, and what's more I—'

'Nevertheless,' Inspector Hooter interrupted, 'I must insist that you leave these good ducks alone, so if you don't mind, sir, please go now while you still can.'

'Tut, tut, tut.' The grey beast slowly shook his head from side to side. 'Don't you know it's bad manners to interrupt? And suppose I don't want to go just yet, eh, then what will you do?' The tail reappeared, menacingly waving from side to side behind his head. 'Well, I'm still waiting – and so are all these ducks. I'm sure they want to know what you are going to do, so why don't you tell us.'

'Very well, sir. You leave me no choice but to arrest you and take you into custody.' Hooter maintained a very calm and proper manner throughout the conversation, but he was secretly very worried indeed; this was a culprit who clearly had no respect for the law. 'So if you don't mind, sir, be on your way now and save us all any more trouble. After all, there are seven of us and only one of you.'

'Is that so?' replied the pterosaur. His solid eyes of black showed no sign of compliance. He slowly raised his head and aimed his beak skyward. Hooter followed his gaze and was instantly filled with dread. He found himself looking up at another twenty of the creatures circling silently high above them with their vast leathery wings outstretched, and their long tails clearly visible. All had their evil black gaze fixed on the ducks below.

Before the inspector could say another word, the pterosaur standing before him spread his wings high above his head and with one broad sweep he was airborne, leaving the ducks coughing and choking in the dust as he took-off. The residents wasted no time in blindly fumbling their way to the safety of their homes, leaving only the seven police mallards standing out in the open. Brave and straight they stood.

'Stand firm, Constables,' called the inspector, gazing up at the twenty-one grey reptiles circling in the deserted sky. Before he could raise his binoculars for a better look, seven of the reptiles separated from the main group. With wings swept back to their sides they rained from the sky like living, breathing spears, keeping their tight formation as they fell. The wind roared across their wings, shrieking hauntingly and proclaiming the inevitable blow they were about to deliver. The pterosaurs passed over the ducks' heads at incredible speed, and frighteningly close. Their grey bodies narrowly missed their targets, but the flattened ends of their tails didn't. They struck the officers' helmets hard, sending them all flying into the air along with Hooter's cap.

Having dealt their blow, the first wave of attackers regained their previous height, and spread their wings to maintain a silent glide separate from the main group.

'Get your helmets back on as quick as you can,' Hooter shouted.

The constables picked up their helmets and dusted them off as best they could, making sure the badges were shining before putting them back on. Hooter looked up again to assess the situation; another seven of the reptiles had separated from the main group, they too swept their wings back to their bodies and straightened themselves out for a formation dive.

'When I shout, "duck," be sure to duck,' shouted Hooter. But they were not quick enough. The grey shadows streaked past them again, the police instinctively ducked without being told, but this time it wasn't their helmets that were in danger. The powerful tails whipped their legs from under them, sending them all to the ground in agony.

Once again the attackers quickly rejoined their squadron high above.

The police lay scattered like skittles, very bruised and hurt – and very dusty. Their hearts were at a loss as to how to deal with such aggression. They staggered to their feet, groaning, coughing and spluttering. They sensed their time was running out. They had barely begun to dust themselves off when six more reptiles mercilessly fell from the sky.

The police ducks didn't see them coming. The grey shadows flashed by in a second. This time their tails were at body height when they struck. Feathers flew from the constables' chests and bellies, white, grey and brown feathers; all beautiful, into the air and lost. Having their helmets knocked off was bad enough, but to have their feathers beaten from them was something that should never happen to a police duck.

The six constables were knocked to the ground yet again; this time they were winded, very hurt and unable to get back on their feet. They lay helpless on their backs looking up into the sky at the only reptile that hadn't yet dived. They recognized him as the one who had confronted Hooter in the first instance. No matter how hard they tried, they were too badly winded to right themselves and protect their leader. A sense of ill-boding swept over the young ducks as they writhed and laboured in the dust, gasping for breath; their chests cried for air while their hearts cried for their inspector.

Inspector Hooter stood in the middle of the yard surveying his brave injured constables strewn all around him, and then he looked up at the pitiless creature who was about to meet him head on. He felt this would be his last stand, but no matter what, he would not desert his post – he was after all 'Hooter of the Flying Squad'.

He stooped and picked up his cap and blew the dust from the badge. 'Must have a shiny badge,' he whispered to himself. 'Must set a good example.' He stiffened his bill to prevent it quivering.

The constables could only look on as their leader stood to attention, completely covered in dull yellow dust apart from his cap which showed a hint of blue and gold as the Sun picked him out standing alone. His bright brown eyes contrasted softly with his dusted green-blue face as he stood with head up and chest out, awaiting the wrath of his adversary.

The pterosaur circled high above, flexing his outstretched wings to gain more height; then higher still he went to be sure of gaining maximum speed before striking the police inspector for the last time. His eyes met Hooter's and stared coldly into them. 'So, you're going to arrest me are you?' he shouted and laughed so high in the sky that his voice could hardly be heard, but those on the ground got his meaning.

'Indeed I am, sir,' Hooter shouted back. He took a deep breath. 'I am arresting you for—' but before he could finish, the grey beast accelerated towards him not wishing to waste any more time listening. He would end this matter there and then. Hooter stopped talking.

The wind screeched over the taut wings, faster and faster towards the ground, towards Hooter. The attacker levelled out at the last second, swooping low over the tree tops; the air in his wake ripped the leaves from their branches sending them flurrying in all directions. The trees cried and waved their branches angrily. The creature had no time for such trivialities; his only thought was to lay the inspector down once and for all.

Hooter stood firm, upright and courageous. He would not falter; he knew he had only a few seconds left before impact, and he knew he couldn't win. His foe was bigger, heavier and harder than he, but he would face the evil reptile to the bitter end. Their eyes fixed on each other. The pterosaur adjusted his height and lowered his clawed feet to tear at his prey. Dust swirled into the air in long spirals behind him as he streaked low across the yard. The constables could look no more, closing their eyes just before impact.

Hooter took a deep breath. This will be my last, he thought, this is it! His entire life flashed before him in the briefest of moments. From fluffy duckling like the one he had just rescued to the brave but frightened adult he had become. His thoughts crashed back to the present to see the pterosaur hurtling towards him, about to strike him down. Hooter's eyes widened in fear – no time left. Firm stood the courageous police duck. At the last moment he shut his eyes tight and waited for the final blow–but wait–from nowhere came the muted thumping of hooves.

'What on Earth—?' mumbled the inspector, still keeping his eyes firmly shut.

Punch reared up on his hind legs with Dick hanging tightly to the horse's mane; they had got between the pterosaur and the inspector in the nick of time. Suddenly confronted by something much more substantial, the pterosaur quickly pulled his feet in beneath his body while working his wings powerfully to gain height. He stretched his neck upwards, narrowly avoiding head to head contact, but his chest crunched into the horse's forehead, and his long beak opened briefly in pain before he veered across the yard out of control. Punch shook his head, amazed to find he was still standing high on his hind legs. *Wow!* he thought. *Didn't know I could do that!*

Travelling too fast to make a safe landing, the pterosaur daren't put his legs down for fear of injuring them, nor could he gain enough height to clear the tops of the caravans. He had no option but to make a belly landing, leaving a furrow in the dust as he careered along the dry unyielding ground with his wings tucked tightly in to protect them. Unable to slow himself down, he bounced and crashed between some rubbish bins before finally coming to rest halfway through a stout laurel hedge.

By now Punch had dropped onto all fours, and Dick had straightened himself up in the saddle. The police constables, still lying on the ground, opened their eyes one by one. They were amazed to see their leader still standing to attention, untouched, in the middle of the yard. They were even more surprised to see the large brown horse standing directly in front of him almost touching noses.

Mounted boldly on the horse sat Dick, wearing his blue tricorn hat and the mask with two holes to see through.

'It's him,' the constables coughed to each other, 'it's the highway duck.'

Inspector Hooter, still in considerable shock, eyed the horse up and down, his bill gently touching the soft pink lips of the Suffolk Punch. The horse looked down at the inspector and gave a quiet huff as if to ask, 'You all right?'

Hooter leaned back slightly to create a little space between them. He then turned his head towards the constables while still keeping one eye on the horse, and said in a calm and quiet voice, 'Right, Constables, up you get. We've got work to do.'

The constables struggled painfully to their feet, groaning and wincing. They gathered their helmets and dusted them off yet again before putting them back on their heads. They then lined themselves up in a perfectly straight line and waited for further orders.

Hooter studied the duck sitting on the horse. He noted the colours visible around the edges of the mask concealing the suspect's face. *Hmm*, he thought, rubbing his bill with his wing. 'Ahem,' he cleared his throat before addressing the rider. 'I notice you have two eyes and a bill on the front of your face, and that you are in fact the same colours as me.'

'Er, possibly,' replied Dick.

'I also note that this horse has a white flash down its nose.'

'Er, you mean down his face – his nose is just the bit at the end – do you see?'

'Hmmm, quite so – may I ask what your name is?' asked the inspector.

'Er, it's Dick, Dick Parsnip,' said Dick, not expecting Hooter to believe him.

'Dick Parsnip, eh? Are you sure it's not Dick the Highway Duck?'

'Oh no, it's definitely Parsnip,' said Dick as he pulled very gently on the reins and tightened his feet against the sides of his horse. Punch knew this to mean get ready for a quick getaway. The inspector took his time to look the horse and its rider up and down several more times. He found himself looking into the horse's eyes, big and brown, with a certain friendly twinkle to them. Punch flicked his ears and winked while carefully moving backwards one small step at a time.

The inspector's train of thought was interrupted by a rustling sound behind him. He turned to see the crashed pterosaur being pulled through the hedge by some of his subordinates who had landed under the cover of the dust.

'Quickly, Constables, grab him, don't let them take him away,' shouted Hooter.

All seven police ducks grabbed the pterosaur's feet with their bills and tugged for all their worth. Meanwhile, on the other side of the hedge, many strong hands had no intention of letting him go, their clawed grip being far superior to that of any duck. One huge heave was all it took, and the police ducks lost their hold. They stared in dismay at the creature's tail disappearing through the hedge. Within seconds the beasts were airborne with their leader hanging limply in their grasp. He stared down at the inspector with glazed eyes of black. Inspector Hooter returned the stare. He had an uneasy feeling they would meet again.

'Oh well,' he said, returning his attention to Dick and the horse. 'What the—? Where have they gone?'

Dick and the horse were nowhere to be seen.

'They slipped away while you were playing tug of war with that ugly bird-thing,' said Marvin Plimsoll-Line, rubbing his sore head. Hooter flopped down in the middle of the yard joined by his six constables; they all let out a tired sigh, thankful to still be in one piece.

Before long they were enjoying the tender care of the grateful residents, who gently dusted them off and gave them cups of tea and cakes, and admiring glances.

'You don't happen to know where that duck and his horse live do you?' asked Hooter with barely enough energy to finish the sentence.

'No,' said Marion Waters-Edge, 'we've never seen him before. He's not from around these parts, I'm sure.'

Within a few minutes the seven police ducks were fast asleep, exhausted, and resting in the wings of the lady ducks who still thought they were truly wonderful.

4

Another day dawned. The song of the blackbird, robin and thrush had returned with the early morning Sun. The five o' clock chorus woke the constables from a healing sleep, their eyes dreamily letting in the light of a new day. Soft sunlight shone through the small panes of a solitary window, filling the room with a comforting half-light. They were in some sort of storeroom where walls of crudely sawn timber planks met in shadowy corners, and spiders' webs patiently waited for unsuspecting flies to happen by. The hay bales on which they lay had been covered with blankets, a basic affair but dry and warm, for which the constables were very grateful.

Battered and bruised, they rested for a while longer, staring up at the rafters and recalling the events of yesterday, especially the monstrous pterosaurs. *How could someone have so little respect for the law?* One by one they swung round on their beds, wondering what would take the longest to heal, their bruises or their pride. Inspector Hooter had spoken to them previously about how pride can be a bad thing, 'Respect and dignity is one thing,' he would say, 'but pride simply gives you a place to fall from.'

They took their time to peruse each other before groaning in unison. It was clear that someone had dusted them off before putting them to bed, but their feathers were still in a poor state, some bent, and some missing altogether.

The subdued light in the room brightened when the door from the yard opened. The young constables raised their heads expecting to see the inspector standing there, but it was a very different sight that greeted their weary eyes; silhouetted in the doorway stood the rounded form of a female duck. At first her features weren't clearly visible with the daylight immediately behind her, but when she waddled quietly across the room six bills dropped open and six pairs of eyes widened. Her colours weren't as spectacular as a male mallard, but she was a very pleasant sight for sore eyes, as was the washing kit she carried under her wing. Her fawns and browns softened her smooth curves as she made her way to the nearest of the young police ducks. The constable in question was PC Thomas.

She stood over him. 'How are you feeling this morning?' she asked. Her words floated from her bill and stroked his aching head. Before he could answer her, another five females entered the room and made their way to each of his comrades.

'Well?' she said, regaining his attention.

'Sorry?' replied the dumbstruck Thomas.

'How you are feeling this morning?'

'Oh, er, I'm not sure really. A bit dazed – you know.' He looked down at his chest, too shy to let his eyes rise and meet hers.

'Aren't you going to tell me your name?'

'Oh yes, miss, its Police Constable FS6 Thomas.'

'I see, and is Thomas your surname?'

'Yes, miss,' he replied, still shyly trying to avoid eye contact.

'And is FS6 your first name?'

'Oh no, miss, FS6 is my number.'

'I see, and what might your first name be?'

'I don't know if I should tell you, miss, what with me being a police constable, and you a lady duck and all that.'

She gently wiped Thomas's face with the damp sponge. Her touch tested his composure while new sensations raced through his body taking his youthful demeanour into new territory. He recalled his mother's touch when he was a duckling, she would delicately clean him from top to bottom as a loving mother should. But this was not his mother, this was a stranger…and it felt very strange.

'Well, my first name is Fay,' said the young female, 'and I'm happy for you to call me that, if you think it appropriate.' Her warm breath soothed his every ache as she continued to clean his feathers, ensuring each one was correctly placed. Occasionally, her gaze would wander and fall upon the young constable's face. Fine dark blue feathers with an emerald green hue swept from his eyes over his rounded head to the back of his neck, underlined by his crisp white collar. He was truly a charming mallard, as were all the young constables in the room, each one being tended to in the same meticulous manner. Fay was mindful not to let her brief gaze become a stare, for fear of causing him even more embarrassment.

The conversation fell into a dreamy silence while Fay continued her welcome task. She cleaned and groomed Thomas's back, and then each wing and top tail feathers. Every stroke of the sponge set a thousand tingling ducks loose inside him. He desperately wanted to talk to her but he didn't know what to say. He had never spoken to a female on a personal level before, apart from his mother of course, but that was different. He was very good at telling others to 'Move on', or to 'Stop, in the name of the law'. But to talk to someone socially was altogether tricky, especially when that someone happened to be the most beautiful duck he had ever set eyes on. His nerves wanted this to be over so that she would leave and he could relax, but something inside him wanted her to stay.

Her touch with the sponge was difficult enough to deal with, but every now and then she would resort to using her bill to rearrange his feathers. Each time she did this, Thomas's thousand miniature ducks would tap dance up and down his spine. No matter how hard he tried, he couldn't stop his eyes from widening each time she did it.

She had cleaned and groomed everywhere she thought she should, leaving the more private parts for the young constable to deal with himself.

'There you are then – you're all done,' she said, in a voice as soft as down.

'Thank you, miss.'

'Just one moment – your bill is still a little dusty.' She dipped the sponge in the water and squeezed it until it was just damp, and then she carefully wiped Thomas's bill, taking extra care to keep her gaze away from his eyes.

The constable stared straight ahead, dumbfounded. *Nearly over,* he thought. He was about to let out a concealed sigh when he sensed her eyes moving up his bill.

Fay wanted to be sure there was no dust in the very fine feathers just above his nostrils where his bill joined his face. 'Just one last little stroke,' she whispered. 'Perfect.' But that was one stroke too many. She found herself looking straight at the perfectly groomed young mallard who was still staring blankly, trying to pretend nothing was happening. But it was. She loved the way his finest feathers formed an arc around the base of his bill, glistening and reflecting light from every angle, shining and shimmering as they swept over his head in a blaze of fabulous iridescence. Fay didn't care if she was staring at him or not; she was drowning in his handsomeness, and enjoying every second. Like PC Thomas, she too was aware of an unknown feeling somewhere deep in her heart, and it felt wonderful.

Thomas tried not to notice Fay's attention, but his wide angle of vision made it impossible to avoid her eyes any longer. He slowly tilted his head to one side. Fay tilted hers likewise. Her eyes were the most beautiful brown, so clear and bright that the whole world reflected in them. Constable Thomas had never noticed that before. Neither wisp nor feather was out of place on her perfect head. The longer he looked into her eyes the warmer he felt inside. The longer he looked at her, the wider his mouth gawped.

Fay placed her wing beneath his bill and gently closed it. Dignity restored. *Oh my – so handsome.* She wasn't sure if she had thought it or said it out loud. For a brief moment she didn't care. Never before had she felt such chemistry by simply being close to another duck. She cleared her throat. 'Ahem,' and then asked in a voice so soft that the words were formed solely from her breath. 'Well, are you ever going to tell me your first name, or do I have to guess it?'

The constable just sat there, his mind floating high above with the fairies. Fay slowly touched her bill on his. Thomas jumped with a start. 'Oh!' he exclaimed with a sharp intake of breath. 'I'm sorry, I seem to have drifted off for a minute – I must be tired or something.'

'Hmm – or something,' Fay replied with a knowing tone far in advance of Thomas's.

'Now will you please tell me your name?'

'It's Thomas.'

'No, not your surname; what's your first name, you silly thing.'

'That's it,' he said, 'it's Thomas.'

'So your name is Thomas Thomas?'

'Yes, miss, I am Police Constable FS6 Thomas Thomas.'

'That's a bit odd isn't it?'

'Not really, miss. There's PC Peter Peters; PC Howard Howard; PC James James—'

'Enough,' Fay interrupted, not wanting her thoughts to

become muddled by such things; she only wanted to talk about her patient – her Thomas Thomas.

'What does FS6 mean?'

'FS is short for Flying Squad, and number six is my flying position. We number from the left, so number six is furthest out on the right when we're in flying formation.'

Now it was Fay's turn to drift off with the fairies; she imagined the constables soaring across the sky looking more wonderful than anything else in the world, and from the look on the other females' faces, they all felt the same way.

The air of gushing and admiring glances was brought to an abrupt halt when Inspector Hooter's voice called from the doorway. 'Good morning, Constables, how are we feeling today? Not too bad I hope. Is anyone unable to fly?'

The room fell silent. The young lady ducks each looked at their own patient, thrilled to have helped restore them, and secretly hoping to continue their new-found friendship.

Inspector Hooter took the silence to mean they were all fit and able to resume their duties. 'Excellent,' he said with a spring to his voice and an uncommon glint in his eye. 'Our hosts have kindly offered to give us breakfast before we continue our pursuit, so enjoy it, and I'll see you on parade in an hour from now.' He turned and made his way back to the caravan belonging to Marion Waters-Edge where he had been tended to and had spent the night on the sofa. The constables weren't sure, but they thought they heard him whistling to himself as he went.

Now that **is** odd, they thought to themselves. Normally he'd be far too prim and proper to let slip a whistle while in uniform.

'Probably the shock from yesterday,' said PC Robert Roberts.

'I guess so,' said PC Howard Howard.

The lady ducks just smiled.

And so the Flying Squad settled down to a hearty breakfast in a most convivial atmosphere in which conversation and mutual admiration flourished – and seven thousand miniature ducks continued with their press-ups. There was no telling what the day would bring, and so, like all animals, they enjoyed the moment while they could.

5

Little did the police ducks know, but Dick and his faithful horse were only a couple of miles away, also preparing for the new day. The early Sun warmed the dew-laden grass while Dick bathed and preened himself at the edge of a shallow stream by which they had camped. Punch had finished grazing the lush vegetation of the meadow, and was now stooping at the water's edge, upstream from Dick. The water sparkled like fine crystal glass as it rippled over the rounded pebbles in the stream bed. Punch amused himself by watching his wobbly reflection in the water. Dick looked across at him affectionately, watching the horse's plump lips of pale pink delicately touch the water's surface, silently supping the cool refreshing drink. *Such a huge animal, yet so delicate.* The young mallard had never really fathomed the horse's mind; he knew Punch to be the most dependable and loyal friend a duck could ever have, but there seemed to be a hidden depth way beyond Dick's understanding. *There's something going on inside that head, but I'm not sure what.* Dick pondered a while longer until the drinking was done, and then he looked up to the sky for inspiration as animals often do, but the heavens were busy piling up the heavy clouds which seemed to be coming from every direction. It wasn't long before the dark, ominous clouds were smothering the tops of the distant hills, leaving the Sun with nowhere to shine.

'We'd better be on our way, old fella,' said Dick, stroking Punch's cheek. 'To tell you the truth I don't really know where to go, but I think we should keep out of the way of the police for a while.'

Punch gave an agreeable snort and nodded his head. Dick squeezed his webbed foot into the left stirrup and swung himself up into the saddle. Another of those thoughtful moments popped into his head. *If I'm a duck, why don't I fly up into the saddle instead of climbing up?*

Likewise, Punch wondered, Why doesn't he fly all the way instead of riding a horse?

Dick sorted the reins and scanned the distant horizon where the heavy clouds were landing. He had never been so far from home before and was a little worried about going any further, but with the police hot on his heels he felt he had no choice. 'I've always wondered what was the other side of those hills,' he said, 'perhaps now's a good time to find out.'

Without any guidance, Punch moved off at an easy walking pace. He held his head high to show off the posh white blaze on his big loveable face; sadly there was no one there to see it apart from the occasional rabbit and early morning butterfly, but that was enough for Punch. Preferring the soft grass to the unforgiving gravel track, he kept to the verge wherever possible and soon stepped up to a slow trot, mindful of Dick's limitations. They both settled their eyes on the distant hills, wondering what mysteries might lay on the other side.

***

In Smallbeef, having finished their breakfast, the police ducks were sitting on a row of straw bales in the yard. They busied themselves cleaning and polishing their helmets and checking for any feathers that might have slipped out of place. Inspector Hooter insisted they should always be above reproach as far as appearance was concerned, something that hadn't gone unnoticed by the female ducks.

The Sun warmed the constables' backs while they contemplated recent events. They recalled the skirmish with the pterosaurs, and how brave their leader had been in the face of overwhelming odds. Inevitably, they ended up thinking of the young females who had tended to them after the fight. They couldn't help smiling when something tingled deep within them, something warm and strong; a feeling somehow expanding beyond their physical size, each of them feeling as though they could take on the world and win.

On the end bale sat the inspector. 'Oh dear,' he sighed, noticing a small dent in his brass hooter. 'No time to do anything about it now,' he said, polishing it with utmost diligence. 'Those beastly reptiles, I bet it was one of their confounded tails that did the damage.' He paid the same attention to his binoculars, huffing onto the lenses and polishing them with a soft cloth which he kept solely for that purpose; after making quite sure they were hanging perfectly straight around his neck he gently rubbed his wing tip over the dent in the hooter, and sighed again.

A female voice spoke softly in his ear. 'If that's the only damage done, I think you should count yourself very lucky, don't you?' Marion Waters-Edge, the lady duck who had cared for him during the night, gently stroked his cheek.

Hooter paused for a few moments, thinking back to yesterday. He pictured himself standing alone in the middle of the yard with his constables injured on the ground. He recalled the evil look in the eyes of the pterosaur as it screeched towards him. He shivered and replied ruefully, 'You know, Marion, I really thought I'd breathed my last, yesterday.'

'I know,' she said, affectionately stroking his forehead, 'but you stood your ground like the brave police duck that you are, and you prevailed. The pterosaur did not.'

'Yes, but what have we got to show for our efforts? The pterosaur got away, and then to top it all so did that highway duck and his horse.' He stared down at his feet in despair before continuing, 'And who knows where they are now, or what they're up to. For all I know they could be robbing someone else at this very moment.'

'Oh, calm yourself,' said Marion, still stroking the inspector's head. He found this a little embarrassing in front of his squad, and hoped that none of them had noticed her attention. They all had of course, but said nothing; the beautiful young females sitting opposite them saw to that.

'Anyway,' Marion continued, 'what do you really know of this so called highway robber and his great big horse?'

'Well, the fact is, he's a robber and I'm a police duck, so it's my job to catch him and see that justice is done; that's what police do.'

'Of course it is, but has he ever actually robbed anyone?'

'Well, er, I don't know really, that's what I have to find out.'

'And did he not save you from certain death yesterday?'

'Er, well, yes.' Once again Hooter looked up to the sky. 'I don't understand why he did that. He could have just ridden away and left us at the mercy of the pterosaurs.'

Hooter slowly but surely succumbed to Marion's aura, her eyes exuding such strength and yet so much compassion at the same time. Like his younger constables, he too was experiencing feelings from a secret place within, but being older, he knew what those feelings meant and why they were there. But he had a job to do, he was a police inspector and couldn't allow himself to be distracted from his duties, or his constables, for whom he felt a responsibility. Marion's breath warmed his cheek; his pulse quickened. Judging by the look on the constables' faces, they too were in the same state of mind. Utterly and hopelessly besotted.

Marion went on, 'Then perhaps the young mallard and his horse are not villains after all, hmm, what do you think?'

The inspector stole himself from her eyes, and then said with a deliberate air of urgency, 'I think I'm losing time, that's what I think, so I shall get my squad together and be on my way.' His words were tainted with sadness, but he had to say them because that was his job, and that was all he cared about…until now. He so loved talking to Marion who had shown him such tenderness, but he had to lead by example, and so he straightened his binoculars and his slightly dented but shiny hooter, and took a deep breath.

Marion whispered in his ear. 'Well, Inspector Hooter, you are a stubborn mallard and no mistake, promise me you will be careful.'

The inspector quickly raised his voice to divert his constables' attention from his predicament. 'Squad – attention, eyes front, heads up, chests out!'

The constables instantly stood to attention with their gaze duly fixed ahead, away from the female eyes that would have them stay. Marion leaned forward and gave Hooter a gentle peck on the cheek. The six young lady ducks did the same to each of the handsome constables.

The inspector cleared his mind of his own thoughts and paced slowly along the line of immaculate police ducks. He was very pleased with the way they had cleaned up, largely thanks to the efforts of the residents who were so happy to oblige. He then stood smartly to attention himself and sorted the day's activities in his head; these being to pursue and apprehend the pterosaurs, or the duck and the horse, whichever came first.

He was about to begin his address when he noticed the shed door in the far corner by number seven swinging back and forth.

'PC Thomas, go and shut that shed door properly will you.'

'Yes, sir.' Thomas turned about and waddled his way towards

the shed. He was barely half way up the path when he noticed Marion Waters-Edge following him anxiously.

She tried to jostle her way past him. 'It's all right, my dear,' she said, 'I'll close it, don't you trouble yourself.'

'It's no trouble,' replied the constable, reaching the door just ahead of her. He was about to push the door shut when something caught his eye from within.

'Please,' said Marion in a desperate tone. She kept her voice down to avoid being overheard by the inspector, but to no avail. The inspector made his way towards the two of them, curious to know what was going on.

PC Thomas glanced inside the shed. A bucket of water stood just inside the door, and in the far corner two large brushes hung from a hook on the wall – brushes big enough to care for a large horse. In the few seconds that followed, PC Thomas grew up a lot. He looked Marion in the eye, and then briefly took another look into the shed at the horsey paraphernalia. Upon hearing his inspector closing up behind him he pushed the door shut and quickly fastened the latch.

'Is everything all right?' asked the inspector.

'Oh yes, sir, no problem, just a wonky latch.' Thomas never thought the day would come when he would lie to anyone, and certainly not while wearing his police helmet, and even more certainly not to the inspector.

'Oh well, perhaps we can fix it on our return,' said Hooter. He sniffed the air inquisitively and caught the scent of something out of place, he sniffed again. *Horse smell.* He kept this thought to himself, but then he noticed the horse dung on the ground. *Fresh horse dung.* He continued to turn unabated, not wanting his expression to give away his suspicions.

'Fall back in line, Constable,' he commanded. Thomas and the inspector avoided eye contact, neither wanting to deal with their emotions at this time. They had both just done something that was wrong, yet it felt like the right thing to do. *Sometimes life isn't black and white.*

***

Dick and Punch had been travelling for a couple of hours, mostly at walking pace but occasionally stepping up to a working trot to allow Punch to stretch his muscles a little. So far nothing untoward had happened, but Dick had an uneasy feeling about his surroundings. He stretched up high on the horse's back, searching for anything not quite right.

The track beneath them had become coarse and uneven, bound on each side by a dilapidated wooden fence of petrified gnarled grain. Beyond this, a few bushes sparsely occupied the vast expanse of dark green moorland. An observer would be forgiven for thinking the entire landscape had been colour-washed with puddle water.

To add to the dreariness, there were no animals. No rabbits bobbing. No birds darting. All gone.

Whispers stirred from within Punch's soul. *Take care,* they said, *be careful, things are not quite right.* His hazel eyes opened wider than ever, his ears inclined forward and his nostrils flared. The slightest sound or movement or scent would not go unnoticed.

The dull gravel track stretched out ahead of them, straight and featureless. Only the ground beneath them broke the silence as it yielded a lifeless thud from each hoof as the horse made his way onward.

A mile or so along the track they passed between two unfinished stone towers, singular turrets standing head high on each side of the track. It seemed a strange place for such buildings, in the middle of nowhere. Beside each turret, rocks were piled, waiting to be added, but there seemed to be no one around to add them. *Strange.*

'Looks like a bridge and a stream up ahead,' said Dick, stroking Punch's mane. 'We'll stop there for a drink and a rest, mate.'

Punch continued his rock steady, easy pace, his head gently moving up and down in time with his muffled reassuring steps. He concentrated hard on the situation. He may not have been the most intellectual creature on Earth, but he had whispers, and an instinct founded two thousand years ago which would always tell him when he should be worried. They were telling him now.

6

The residents had gathered in Smallbeef to wave goodbye to the Flying Squad. Such a spectacle was not to be missed, especially by the youngsters who dreamed of one day becoming police ducks themselves. PC Thomas had joined his colleagues in the yard. Inspector Hooter stood before them; he looked down at his feet and pondered for a few moments, and then he looked up to the heavens for inspiration – none came. He needed everything to be just right in his head, but it wasn't. He was confused. *Why would they hide the highway duck and the horse from me? And why would Marion lie about knowing him?*

Everyone expected him to give the order to take off, but instead, he muttered in sombre tones, 'Squad dismiss, stand down and await further orders.'

The constables were saddened by the sorrowful look on their leader's face. *What can be the matter?* PC Thomas knew what the matter was and felt he should say something, but he was unsure about approaching the inspector while he was so troubled.

Hooter walked slowly to one side of the yard to be alone with his thoughts. PC Thomas followed with some trepidation and stopped by his side.

'Excuse me, sir,' he said, rather nervously.

'What is it, Constable?'

'It's about this affair in the shed, sir, I mean, I'm not really sure what I saw, sir.'

'You are a bright police duck, PC Thomas, I'm quite certain

you know what you saw – you saw horsey things. The question is, what is to be done about it?'

'Yes, sir, but they've been so kind to us here – and after the way the duck and the horse fought off the pterosaur it seems—'

'That's enough, young duck,' Hooter interrupted, 'we are police ducks first and foremost, and as such we have a duty to do.'

'Yes, sir, but—' Thomas tried to interject, but was cut short again.

'No buts, Constable,' was the firm response, 'if we decide who we subject to the law and who we do not, we risk becoming corrupt ourselves, and that would never do.'

PC Thomas struggled in his reply. 'Yes, sir.'

'You are not to burden yourself with this predicament; it is for me to deal with. I think you should return to the others while I do my duty.'

'Yes, sir.' PC Thomas turned mournfully, but found his way blocked by Marion Waters-Edge who had come quietly upon them in the hope of making things better. Hooter found it difficult to look her in the eye; he felt betrayed and untrusted by the one person he thought he had made a real connection with.

'Please, look at me,' said Marion. Her eyes were tearful, and she had a look of vulnerability about her.

Hooter replied sadly, 'You ask me to look at you? I should be arresting you for aiding and abetting a villain,' his voice wavered, 'and for interfering with a police duck to prevent him carrying out his duty, that's what I should be doing, madam.'

PC Thomas slowly moved away, hoping to leave the two of them to settle the dispute on their own.

'Don't go, Constable,' said Marion.

'Madam,' Hooter retorted, 'it is for me to tell my constables when to go and when not to go.' He did his best to remain authoritative and detached, but a thousand little ducks wept secretly into his heart.

Marion went on, 'Please hear me out, then if you still think it the right thing to do, you can arrest me; I won't resist or cause any trouble.'

The inspector drowned a little more in her eyes. 'Very well,' he said, beckoning PC Thomas to stay and hear what Marion had to say.

She took a deep breath. 'The duck on the horse you are looking for,' she paused to bolster her emotions, 'he isn't a bad duck, he would never hurt a fly. He loves his horse, and his horse looks after him.'

'But that is not the point – he is a robber, madam – a robber. How can you say he is not a bad duck when he goes around robbing everyone?'

'But that's just it, he hasn't robbed anyone, and he never will.'

'That's what you think, but how can you possibly be sure?'

Marion's chest rose and fell heavily as she struggled to control her feelings. 'You can ask anyone who knows him. You see, he isn't quite like other ducks.'

'What on Earth do you mean by that?' A puzzled expression settled on Hooter's face. 'He looks just like any other duck to me.'

'He's a lovely young chap,' said Marion. 'He's bright and intelligent, but he has an overactive imagination, and sometimes…' the tears welled up and ran down her cheeks. She pushed on with her explanation, her voice trembling and her heart aching. 'Sometimes his imagination gets the better of him, and he acts out his dreams, but he never hurts anyone. One day in his mind he might be a highway duck, the next he is a pony express rider racing across the moor with an imaginary message for someone.'

'I've never heard of such a thing before,' said the inspector, somewhat confounded by what Marion was saying.

She continued, 'He's just different from most of us, and when he comes into contact with those who don't know him he gets misunderstood, but that doesn't make him bad.'

Hooter stared into the sky once more before replying. 'Do you mean to tell me that this juvenile duck has never actually carried out any of these crimes people talk about?'

'That's exactly what I mean,' Marion replied, gathering her composure. 'You know what it's like; it only takes someone to exaggerate a little, then the erroneous whispers take over and before you know it things have got blown up out of all proportion.'

'Hmm, that's true enough,' said Hooter, rubbing his bill. 'Doesn't he realize he would be in serious trouble if the Armed Response Ducks caught up with him; they would act first and ask questions later, they're a very mean lot.'

'I know, but he's learned his lesson, and has promised me he'll curb his imagination.'

'Do you believe him?' asked Hooter.

'Yes I do…I know him.'

As those words left Marion's mouth, a ray of understanding shone upon the inspector. He turned and looked her squarely in the eye. 'I dare say you know his name too, don't you?'

'Yes.'

'What is it?' asked Hooter. He already knew the answer but needed to hear Marion say it.

Marion took a deep breath. 'His name is Dick Waters-Edge…and he is my son.'

The inspector's eyes filled with tears. 'And what of the boy's father?'

Marion explained, 'He went out flying one day last summer with some of his friends, and none of them came back. Others went out searching for them for weeks after, but there was no trace of them anywhere.'

'Last night you walked down to the bottom of the lane, alone,' said the inspector, 'were you waiting for someone?'

'Yes,' Marion replied, 'every day at dusk I gaze into the far off sky to see if my husband is coming home, but he never does,' she sobbed.

The inspector turned to PC Thomas. 'I think you should go and say your farewells to your friend now, Constable.'

'Yes, sir,' replied Thomas, promptly turning to hide his own tears. With great relief he eagerly waddled back to his Fay, who was still waiting patiently on the bench.

'What will you do if you find Dick?' asked Marion.

Hooter rested a gentle wing around her. 'Don't worry, my dear, we will find him, and when we do we will make sure he comes home safely.'

Fay stood up when Thomas returned, and rubbed her cheek on his.

'Do you know when you will be back?' she asked.

'No, we never know where we will be from one day to the next.'

'I don't suppose you will have time to think of me when you're gone.'

Thomas felt that warm feeling again. 'My dear Fay, you've been so kind to us, and you're so beautiful, how could I not think of you?'

Fay gently pressed her cheek against Thomas's and rested there for a moment. 'I will think of you every single day you are away,' she said. 'I promise I will wait for you, however long it takes for you to return.' She put her wing on his shoulder. 'You're going after those awful pterosaurs aren't you. There are so many of them and they're so big and strong, it's not fair.' Her bill quivered and tears gathered in the corners of her lovely bright eyes. Thomas carefully wiped them away.

'There's no need to worry,' he said, 'I'm sure everything will be all right. After all, we've got Inspector Hooter to lead us, so what could possibly go wrong?' That remark didn't entirely fill Fay with confidence. There was no doubting the bravery of the inspector or any of the constables, but the odds were not in their favour. Thomas continued, 'And besides, the pterosaurs are evil, and we're good, so we're bound to win in the end, aren't we. Aren't we?'

'Of course you are, my brave mallard, of course you are.'

Waddling across the yard towards his squad, Hooter was a little taken aback to see all six constables in the same cheek to cheek embrace with their new-found lady friends. He had never had to deal with such a situation before. *My word, they grow up so fast.* He gave a loud, 'Ahem,' as he approached. The constables immediately broke off their embrace and stood in a perfectly straight line in readiness for the inspector's address.

'Attention!' he called out, using his most important voice. The constables sprang to attention, heads and helmets at precisely the correct angle and chests out, as smart as the smartest duck they could imagine. Hooter walked along the line. He paused in front of each young officer and looked him up and down, looking for anything not quite immaculate, but as usual his squad had not let him down. They were in surprisingly good order considering the ordeal they had all gone through the previous day. His soul had been lightened and his head sorted by Marion's motherly love for her son. Now he was glad of the task of finding him and bringing him home safely.

He was about to congratulate his squad on their efforts but was interrupted by a clatter and a crash at the park entrance. Everyone turned to see what was going on. Lying flat on his back in the dust with his bicycle on top of him was the village bobby, also a mallard. The wheels of the upside down bicycle spun slowly in the air, making a ticking noise as they did so.

Hooter quickly waddled to his assistance. 'What on Earth happened to you, are you all right?' he asked, helping the sorry looking constable to his feet. The constable patted most of the dust from his feathers and put his helmet back on his head, albeit not very straight. He was never the smartest police constable, and no matter how hard he tried, he found it extremely difficult to ride his police bicycle. Being a duck, his webbed feet were too big to fit properly on the pedals, which meant that every time he turned the handlebars to go round a corner, the front wheel would strike his feet and knock him off. His solution to the problem was to ride along the straight bits and then get off and push his bike round the corners. However, on this occasion, he was in such a hurry to catch up with the inspector that he forget to get off before turning into the park, and so off he came.

'Why the rush, young fellow?' asked Hooter.

'I have a communication for you, sir. It's from headquarters – very urgent it says,' said the bobby.

'Well, let's have a look shall we?' All was quiet for a few moments while Hooter opened the sealed envelope and read the message to himself. Consternation got the better of him, and as soon as he'd finished reading it he blurted out, 'What the—? I don't believe it!' He paused and composed himself before turning to address his squad.

'Constables, we have work to do. It seems the stagecoach we rescued yesterday never arrived home; it was found this morning at the side of the road, half a mile from where we left it.' He took a moment to read the last part of the message aloud. 'There was no one on board – no sign of anyone – all gone.'

The crowd gasped. Hooter concealed the communication

beneath his wing to ensure no other eyes would see what else was written on it. 'Stand ready, squad, I shall be back in just a moment.' He waddled anxiously towards Marion and guided her to one side.

'What is it, what's the matter?' she asked.

Hooter explained. 'This picture was found on the stagecoach, probably drawn by one of the passengers.' He discreetly held the piece of paper for Marion to see. On it was a child's drawing of a duck wearing a mask and sitting on a large horse.

'Oh no, that's all we need,' exclaimed Marion. 'You know Dick isn't responsible for all those ducks disappearing, don't you?'

'Of course I do, but it's like you said, my dear, others will jump to the wrong conclusions.' Hooter handed the drawing to Marion and suggested she dispose of it as soon as she could. 'No one else must see it,' he declared.

'Of course,' said Marion, 'is there something else worrying you?' she asked.

'Yes there is,' replied Hooter. 'I'm worried that this matter might catch the attention of the Armed Response Ducks – that will only make matters worse. We shall have to get moving right away if we are to find Dick before them…' he paused for a second. 'You may well get a visit from them after we've gone. Their leader is a duck named Orange, Alan Orange, and he is not to be messed with, but you must stall him for as long as you can to give us a good head start.'

'Don't worry, we'll distract them all right,' she said, with a hint of mischief in her voice.

They touched bills affectionately, and dwelt in each other's eyes for a few precious moments. The inspector then returned to his squad. They all knew they were about to embark on a very dangerous mission, but now every heart had good reason to come back.

The inspector took his brass hooter, and after giving one 'honk' he shouted, 'Onward and upward, Constables.'

Within seconds the Flying Squad was airborne in perfect formation as always, gleaming in the morning sunshine with wings beating in precise time with each other, and helmets in perfect alignment, tilting slightly forward.

The young lady ducks gave a long sigh as they watched their brave constables slowly disappear into the distant Hampshire sky.

7

A long way across the common, almost at the bridge, Dick and Punch stared up at the inky black clouds squeezing into a sky that wasn't big enough. The fence that had accompanied them came to an abrupt end, leaving the two of them alone thirty paces from the bridge. For its part the bridge was a stone built humpback affair, wide enough for the passage of a single cart and nothing more.

Punch's ears pricked up; he sensed a faint voice from the other side. Dick stretched up out of the saddle to improve his view over the hump while Punch walked steadily onward with the whites of his eyes clearly showing concern. The temperature had dropped, exposing the horse's breath as it flew from his nostrils animating the otherwise dormant air.

The voice grew louder – a female, a bird probably and definitely in distress. 'How could this happen, how?' cried the voice.

Dick stretched up a little more but the hump still obscured his view.

'Oh dear, all is lost, all is lost,' the voice teetered on the edge of breaking down.

Then came another voice, one which Punch recognized immediately. 'Hee-haw, haw, hee-haw.' The desperate braying prompted Punch to quicken his step.

From the top of the hump the two of them looked down on an agonizing sight; part way up the other side stood a donkey quaking and braying, his heart broken. He was once a white donkey, but now he exhibited all the signs of an abused and neglected beast of burden; a dirty donkey with legs soiled by the dark gravel track. His hooves curled upwards, overgrown and painful, and his face was marred by umber stains from tears of pain. Two large wicker baskets lay on the ground by his sides, they had fallen from his back with their load of rocks now scattered all over the track. In front of him stood a female moorhen, about the same height as him but coloured a dusty black with a red flash down the centre of her face. She pulled gingerly on a piece of rope tied around the donkey's neck. 'How could this happen?' she repeated.

Dick jumped down from the saddle and waddled quickly to her aid. 'Oh blimey, what's happened to your donkey? Look at the state of him.'

The donkey's dark blue eyes stared, but saw nothing. He brayed again, 'Hee-haw, haw,' utterly exhausted and unable to move another step.

'Please help me,' the moorhen cried. 'His harness has snapped and spilled the rocks all over the ground; I must get them loaded back up and onto his back, quickly.'

The donkey's head dropped and his long ears lay flat on the back of his head. His expression was one of total sadness and pain. The moorhen cried again. 'Please, please, help me.'

Dick raised his voice. 'You can't do that, it's cruel,' he insisted. 'Look at the state of his back, its cut to pieces and bleeding everywhere.'

Punch clomped his way closer and then neighed into the air. *Someone help him!*

Realizing the hopelessness of the situation, the moorhen finally broke down in tears. 'Oh, my child, my child,' she cried, 'I'll never see him again.'

Dick puzzled at the meaning of her words. *What's she talking about?*

Punch rubbed his cheek on the donkey's face; he then whispered and let himself in through the sad eyes to caress and hold the tired soul he found within.

The donkey's heart warmed; at least he would briefly know love while in the soulful embrace of his peer. The pains from the sores on his back grew, the stains beneath his eyes brightened when fresh tears ran down his cheeks. He felt the tender touch of Punch's muzzle on his face and drew solace from the company of the big chesnut horse.

'Has he got a name?' asked Dick.

'Yes – it's Lucky,' replied the moorhen.

During the frantic activity, the darkness had crept up unnoticed. It wouldn't have been so dark were it not for the heavy clouds warding off the sunlight and bringing the day to a premature end.

'We need some wood for a fire,' said Dick.

'No, you can't do that,' the moorhen cried, 'you can't make a fire, they will see it.'

'Who will see it, and what if they do?' replied Dick.

The moorhen lowered her voice, as if others might be listening. 'The Bogs,' she whispered.

'Bogs, what are Bogs?'

'The Bogs are in charge, they rule us and make us work for them and they punish us if we don't do their will, and they always know if we're slacking and—' She paused for breath, giving Dick a chance to get a word in.

'How many of these "Bogs" are there?'

'Oh, far too many, far too many.'

'Well, why don't you fly away and make a fresh start somewhere else?'

'Because they have my child and my husband, and if I don't do as I'm told they say they will send them to oblivion, wherever that is. And I'll never see them again.'

'Oh dear,' sighed Dick, 'Is Lucky your own donkey?'

'Yes,' replied the moorhen, 'poor Lucky, I couldn't have done any more for him. The Bogs only allow us to give our donkeys water first thing in the morning and last thing at night; they say water makes them slow and lazy, and is bad for them.'

'That's ridiculous, everything needs water,' said Dick, looking across at Punch who was still gently touching the donkey to let him know he was there.

'And who let those baskets cut into Lucky's back like that?'

'The Bogs do that, and they check the harnesses at the end of each day to make sure they're still tight.'

'Do you mean they never take them off?'

'That's right, the Bogs don't care about anyone else, especially donkeys; they think they're stupid animals and don't deserve any better.'

'Hmm, well, first things first,' said Dick, taking a small pot to the stream to fill with water. 'We need to clean his wounds before we do anything else.'

'Of course,' said the moorhen.

Lucky settled down at the side of the track. Dick soon set about tending the wounds while the moorhen carefully trickled water over Lucky's dry lips. The donkey lapped feebly at it, desperately drawing in as much as he could.

8

While the stricken donkey struggled beneath weighty skies, Inspector Hooter and his faithful squad were flying through clear skies of the richest blue. The inspector knew he only had two hours of good daylight left, but so far had found no clue as to the whereabouts of Dick or his horse. He called out to the constables each side of him, 'If you were trying to hide a large horse, where would you go?'

PC Roberts replied, 'Not out in the open, that's for sure, sir.'

'How about the town?' said PC James. 'There are plenty of buildings to hide a horse in.'

'Hmm, I think you might be right,' replied Hooter. 'Davidsmeadow is the nearest town; we'll start there and see what we find – head west, Constables.'

Surrounded by rolling hills and open fields, Davidsmeadow was an attractive town situated towards the western end of the South Downs. It wasn't a large town by any means but able to sustain the needs of the surrounding localities.

Within five minutes the police ducks were circling above the streets and shops. The inspector soon realized the hopelessness of his task. To find one particular mallard among several hundred milling about the streets below would be virtually impossible.

'We shall have to land,' he called, 'follow my lead.' A large pond on the heath at the southern edge of the town caught his eye. He couldn't think why the water held such a strong attraction, but it was as good a place to start as any.

All manner of birds were enjoying the afternoon sunshine around the pond.

Baby moorhens, coots and ducklings were having a fine time in the play area under the watchful eye of their parents. They soon stopped swinging and sliding when the seven mallards approached to land beside them. By the time the Flying Squad had landed a considerable crowd had gathered, curiously looking them up and down.

'Cor,' said the youngsters, beguiled by the dazzling helmet badges.

'Ooh, wonderful,' the mothers sighed.

Very conscious of the onlookers' attention, Hooter felt slightly embarrassed by what he was about to say. He looked around at the growing crowd, comprising families of moorhens, coots, and geese; even a swan family had come to gaze. *I need to address my constables in private.* He cast his eye along the water's edge and spied a rowing boat beside a small jetty, normally for use by the lifeguard to rescue any bird who might fall in the water.

Aha – I'll commandeer the rowing boat and row out to the middle of the lake and hold conference with my squad there, out of earshot of the locals. The inspector stood smartly in front of his squad. 'Attention, right turn, quick-waddle.' The constables briskly waddled in line behind the inspector and made their way to the jetty.

'Squad, halt,' called the inspector. 'Are you the lifeguard?' he said to a fit looking white goose wearing a vest with 'Lifeguard' written on it. The goose looked at the inspector, and then looked down at his vest. The six constables, not impressed by his sarcasm, leaned forward as one, and gave the goose as mean a look as they could muster, which wasn't very mean at all.

'Yes, that is me,' said the goose.

'I am Inspector Hooter of the Flying Squad, and I am

commandeering this rowing boat in the name of the law.'

'I don't think that would be a very good idea,' said the goose in a matter-of-fact kind of way.

'Well, I'm sorry if that's what you think, sir, but I must insist,' said the inspector.

The goose looked at the constables who were still doing their best to look menacing. 'Okay then, if you put it like that, I suppose you had better take it.'

'That's more like it, my friend,' said the inspector. 'Now, if you would be so kind as to hold the boat steady while my constables and I get in, I would be most grateful.'

The goose did as he was asked and duly held the boat steady while the inspector carefully stepped aboard and took up position facing forward at the bow, (the pointy end). The constables then sat two to each seat behind him, facing to the rear, (or stern in boaty terms.)

'PC Roberts and James, have you got hold of the oars?'

'We're ready, sir,' came the reply.

'Right then – cast off if you please, Mr Lifeguard,' shouted the inspector. The goose set them free from the jetty and gave the boat a gentle push away from the side.

'Nice and steady, Constables, in, out, in, out,' called the inspector. The squad's colours glistened in the sunlight as the boat made steady progress away from the shore.

'Ooh, how wonderful,' gushed the mums. 'So brave.'

'Yeah, yeah, very clever,' grumbled the dads.

The lifeguard said nothing, but he couldn't conceal the wry smile on his face.

It wasn't too long before the squad reached the centre of the pond, and the inspector said in a low voice, 'Stop rowing, and ship the oars.' The oars were swivelled round in the rowlocks and rested on the sides of the boat.

'Right, now listen up,' the inspector went on, still keeping his voice down to be sure no one on the shore could hear him. 'The fact is this, I have reason to believe that the mallard you suspect of being a highway duck is in fact quite innocent of the crimes levied against him. His real name is Dick Waters-Edge.' The constables looked bemused, except PC Thomas who was already aware of the situation. Hooter spent the next ten minutes explaining how they had to find Dick and his big horse and help them keep a low profile, at least until the perpetrators of the stagecoach kidnapping had been found.

The constables had never relished the prospect of arresting the big horse with the soft eyes, but now, relieved by the inspector's revelations they looked forward to meeting him once more.

'The horse is our best hope of finding them,' said Hooter. 'Finding the mallard would be like looking for an ant in an ant hill, but the horse will stick out like a sore thumb in these surroundings.'

'How much time do we have to look for them, sir?' asked PC Russell.

'A good question, Constable; we must resume our hunt for the kidnappers tomorrow, so we must try hard to find young Dick and his horse today if possible. I suggest we make our way back to the shore and start our search right away.'

The inspector had barely finished what he was saying when PC Howard spoke up alarmingly. 'Sir!'

'What is it, Constable?'

'It's our feet, sir; they seem to be getting wet.' They all looked down to see three inches of water swilling around in the bottom of the boat.

'Good heavens,' exclaimed Hooter, 'that's pond water; this boat must have a leak.'

Sure enough, the boat had a hole in the side; a hole which was above the waterline when the boat was empty, but with seven large mallards aboard, the water was now above the hole, and slowly but surely filling the boat.

'Quick as you can, turn the boat round and row for all you're worth.' A flush of embarrassment washed over the inspector at the thought of sinking in the middle of the pond. *Whatever should we do if that happens?*

Roberts and James called the time to each other and rowed as strongly as they could towards the jetty. 'In, out, in, out.'

With one hundred yards to go there was now six inches of water in the bottom of the boat. PC Howard squashed himself against the hole in an effort to slow the ingress of water, but with little effect. With seventy-five yards to go, the top of the boat was only six inches above the waterline. As the boat filled so it got heavier and more difficult to row.

'In, out, in, out,' called Roberts and James, vigorously. They were now up to their knees in water. Fifty yards to go, the onlookers watched from the shore with utmost concern.

'Oh my, do you think the police can swim?' asked one lady mallard.

'Oh, I don't really know, why would they ever need to?' replied another.

Only twenty yards to go. 'Well done, keep it up, we're nearly there.' Hooter did his best to encourage Roberts and James in their valiant effort. Sadly, they were just ten yards from the jetty when the boat finally succumbed to the weight of the water and sank beneath them. The onlookers gasped in amazement to see the seven mallards floating on the surface, and maintaining the same positions they had occupied before the boat sank. Roberts and James still had hold of the oars, but they were of little use without a boat to row.

'Listen very carefully, here's what we shall do,' whispered the inspector, trying not to sound flustered while a thousand miniature ducks frantically did the breast stroke in his stomach. 'I want you all to turn round so that you're facing the same way as me, and then very carefully move your feet back and forth in the water – I don't know why but I've a feeling that might help.' The constables had never heard of such a thing before, but in true disciplined fashion they did as they were told without question. They were amazed to find themselves slowly moving through the water, pushing their inspector ahead of them. *Weird!*

The crowd applauded and cheered as the police waddled ashore in pairs, helmets at precisely the correct angle of course.

'Right, where's the lifeguard?' said Hooter in a stern voice.

'Here I am,' said the goose.

'Ah, yes, well there seems to be something wrong with your boat.'

'I know,' said the goose, 'it's got a hole in it.'

'Then why didn't you tell us that before we put our lives at risk?' said Hooter.

'I tried to, but you wouldn't listen,' insisted the goose. 'And your constables looked a bit mean if you asked me.'

The inspector could see the goose's point, but he felt he had to say something more to bring the matter to a conclusion without losing face.

'Good heavens!' he said in a raised voice for all to hear. 'You're very lucky it was us in that boat and not some untrained buffoons who might well have gone down with it.' It was then that he noticed the large number of ducklings and other youngsters watching and listening to him. He turned to them and said in his most expert voice. 'Now listen, children, it's important that you don't try this at home; swimming is only for the experts, and for fish of course, do you understand?'

'Yes, sir,' the youngsters squeaked, much to the relief of their parents.

And so, with no time to waste, the squad headed off in the direction of the town centre to start their search for the big brown horse.

The goose stood on his jetty looking at the two oars floating on the water, marking the spot where his rowing boat lay beneath. *Bloomin' ducks, daft if you ask me.*

***

The night crept over the horizon by the stone bridge. Lucky had recovered slightly. He raised his head from the ground and shifted himself to get more comfortable. Punch laid down next to him, and before long Lucky was resting his head on Punch's warm belly, rising and falling gently with each comforting breath of his giant friend. Dick and the moorhen soon followed suit by snuggling up to the horse's substantial neck.

So ended their day with all four of them under a blanket, cuddled up together for warmth in what seemed a very unwelcoming land. They slowly drifted into sleep, each with their own thoughts. Punch hoped Lucky would be better in the morning. The moorhen thought about her family and wondered where oblivion was. Meanwhile, Dick tried to figure out what a 'Bog' was. As for Lucky, he was still in pain, but he knew he was among friends, and sometimes that's all a donkey has.

***

The efforts of the Flying Squad to find Dick and the horse by sundown had proved fruitless.

Little did they know they were searching in completely the wrong place. As daylight faded over Davidsmeadow the seven very tired police ducks settled down for the night in a local hostelry. The news of them floating on the water had gone before them, and they found themselves having to field many questions as to how they had learned to do such a thing.

'Oh,' the inspector would reply, 'it was nothing really, it just came naturally.'

Having retired for an early night, they soon drifted off to sleep while more not-quite-right moments filled their heads. *Strange how the water held us up from underneath – how did it do that?*

9

A new day dawned. Dick stirred. It was about five o' clock, but it didn't look like it. A deep purple sky grew along the horizon where the Sun tried in vain to penetrate the cold depressing air. A few moments later the moorhen roused. She began fretting almost before her eyes were open. 'Oh dear, oh dear.'

Dick took a bag of pellets from his saddlebag and mixed them into a mash with water from the stream. It didn't look too good but tasted okay, and so the two of them sat and ate, and chatted.

'I hope you don't think I was rude to you yesterday,' said Dick.

'Oh, no, not at all,' replied the moorhen. 'I don't know what I would have done if you and your horse hadn't come along when you did. I hate to think what would have happened to my poor donkey.'

'In all the commotion I didn't even ask your name,' said Dick, chewing on the stodgy mash.

'It's Maywell. Mrs Moira Maywell.' A solitary teardrop slipped from the corner of her eye. 'And I have a husband named William and a young son, a chick named Bill. I'm so worried I may never see them again.' She began crying openly, letting go of all the anguish she had been carrying for the past year.

Dick comforted her with a wing around her shoulder. 'Things will get better, don't you worry,' he said, giving her a gentle squeeze of encouragement which felt rather odd, him being a relatively young bird and her an adult. *But sometimes adults need a cuddle too.*

Moira's voice trembled. 'You've been very kind to Lucky and me; it's so nice to talk to someone. The Bogs discourage talking in the fort.'

'They have a fort?'

'Yes, with stone walls to keep us in and others out. Inside the fort are huts where they keep all the workers locked up. They only let us out to work for them. All I seem to do is fill Lucky's baskets with rocks, and then walk him to the two turrets further down the road.'

'Will the Bogs notice your absence?'

'They will if I'm not back by the end of today. I must get Lucky up and be on my way.' She moved to get up with tears dripping from the end of her bill, but Dick pressed down on her shoulder to stop her.

'You can't possibly go back there. Look in the other direction; do you see the brightness in the morning sky? That's where I come from. You could be happy there with no nasty Bogs to worry you.'

'You don't understand,' she said, 'if I don't go back to the fort I'll never see my son or my husband again, and the Bogs will probably come looking for me. Wherever I go they will find me and punish me to make an example of me; I won't be safe wherever I go.'

'How many workers do they keep in the fort?' asked Dick, getting more concerned with every passing second.

'Oh, too many to count...a hundred I guess. I must go back before something dreadful happens to my family. Don't you see?'

While the two of them talked, Punch lay quietly. His hazel eyes were watching them, and his furry ears were listening. He didn't understand spoken words because he was a horse, but their aura was plain to see. He watched their expressions and their gestures, and heard the tone of their voices. His whispers spoke to him.

There, you see, the moorhen is a victim just as the donkey is a victim; she also needs your help.

The whispers calmed his mind. He didn't enjoy the feelings of discord which he'd felt towards the moorhen the day before, and was relieved to know she was in no way to blame for this predicament. From that moment a strength gathered pace inside him, a desire to put things right.

Lucky began fidgeting. His first sensation was that of warmth. With his head resting on Punch's belly he drew comfort from the slow rise and fall of the big horse's ribs. Punch kept perfectly still, a rock for Lucky to lean on while he struggled to get up. Slowly, the feeling came back to the donkey's legs and he was able to stand alone. 'Hee-haw, haw, hee-haw,' he brayed in celebration at being back on his feet, albeit in a very wobbly way. A thousand little donkeys danced inside him before finally retaking their rightful places and restoring his balance. Punch vented a loud fluffy huff while Dick and Moira cheered excitedly. The hee-hawing was clearly getting a little out of control, so Punch carefully raised his muzzle beneath Lucky's chin. The donkey stopped braying immediately. They stared into each other's eyes while something passed between the two of them. After a few moments Punch took a couple of steps backwards. Lucky gave one little 'haw' and settled down.

Not quite understanding what had just gone on, but happy to leave Lucky in Punch's care, Dick and Moira continued discussing what to do next.

'What will happen to you if you go back to the fort without the wicker baskets?'

'I will be judged for disobeying the Bog's orders, and then I'll probably be fired; that's what happens to anyone who is found guilty.'

'If they fire you at least you won't have to do anymore horrid work for them.'

'I don't mean fired like being given the sack, I mean fired like from a huge catapult into nowhere.'

'Oh, I see,' said Dick not really understanding what she meant. 'What if you're not found guilty?'

'Everyone is found guilty.'

'In that case, we've no time to lose. We must check Lucky's wounds and then you can head for Smallbeef where I come from.' He thought for a moment and then added, 'I'm pretty sure the police aren't far behind me, so they may well find you and help you. In the meantime, Punch and I will make our way to the fort and see what we can do for your husband and son.'

'You must be very careful, the Bogs are very suspicious of strangers,' said Moira, fretting as only she could.

Dick continued with the questions while they cleaned Lucky's wounds. 'What do the Bogs look like?'

Moira stood on tiptoe and stretched a wing as high as she could. 'They're a bit higher than this,' she said, 'and sometimes they wear grey cloaks to hide themselves.'

Dick looked up at her wing tip and imagined a creature a good deal taller than him. *Wow*, he thought, *they must be eight feet tall at least*...and then a thought escaped his bill. 'Oh crikey, I think we've already met them back in Smallbeef.'

'Did they have dreadful eyes and a long beak? Moira asked.'

'Yes, and I don't think their boss will forget me or Punch in a hurry, we bumped into him and made him crash into a load of bushes. They were beating up the police at the time, really nasty they were.'

'Oh dear, that sounds like them. You mustn't go near them, you really mustn't.'

'As I see it, we don't really have much choice. Your husband and son, and all your friends, are in a bit of a pickle' Dick replied.

'Me and Punch might be able to delay things until help arrives. I'm sure the police will find you, and then you can tell them all about it. With any luck they will catch us up before long.'

'I do hope you're right,' Moira fretted.

Dick gently stroked the donkey's neck. 'There you are, my friend, that's the best we can do for now. Just make sure it's kept as clean as possible, and when you get to Smallbeef you must find Mrs Waters-Edge; she'll get the farrier to look at your feet.'

Lucky didn't understand the words any more than Punch did, but he knew they were kindly, and he sensed a renewed vitality in Moira which he hoped would see them through their ordeal.

***

Inspector Hooter was running out of time. He and his constables had scoured the town, looking in every possible hiding place where a horse might fit. 'Dear me, where can he be?' He knew he'd already spent more time than he should searching for the mallard and the horse. Reluctantly, he turned to his squad. 'We can't spend any longer here, we shall have to make our way back to the stagecoach and take up the search for the kidnappers before they get too much of a head start on us. For all we know, Dick and the horse may well have gone in that direction anyway.'

Without further delay Hooter led the Flying Squad into the air and headed east in the hope of picking up a trail – either trail would do.

***

'Thank you so much,' said Moira, wrapping her wings around Dick's neck in a farewell embrace. 'You're a lovely duck.' She picked up the piece of rope to tie around Lucky's neck. The donkey flattened his ears tight to his head at the thought of being tethered again. Moira looked at him, and then she looked at the rope before throwing it as far away as she could. 'You won't need that anymore,' she said. Lucky brayed, and Punch huffed his approval.

As soon as Punch was saddled and ready, Dick turned to Moira, saying, 'Just follow the road towards the blue sky and you'll be in Smallbeef before you know it, and remember to ask for Mrs Waters-Edge.'

Moira turned to Punch and stroked his cheek, and then she turned again and rested her wing on Lucky's shoulder as the pair of them set off in the hope of getting help.

Dick couldn't see her face, but he knew she was crying silently. He swung himself up into the saddle, and without a word being said, Punch moved off towards the unwelcoming land of the Bogs. Occasionally Dick would turn his head to see the moorhen and donkey shrinking into the distance. Likewise, Moira looked back to see the rounded rump of the horse and its rider fading into the murky lifeless mist that hung in the air, until finally, they could be seen no more.

10

Keen to get on, Punch picked up the pace to a brisk trot. Dick found this to be the most difficult to maintain. His legs being relatively short made it difficult for him to rise with Punch's movement; occasionally he would go out of time with the motion of the horse's croup, resulting in a substantial blow to his soft rump.

Sensing Dick's discomfort, and wanting to ease the strain on his own back, Punch took the initiative and broke into a canter. Dick gladly adjusted his posture and soon settled into the smoother rhythm of the Suffolk's gait. The landscape grew evermore barren, the grass and gorse cowering beneath heavyweight skies.

They both sensed they weren't alone. It wasn't long before their suspicions were realized. A fine wisp of smoke could be seen rising from beyond the horizon directly ahead, a chimney or a campfire perhaps. The smoke had barely found its freedom before mushrooming against the underside of the cloud which lay like a dirty quilt over the land.

The horse cantered onward through the desolate countryside, his heart and soul undaunted by so unfriendly a place. Eventually, the roof of a building appeared; Dick stretched up out of the saddle to extend his view. *Is it occupied? Is it a Bog outpost?*

Dick couldn't imagine a more depressing place on Earth than where he was right now. Being a duck he was generally of a cheerful disposition, but try as he might the foreboding atmosphere around him was beginning take its toll. He wished he could turn round and head for home. His eyes wetted at the thought of his mother waiting and worrying for him back at Smallbeef, and of his father who had been missing for more than a year.

Punch broke the rhythm of his canter and slowed to a walk, bringing Dick out of his sombre thoughts. Dick couldn't see what had caused the horse to change so abruptly without warning, but he was sure Punch knew best. His trust was justified when two figures came into view standing in the fug which crept eerily over the ground.

The heavy mist felt its way around Punch's legs at knee height, cool to the touch and potentially hazardous to a horse. From thereon he progressed with extreme caution, feeling uneasy on ground he couldn't see. Dick gave him free rein, quite amazed at how delicate a huge horse could be when necessary.

The two figures were now twenty paces ahead of them, standing quite still on each side of the track. Their lack of colour afforded them excellent camouflage, making it difficult to see any of their features.

They're not small, Dick cast his mind back to his confrontation in Smallbeef recently. *Are these the same creatures, are these Bogs?* He also remembered the description Moira had given when asked what the Bogs looked like. Now ten paces from them, he could see the figures were wearing heavy cloaks from top to bottom, with a capacious hood shrouding their heads and faces completely.

Punch drew level with them and stopped. Through wide eyes he tried to see into the hoods. There was nothing to see, all signs of life hidden. For a moment Dick thought perhaps there was no one in the cloaks at all. *Maybe they're just dummies, like scarecrows, there to frighten off the less determined visitor.* Punch wasn't about to be fooled; he turned his lips inside out to heighten his sensory perception, not a pretty sight but extremely effective. He couldn't see whatever was hiding within the hoods, but he could certainly smell and taste them in the air. He relaxed his lips and breathed steadily through his nostrils, his breath contrasted white against the cold grey air. The two figures leaned back as if to distance themselves from the uncouth creature polluting their space. *Horse, ugh.*

After a few silent seconds Dick spoke up. 'Erm, hello, excuse me?' No response, no movement, no sound. 'I was wondering if there was somewhere I could rest my horse and get some food.'

Very slowly both sentinels raised an arm, and without uttering a word they gestured towards the single building ahead, taking care not to let their cloaks slip.

'Thank you, sir,' replied Dick, being very careful not to say anything that might offend them. Punch moved on without being asked, his unshod hooves gingerly feeling the way. The grey figures lowered their arms and resumed their statuesque pose.

Punch could sense Dick's anxiety but his heart longed to do the right thing. He knew the injustice to Lucky and all the other donkeys in this awful land had to stop.

The building, standing close to the left hand side of the road, presented a ghoulish appearance; its ancient grey timbers beneath an equally grey shingle roof did nothing to relieve it of its grim complexion. Smoke vented lazily from the chimney only to press up against the cloud so low that Dick could almost reach up and touch it.

A dim light filtered through the front window, casting a feeble yellow tint onto the veranda which ran along the entire front of the building. On the veranda sat a solitary figure in a wooden rocking chair. He too was grey, cloaked as the others were with his features concealed, slowly rocking back and forth. Even when sitting down he looked tall.

Twenty paces beyond the building stood a pair of donkeys harnessed to a small wagon, both were filthy and neglected; they turned their heads and brayed despondently at the newcomers. Punch huffed in reply, but his progress was halted when the sound of faint laughter and music could be heard coming from within the building. Dick's heart lifted, *Thank heavens, some friendly company perhaps*. Punch kept his gaze on the donkeys while Dick dismounted. After a good stretch and a ruffle of his feathers he whispered, 'This must be an inn or a hostelry of some sort'.

Punch was not at all convinced he was welcome.

Keen to get inside and mingle with the locals, Dick muttered quietly to himself. 'Perhaps this place isn't as bad as Moira Maywell made it out to be.' He waddled a step closer to the character in the rocking chair. 'Excuse me,' he asked, 'is there somewhere I can stable my horse?' The grey figure slowly raised an arm without revealing himself. The cloak pointed to a stable behind the inn, barely visible through the murky fog.

'Thank you, sir.' Dick took the reins and led Punch towards the rickety stable doors, above which hung a single lantern. The light from it struggled to illuminate a faded sign which read, 'Stables – No donkeys.'

Punch huffed disconsolately, but before either of them could change their minds the stable doors opened and a voice came from inside.

'You'll be wantin' to stay the night then?' From the shadows stepped a duck, a dull dowdy duck. At first Dick thought it was an older female because it had none of the colour of a male such as himself. However, as the bird drew closer he realized it was a male mallard just like him, but of indiscernible age, with colours lost beneath a covering of dirt and dust. Dick couldn't understand how a duck could let itself get in such a state; one thing ducks do well is clean themselves, but not this one. Dick was relieved when the dirty duck stopped short, saving him the embarrassment of having to step away.

'He's a 'andsome beast and no mistake,' said the dishevelled mallard. 'I don't think we've ever 'ad a 'orse the size of this one 'ere before – like a mountain 'e is. By the way, I'm the stable-keeper on account of I looks after the stable y' see.' He reached forward to take the reins from Dick's grasp. Dick resisted at first but didn't want to appear rude. Once the keeper had hold of the reins he led Punch into the stable with Dick following close behind.

Beyond the reach of the outside lantern little could be seen within, until a soft glow came to life in the far corner. The source of the light was hidden behind a timber partition with no hint of who had lit it.

'I'll just fetch that,' said the keeper. He let go of the reins and waddled to the back of the stable where he disappeared behind the partition and could be heard to mutter, 'Thank you, sir, thank you.' He soon reappeared holding a hurricane lamp which, although wasn't overly bright, did at least lend a pleasing glow to the surroundings. Moments later another lamp was lit from behind the partition.

Dick piped up, 'I'll get that,' eager to see who or what was hiding from them.

'No, sir, no, 'tis my job and mine alone – I must get the lamp, thank you.'

The keeper jostled his way ahead of Dick and quickly produced a second hurricane lamp. Each lamp was then hung from one of two large ornate iron hooks, one roughly in the centre of the stable and the other just inside the entrance doors, leaving the back of the stable in dark shadow.

Despite his initial worries on entering the stable, Dick didn't feel so bad once he'd got used to the warm orange light. He could see only one cubicle for a horse to rest in, but it was well tended to, with clean straw bedding and plenty of fresh hay held in a manger, and a large bucket of drinking water on the floor.

The keeper uttered a few comforting words to Dick while leading Punch into the cubicle. 'Now you just go an' get yerself a liquid refreshment an' some food inside you, sir, and leave me to tend to your 'orse – and marvellous 'e is too, an' no mistake.'

Dick gave Punch a long hug. 'This doesn't seem too bad, old friend. You rest here and I'll see what I can find out in the inn. I won't be too long.' On his way out he tried to sneak another look into the far corner where the lamps had come from, but the shadows concealed their secret well, giving no clue – nothing.

As soon as he was outside, Dick turned to see the mallard dragging the stable doors closed. Swirling eddies of fug soon covered the marks carved in the dust, hiding the evidence of them ever having been opened.

Dick cast his gaze toward the donkeys as he crossed the yard, they were still harnessed to the cart at the side of the inn, waiting, unmoved. *Hmm, I wonder if I should say anything about their condition.* He continued on his way, feeling vulnerable without his trusty horse by his side. *He's a big fella, and clever with it, if he could talk he'd probably be cleverer than me. Perhaps I should tell him that some time, perhaps he already knows. Anyway, let's see what's going on in here.*

He stepped up onto the veranda. The lone figure was still there rocking slowly back and forth. There was only one entrance door and that was closed, no doubt to keep the damp mists out. Dick paused outside for a few moments to peruse a sign above the door, a roughly cut piece of wood with words carved equally roughly in it. He couldn't quite make out what the sign said, partly because of the poor light and partly because of the generally grubby state of the building. He squinted and tried to read it quietly to himself. 'B – of – something,' he concentrated hard, 'are welcome to stay.' The remainder of the writing was completely obscured by shadow and dust-laden cobwebs. After a few seconds he gave up trying to read it.

'Ah well, at least it looks like birds are welcome.' The door opened with a rusty squeak. He cautiously stepped over the threshold and waddled three paces inside and paused again. The door swung shut behind him with such force as to let loose the sign outside and send it clattering onto the veranda. Now it could be read, but Dick was in no position to see it.

His feet remained planted on the dusty wooden floor, and he slowly turned his head in a full arc as ducks do, surveying the entire room. He was puzzled; he'd expected to see others drinking and laughing, but there was no one to be seen. He noticed the unusually high ceiling. *No doubt because some of the patrons are quite tall, like the one outside.* He could still hear the laughter and the voices, and the chinking of glasses, but the room seemed empty. He shuffled across the floor, hungry for clues. At the far end of the room was a bar, but no bartender. The laughter seemed to be coming from that direction, but he could still see no one.

At the bar he stood on tiptoe to see over. At first he could see very little of note, but after a few seconds the poor light yielded an old wind-up gramophone player resting on top of a bar stool; it whirred round and round with the crude needle wavering in the grooves of an old record. It was from this that that jovial sounds were emanating.

'What on Earth?' He had no more time to think before the sign from outside slid across the floor, coming to rest at his feet. He looked down at it; now he could read it quite easily. *Beasts of Grey are welcome to stay, all the rest shall become our prey.*

He shivered and turned to see how the sign had come to be at his feet. In the doorway stood the cloaked figure from the rocking chair, his head almost touching the ceiling. The door creaked its way shut behind him, creating an atmosphere of confinement. The figure remained silent, his cloak concealing his gaze.

Realizing the creature was not going to move aside, Dick looked over his shoulder hoping to see another way out, but another two figures were now standing in each of the far corners, blocking his exit.

Dick was still unsure if he should be scared or not. *After all, these chaps might be quite friendly for all I know. Perhaps they're just shy.* But the little ducks in the pit of his stomach quaked with dread.

The talking and laughing became slower and slower, distorted and lower in tone as the gramophone unwound itself. Finally, it ground to a halt leaving an unnerving silence to fill the room.

The figure at the door grumbled deeply. The coarse tones brought back recent memories. Now Dick was in no doubt. His thousand miniature ducks ran for cover, turning his stomach over as they went.

The figure's cloak parted at the front. 'Well, well, if it isn't my little duck in the fancy blue hat. Remember me?'

Dick slowly raised his eyes from staring at the floor. The clawed feet; the scaly bowed legs; the barrel chest, and the wings that made the air scream as they dived from high above, they were all there. The wings were folded against the sides of the body, the clawed hands clearly visible resting on the floor. Then there was that face, the razor sharp serrations of the long beak, and most menacing of all, the black lifeless eyes of no reflection.

Dick craned his neck way back to meet the gaze of the giant reptile looking down at him. With their eyes fixed on each other, the creature tilted his head slowly to one side to reveal the spade-like tip of his long tail.

'Do you know what I am?' the gruff voice asked.

'Yes,' replied Dick with a slight waver, 'I think so.'

'Oh, you only think so, do you? Well let me clarify the matter for you, hmm, shall I?'

'Er, yes please.' Dick hoped so much that Punch would come thundering through the door to his rescue, but it was not to be.

'I'm a pterosaur, a Beast of Grey, that's B – O – G, Bog, and so are my two colleagues standing behind you. But you know that don't you – because we've met before haven't we.' The Bog's voice rose to a dreadful piercing screech. 'You and your ugly horse, we've met before!'

Dick stepped back a pace to avoid the creature's breath, and then for the first time in his young life he stood square on and stretched himself as tall as he could, puffing up his chest feathers to complete his brave posture. His thousand miniature ducks did likewise, empowering his heart with courage far beyond his weight.

Dwarfing the duck, the Bog sneered cruelly before continuing. 'And we have a score to settle with you because we can't have birds thinking they can get the better of us.' He paused for two seconds before bellowing so loud that it hurt Dick's ears. 'Can we!'

The ferocity of the Bog's outburst sent Dick staggering backwards into the grasp of the other two Bogs. His wings were held firmly at his sides while a sack was pulled over his head. He struggled as best he could but he was no match for the hardened reptiles holding him. The sack had a strange smell, like something a doctor would administer. He quickly felt drowsy; his mind began swimming and turning within his head. His legs turned to jelly.

The Bogs strengthened their grip to prevent him falling to the floor.

'Bring him now,' the leader scowled, 'put him in the crate on the cart outside and take him back to the fort tomorrow.' His eyes narrowed. 'I'll deal with his horse later.'

Those were the last harsh words Dick heard as the volume faded from his ears, and total darkness filled his head.

11

If you've ever seen a moorhen walking you'll know why they have wings and live on the water. With somewhat oversize feet resembling those of a circus clown, Moira found walking such distances very tiresome. Every so often Lucky would have to slow down and wait for her to catch up, this in spite of his own progress being slowed by his deformed hooves.

'It's no use, Lucky, I'll have to rest for a while, my legs are killing me,' said Moira, parking herself on a dry clump of grass at the side of the track.

'Ooh, my poor legs,' she sighed.

The dismal light hung relentlessly all around them. The few gorse bushes and the dull grass sprouting from the grey sand did little to lighten the ambience.

The stillness lulled Moira into a state of day-dreaming, and she soon found herself reminiscing times gone by; times when she lived in a land of sunshine and colours like the one she was hoping to find at Smallbeef.

Lucky recognized the look in her eye and realized he might be in for quite a wait, so he too relaxed and sat down as best he could to rest his legs. His emotions were as mixed up as Moira's; after a life of slavery and punishment he was unsure of how he should feel about his freedom. He knew he wanted to get as far away from Fort Bog as he could, but most of all he felt relief at not having the awful burden of rocks on his back. The air resting over him was a revelation; Mother Nature's own hands soothing and cooling his injuries.

Moira stared into the clouded sky. Her mind slowly filled with memories which had been kept locked away for many moons. She remembered growing up among reeds and long grasses. She recalled foraging in the undergrowth for seeds, small fruit, and snails. But she couldn't remember walking far. *So why am I walking now?* Something ruffled her memory; the veil that had shut out all thoughts of her previous life slowly lifted, no more her gaoler.

'That's it – of course.' A hint of excitement crept into her voice. 'I couldn't possibly, could I?'

Lucky had never seen such a look of enthusiasm on her face. Unsure of what to expect next, he watched, bemused, as Moira got to her feet.

The moorhen looked up the road, and then down the road. 'There's certainly enough runway,' she muttered, 'but these are so stiff.' She stretched her wings as wide as she could. 'I can't remember how to do it, I'm sure I'll get it wrong, but I must try.'

She positioned herself facing straight down the road and flapped her wings up and down a few times for practice, a lot of dust issued from her feathers in the process. In comparison to her body her wings were overly long and wide. 'They do work!' she exclaimed. 'Oh, that feels so good, but, oh my, what next?' She looked at Lucky, and he looked at her, then they both looked down the road; it seemed very straight with very little to crash into and no wind to consider.

'This is it!' She took a deep breath, tucked her wings in by her sides and began to run, quite slowly at first, lifting her feet up higher than she really needed. *Don't want to trip over my own feet.* Next she opened her wings and began stroking the air as it slipped past her body. No difference at first, until she instinctively swept her wings in more of a circular motion to pull the air towards her. Lighter and lighter she got. After twenty paces she was still on the ground, but things were improving by the second. Faster went her wings. Faster went her legs. She stretched her neck forward as far as she could; her body was now going faster than her legs could manage. Her heart filled with vitality such as she'd never known. Her legs were running in the air. She was airborne and moving faster than she could ever remember, only as high as two donkeys, but she was definitely flying. Mother Nature cradled her in her effort, guiding and steadying her until finally letting go. Up Moira went, with unfettered exhilaration coursing through her veins.

Cruising through the loaded sky her confidence grew with every stroke of her wings. The underside of the gloomy clouds wiped against her back, but she had no regard for their cold touch, nor a thought of what might be lurking above them. Onward she flew with a light in her eye, singing at the top of her voice for all to hear. 'Oh, how wonderful, I'm wonderful, I'm a bird and I can fly – look at me, Lucky – look at me, I'm really flying!'

Lucky struggled to his feet, wincing in pain and braying loudly. Hearing his call, Moira stilled her wings and turned gently to retrace her course. For the first time in a long time she dared to think things might turn out right after all. With a beautiful smile on her face she glided towards her braying companion, but her joy was short lived — Thud!

Something struck the back of her head. Her senses reeled, her vision blurred, and she went into a spin with one wing stuck out and the other folded halfway awkwardly in. Her flight was over, her smile gone. She was dazed, but there was no mistaking the dreadful shape that circled and watched her plummet towards the ground. It was a Bog. He'd come from out of the clouds and struck her with his tail. Now he simply followed her down – all the way to make sure his job was done.

Lucky hollered frantically. 'Hee-haw, hee-haw.' He ran to where he thought his friend most likely to land, stumbling over his feet and forgetting about his own pain. *Please, not now. Don't let her crash.*

The Bog had the strength to catch and carry Moira if he wanted, but he didn't. Moira stretched her good wing as much as she could in an effort to slow her fall. It had little effect. She spiralled towards the ground, the wind conspiring to take her breath away.

Is this it, is this how it ends? My last flight nearly over? Her nostrils tingled with emotion, tears of sadness welled up in her eyes.

'Not so fast, Moira Maywell.' A voice spoke in her ear; a grip around her sides, firm and strong. 'The next world will wait.'

Moira peered beneath her belly to see two bright yellow hands gripping her, or were they feet gripping her? It was hard to tell, but they had amazing claws curling tenderly around her. Then she looked from one side to the other to see the longest wings in the world stretched out, carrying her calmly through the clear warm air.

'Now what's happening?' she cried, fully expecting to be carried off to a nest high on a cliff top to be fed to a family of hungry Bogs. Emotionally exhausted Moira tried to wriggle her way free, but the grip was unassailable. She looked to her right, mesmerized by the vast wing as it equably caressed the air beneath it, powering the pair of them swiftly along. Then she looked to the left. 'Oh my word!' she yelled. Right next to her was a face, brilliant red with deep furrows around a sparkling blue eye, looking right at her.

Having shown himself, the red-faced Bog straightened his neck and resumed his flying pose. Every so often the clawed feet adjusted their grip on the moorhen, slightly tightening some digits while loosening others.

Is he trying to keep me comfortable? Moira wondered. Surely not.

'Not long now,' said the voice before enquiring, 'Would you say I was ugly?'

This question confounded Moira; the last thing she expected was to get into a discussion about whether someone was ugly or not, especially someone who was probably about to eat her.

'Er, well er, erm,' she stumbled over her words.

'Please say what you feel. Believe me, it will have no effect on your future.'

'Oh, I see,' said Moira, not knowing if that was a bad thing or a good thing. 'Well erm, I wouldn't say you're ugly, not really ugly anyway.'

'But you think I am a bit ugly.'

'Well it's difficult to say really.'

The Bog craned its neck once again and appeared eye to eye by the side of Moira. 'Does my eye not sparkle with the light of the world and all the flowers and the Sun and the sky?'

Moira gazed into the eye beside her. The feeling of love and warmth gathered strength the longer she looked into it, compelling her to answer. 'Well, I suppose…erm. Yes, it really is very lovely, really it is.'

'And is my face not the colour of the reddest rose in the prime of its bloom?'

Moira looked again at the face alongside hers. She felt no embarrassment or discomfort at lingering in the eye of this strange creature, which she still thought might be about to eat her. 'Yes, I suppose it is,' she replied.

So, you would say the flowers and the Sun and the sky and the rose are beautiful?'

'Oh yes, yes most definitely,' Moira replied without hesitation.

'You think this, and yet you still think of me as ugly.'

'Well, no not really, that is, well, I don't know what I think anymore.'

The Bog cruised on with a smile in his eye and the moorhen in his grasp.

Moira was more than a little confused by the goings-on of the last few minutes. She had just had a bizarre conversation with what was arguably a very ugly flying creature, and yet she had found the experience totally heart-warming and kindly.

'I must put you down now and go on my way,' said the Bog as he carefully lowered his precious cargo to the ground.

Moira stood on shaky legs with her wings in a sorry state. 'Oh dear, these are going to take some sorting out.'

'Let me help,' said the red-faced Bog. With uncanny dexterity his claws set about carefully untangling her displaced feathers until all but one were back where they belonged. The feather in question had broken half way along its length. 'There you are, my dear,' said the Bog keeping the broken part in his grasp, 'I'm sure you'll manage fine without this little piece.'

Moira held her wings wide and looked to both sides. 'That's wonderful, thank you so much.'

Lucky eventually clattered to a halt next to her, braying excitedly. 'Hee-haw, hee-haw.'

The Bog with the red face put his beak beneath the donkey's chin and lifted it gently. The braying stopped. 'Your attacker will probably be back, and not alone. You may be sure of that.'

'What – but,' Moira mumbled, bewildered.

'Hee – haw,' said Lucky, which probably meant the same in this instance.

'I can help you no more for the moment,' said the Bog. 'You must be on your way as quickly as you can. You will reach your coloured land if you don't linger.'

'But, what? Why? Who? I don't understand.' Moira struggled

to get her words into the correct order.

The Bog spread his wings wide, giving Moira no more time for questions. 'Remember to trust in your heart, not in your mind. Your mind does not always see what is there.' His business done, the Bog lifted eerily from the ground in an upright pose. At a height of no more than two trees he brought his body to the horizontal and powered away on wings of immeasurable strength, quickly disappearing into the distant fog in the direction of Fort Bog.

'I think we'd better heed his words,' said Moira,' straightening her wings.

'Hee, hee-haw,' Lucky replied, settling into his painful hobble towards the brighter horizon, now with a glint of hope in his eye.

Moira took to the air in a few strides, this time keeping well away from the clouds. With the cold grey light behind them, the pair continued their way towards the coloured land, each casting a watchful eye skyward, hoping not to see anymore Bogs.

12

'They can't simply vanish without trace,' Inspector Hooter muttered. He paced up and down alongside the abandoned stagecoach, rubbing his bill to aid his thought. 'There must be a clue as to what happened or which way they went.'

The constables patiently waited in line for their orders; they were as mystified as their inspector as to how the passengers could simply disappear.

'Listen up, Constables, spread out and go over the entire area, leave no stone unturned. I don't want anything overlooked, is that clear?'

'Yes, sir.' The constables replied as one and promptly began searching meticulously on and under the coach, in the hedges, under the hedges, around the trees, everywhere they thought a clue might be found.

While rummaging beneath a nearby hazel bush a rustling sound caught PC Thomas's attention. He paused for a moment to listen more carefully. The rustling stopped, but something was there, something trying to elude him. *A hedgehog perhaps.* He reached forward and brushed away a leafy branch. 'Oh, good heavens!' he shouted and fell backwards in shock, his helmet falling over his face.

A family of tiny humans darted out from under the bush and scampered away keeping close to the hedgerow, leaving the constable sitting on his rump at the side of the road.

'Please don't let anyone be looking, please,' he whispered,

hoping to avoid the humiliation of a police duck being frightened by little human beings. He hurriedly straightened his helmet and got to his feet, but unfortunately his embarrassment was complete when he turned to see Inspector Hooter standing before him.

'Oh dear, FS6,' Hooter chuckled, 'we're not afraid of some teeny-weeny humans, are we?'

'No…of course not, sir.'

Hooter couldn't resist another chuckle. 'They don't bite you know, although I have occasionally seen them spit on the ground, and even shout rude words, but they are only human after all.'

No matter how many times Thomas told himself humans are harmless, he couldn't help shivering at the thought of accidently touching one. *All that bare skin, and those little hairy heads and naked bottoms, oooh yuk. Why on Earth would something be made like that?* He shivered again at such thoughts. From then on he took to using a stick to give the undergrowth a careful prod in the hope that any humans would scuttle away before he got too close.

In the meantime Hooter stepped up into the stagecoach and began searching thoroughly between the seats, and then under the seats. 'Hello, what's this?' He pulled a piece of paper from behind a cushion and unravelled it hoping it would help him in his investigation. His heart missed a beat. 'Oh no, not this, oh dear me, no.' He stepped down from the coach. 'Come to me, Constables, quickly, I have some important news.'

The constables immediately stopped their rummaging and gathered round. 'I've just found this on the stagecoach,' said Hooter, holding up the piece of paper. 'I would hazard a guess it was drawn by the same witness who drew the picture of Dick Waters-Edge and his horse.'

Like the other drawing, this one was also a crude affair, probably drawn by a youngster, but there was no doubt of the subject – it was a pterosaur – a Beast of Grey. The constables gulped heavily. The fear behind their eyes was plain to see, a fear which they would have to overcome in their pursuit of an adversary of such overwhelming odds.

'Be brave, Constables, be brave,' said Hooter, bringing them out of their thoughts. 'There's nothing more we can do here, and it's too late to start after them now, so we'll head back to Smallbeef to regroup and prepare ourselves. We'll set off in pursuit of those perishing reptiles first thing in the morning.'

Thoughts of the lovely young lady ducks waiting for them at Smallbeef came to the fore, tempering the sense of dread brought on by the awesome culprits they were about to pursue. With mixed emotions they quickly moved into V formation at an altitude of ten houses, and were soon on their way back to Smallbeef for a welcome respite.

Hazy evening sunshine reached down through the high feathery clouds warming those who hadn't yet sought the refuge of their homes. Perfect flying conditions. Long late shadows cast by trees and hedges lay across the green and yellow land below. Rabbits grazed the grass and dandelion beyond the shadows, stopping occasionally to scan the sky for hawks and the like. Their hind legs would thump out the alarm at the first sign of such an intruder, but the mallards passing swiftly overhead caused them no such concern.

The little humans of that world were a different matter. At the first sign of anything out of the ordinary they would point and argue among themselves, shouting abusively and pushing their way to the nearest hedge to hide under, distrusting everything and everyone.

I wonder why that is? Hooter thought to himself. No one has ever mistreated them. Perhaps they were really horrid in a previous life and they think everyone else is the same. Surely not?

Thankfully, Smallbeef soon came into view. A young lady duck stood in the yard feeding the chickens; she looked up and immediately recognized the sparkle of the helmet badges reflecting the late Sun.

'They're back, they're back,' she shouted at the top of her voice. 'Everybody come and see – our constables are back!' She was promptly joined by the other young ladies, all of whom looked up in deep admiration at the welcome sight.

'Oh, aren't they magnificent!' They all agreed with a long loud gush.

The constables eagerly picked out their sweethearts on the ground below. Even Hooter chanced a quick peek to see if Marion was among the waiting crowd. The squad landed in record time and stood with heads up and helmets vertical, all perfectly in line of course. The inspector's normal routine of debriefing came under pressure when warm feelings stirred in his heart. Marion Waters-Edge waited patiently outside her caravan, looking and loving what she saw, and so was Hooter – and so were all the constables.

'Right, Constables, well done, I'll address you later as to our next move – dismiss.'

The constables were surprised and glad of the inspector's brevity, and hurriedly made their way to their sweethearts' embraces, becoming fonder of Smallbeef by the minute.

'Mmm, come here, my dear Inspector,' said Marion, wrapping her wings around him. She added with a sigh, 'I see you haven't got Dick with you.'

'No, we searched high and low to the west, but there was no sign of him.' He paused tentatively, knowing Marion wouldn't like what he was about to tell her. 'I'm afraid there has been a development in my inquiries.'

'Mmm, and what sort of development is that then?' Marion gently rubbed her cheek on his.

Hooter promptly ushered her into her caravan before continuing, 'We found evidence that confirms your story and clears Dick of kidnapping the passengers on the stagecoach.'

'Well, that's good news,' said Marion with a hint of relief in her voice. 'I dare say the stagecoach simply broke down and they all made their own way home, is that it?'

'No, it isn't,' Hooter continued. 'I have reason to believe it was the pterosaurs who took them.'

'Oh no, do you mean you have to go after them instead?'

'Yes, we have no choice. Those dreadful creatures must be brought to book.'

'But why does it have to be you?'

'Because I am a police duck, that's why.'

'But there are so many of them and so few of you, and you know what happened the last time you met them. They won't forget you in a hurry.'

'I know, but it's my job and there it is; so let's have no more said, my dear, for this might be our last meeting for quite some time.'

With that, they both settled down on the sofa and enjoyed the gentle comfort of each other's closeness, and a cup of tea.

Meanwhile the constables were sitting on the sides of their beds in the makeshift dormitory, each one similarly cuddled up to their sweetheart.

'Oh, my poor brave Thomas, I know you must go, but I really wish you wouldn't,' said Fay.

'But we must follow our leader, it's our job,' replied Thomas. 'Besides, if we don't put things right, who will?'

Fay slowly rubbed her soft cheek along Thomas's bill, neither of them wanting it to end. But they both knew it must.

An hour later they were all sitting at a large rectangular table in the yard, enjoying their alfresco supper. Despite having plenty to say, there was very little conversation going on. Instead, they thought quietly of what the future might have in store for them, and wondered about all the things they might miss out on if the constables failed to return from their quest.

Eventually, Hooter broke the silence. 'I need to speak to the local constable, urgently.'

'That's no problem,' replied Marion, 'we can send for him by carrier pigeon.'

Within minutes the inspector had written a note. *Local Constable, you are to attend Smallbeef Caravan Park immediately, if not sooner, from Inspector Hooter, Flying Squad.*

Seconds later, the pigeon was airborne with the note contained in a small pouch hanging beneath its neck.

'There now, let's finish our meal while we wait for the constable to arrive,' said Marion. And so they finished their day looking into each other's eyes, wishing their mission was over before it had even started.

***

Punch's day was also drawing to an end. The stable was comfortable enough, but he found it difficult to relax. *Where's Dick?* He got to his feet and tugged a mouthful of hay from the manger, looking around as he chewed. The shabby mallard had settled down beneath the central lantern, his head resting on his chest, slowly rising up and down as he dozed.

Punch supped some water from the bucket. He'd grown accustomed to the poor light, but he still couldn't see what or who was loitering beyond the partition in the corner. His train of thought was interrupted when he heard someone approaching from outside. *Is it Dick?*

The stable doors opened, the damp air suppressed any dust that might have risen. The startled mallard jumped to his feet.

Punch raised his head hoping to see Dick standing there. His heart sank when the silhouettes of three Bogs appeared in the doorway. Two stayed outside while the one in the centre stepped forward, flicking his elbow out as he passed the mallard. 'Get out of my way,' he rasped, and gave the forlorn bird a hefty thump on the shoulder, knocking him off his feet and landing him among the pile of dirty hay and manure piled up in the corner.

The Bog then stopped two paces short of Punch, facing him head on. He looked the horse up and down for several minutes without a word being said. Punch stood firm with his head high and his constitution solid and true, comforted by his whispers and a thousand unseen hands.

The Bog eventually broke the silence. 'No one in this land faces me without regretting it, but then few in this land are tall enough or big enough to look me in the eye.'

Punch didn't understand the words, but he understood the meaning of what was said. He remained unmoved, determined not to back down. He sensed this was a bad situation, outnumbered by these hard-hearted creatures who thought nothing of hurting others badly. He remembered what they had done to the constables at Smallbeef, but his heart was bigger and stronger than theirs; this he knew to be true. He knew he could make a good account of himself against the Bogs standing in his way, but then what of Dick? In his head he had only one vision, that of riding away with his friend on his back. That was what he wanted; that was the limit of his plan.

The Bog continued in a low but stern voice. 'You are not like the others, not like the donkeys, the pathetic donkeys. Not like the ducks, or the moorhens and coots. But I warn you, horse, do not stand up to me for I shall unleash a wrath the like of which even your big head cannot imagine; even **your** muscles will fail before me, do you hear? No one stands up to me – no one.'

Every word the Bog spoke had a chilling edge to it. 'You may not know my words, but you understand me, I know you do; so take heed or you will be sorry.' He turned and made his way back to the doorway. The keeper, having just got to his feet was stepping out of the manure pile; the Bog clouted him again, sending him straight back in.

'Remember my words, horse, and remember my name.' The beast rejoined his two subordinates. 'I am **Beeroglad**, leader of the Bogs.' He paused at the doorway and placed a hat upon his head, the nearby lamp illuminated it clearly – it was Dick's blue tricorn.

Grief stricken at the thought of how the Bog might have relieved Dick of his coveted hat, Punch tramped anxiously on the ground and raised his head up and down, huffing loudly. Unusually for a horse, his instinct was to advance and fight, but his whispers had him stay where he was until he'd thought things through.

The doors closed. His soul whispered to him and calmed him; he had a lot of thinking to do. He needed a plan, but he was a creature who lived by his heart's ruling and had no idea of how to make a plan. The situation demanded his head take over, and so he began by surveying his surroundings and taking stock of the situation. Thinking with his head felt very odd to Punch, but that was how it had to be. So he closed his beautiful eyes and started thinking. And then he thought some more.

The mallard groaned and stepped out from the muck pile once again.

13

Early morning light the colour of drain water struggled to cast some enlightenment over the desolate landscape. For the first time in a long time Moira took time to preen herself, sorting her plumage in readiness to take to the air yet again. As for Lucky, he had long since abandoned any regard for his appearance or condition; all he wanted was to be where the Sun shone and where someone might care for him in return for his friendship. *Not too much to ask is it?*

They were soon on their way once more, eagerly following the solitary gravel track towards the distant hills. It wasn't long before they came to the two unfinished turrets at the roadside; the sight of the rock piles reinforced their determination to make good their escape and summon help for all those they had left behind in Fort Bog.

'We'd best be moving on, dear friend,' said Moira. 'Those dreadful Bogs can travel much faster than us, so we mustn't dally.'

Lucky stood fast and brayed in reply as if to say, 'Hang on, something's not right.' He stared wide eyed with ears erect in the direction of Smallbeef, sensing there was something in the air.

'What is it?' Moira followed Lucky's gaze into the far off sky. No matter how hard they tried they were unable to focus through the haze to see exactly what it was, but whatever it was it was coming their way, albeit quite slowly and low in the sky. First one speck, then a second speck came into view, and then a third.

'Oh dear,' Moira fretted, 'who are they, are they friendly do you think?'

Lucky's whispers bade him keep quiet, so he did, silently watching and hoping. Moira reckoned it would be safe enough to get up into the air for a better look, so up she went, spiralling directly above her friend. She remembered what happened the last time she was this high, but now she was much more aware and alert to such dangers.

She climbed to within touching distance of the dark cloud which seemed fixed in the sky like a ceiling. The distant specks were moving very slowly, but now she could count seven of them flying in a circular motion, as if escorting something on the ground.

Before long, a cart of some sort appeared on the far off horizon; it was this that the birds were following. *They must be big birds for me to see them from this distance.* Moira stayed up for as long as she dared, straining to make out any detail. As the specks got closer their shapes became more distinct. Their circular path in the sky made it easy for her to view them from every angle. Their vast wingspan soon became evident, and then as they presented themselves side on, the long beaks and tails became clearly visible.

They're not birds – they're Bogs – seven of them!

'Oh dear, oh my, now what shall we do?' Moira landed as quickly as possible, and immediately began talking things through with Lucky. She knew he couldn't understand what she was saying, but it helped her work things out in her head if she thought someone was listening.

'Now let me think, they'll be here in about thirty minutes at the speed they're going.' She looked all around. 'Oh dear, there's never a bush around when you need one. We must find somewhere to hide while they pass or we'll be caught and taken back for certain.'

Lucky huffed softly to get Moira's attention, but his efforts went unnoticed.

'I suppose I could hide behind Lucky and he could hide behind me at the same time, then we'll both be hidden.' She immediately realized the impossibility of such an idea.

Lucky repeatedly nudged her until she eventually broke from her own thoughts and acknowledged him. He held her gaze with his dark blue eyes while slowly walking behind one of the stone turrets, and then, stepping in through a gap in the unfinished wall, he disappeared from view.

'Oh, you are a clever donkey.' Moira quickly turned and did likewise inside the other turret. Now all they could do was wait and hope the Bogs would not see them.

***

At Smallbeef the constables were finishing their breakfast in the early morning sunshine. As much as they'd enjoyed the attention of their hosts the night before, thoughts of the dangers that lay ahead suppressed any conversation at the table. Each constable looked across at his sweetheart, and she looked back at him. All wished these were better times and that they wouldn't have to part.

'Well, Constables,' said Hooter, 'we can't wait any longer for the local constable. You have five minutes to say your goodbyes before I expect you on parade as smart as ever. Jump to it.'

Constables Thomas Thomas, Robert Roberts, James James, Howard Howard, Peter Peters, and Russell Russell collected their helmets from the dormitory and, after making sure they were all quite immaculate, returned to the yard for a final farewell.

'It's so unfair,' said Fay, holding back a tear. 'How can you be expected to bring those dreadful creatures to justice with only your badge and a helmet?'

'Oh now, don't forget we've all got a whistle as well,' said

Thomas, confidently. He took a whistle from inside his helmet and put it to his bill. It wasn't easy blowing a whistle without proper lips, but he managed somehow. They were all a bit concerned when the whistle produced a 'Quack quack' sound which was not at all what they'd expected.

What a strange noise, they all thought, and yet in the back of their minds a haunting familiarity lingered, another of those not-quite-right moments.

Thomas put the whistle back inside his helmet, feeling more than a little embarrassed. The tear in Fay's eye trickled down her cheek, running quickly over her beautifully oiled feathers and falling to the ground, making the tiniest dimple in the dust. The other young ladies were in much the same state.

'Honk honk', the inspector's hooter broke the silence.

'Come along now, on parade, as quick as you like.'

The young ladies adjusted the helmets on their constables' heads to be sure they were quite straight. Then they stood back and let them pass. The constables paraded as smartly as ever, heads in line and chests out. They looked absolutely splendid, so bright, handsome, and young.

'Right, Constables, I have a map here to show the way to the land where the pterosaurs live. I believe we shall find the kidnappers there.' The inspector held up the map consisting of one piece of paper with nothing on it apart from a single road going straight up the centre of the page. 'Uncharted territory.' With a lump in his throat he reluctantly moved things on and gave the order, 'Prepare for take off.'

The constables braced themselves, but were interrupted by a familiar crash and a clatter outside the park. Everyone looked round to see the hapless local bobby once again entangled in his bicycle.

'Not again,' said Hooter. 'Here, let me help you up.' He lifted the bike while the crumpled constable withdrew his legs from the frame and replaced his helmet on his head, crookedly.

'Sorry, sir, I hope I'm not too late.'

'You're just in time,' said Hooter, leading the bobby to Marion's caravan. 'Now listen to me,' he went on, 'it's of the utmost importance that this communication gets through to Flying Squad Head Quarters as quickly as possible, do you understand?'

'Yes, sir,' replied the constable, excited to have something important to do. He looked as if he wanted to say something more.

Hooter hurriedly prompted him. 'Well, what is it young duck? Come on, out with it.'

'Well, sir, do I have to go by bicycle?'

'Of course you do – it would take far too long if you walked.'

'Well, yes I know, sir, but I was wondering if I could fly, sir.'

'Fly, fly? Have you had flying lessons?'

'Well no, sir, but I'm a du—'

'There it is then, how can you possibly fly if you haven't had flying lessons? So let's hear no more of it, and be on your way. We can't afford to waste any more time here.'

'Yes, sir.' The constable returned to his bicycle feeling rather hard done by. He pushed it back out to the road where he lined it up carefully with the distant bend, and was soon wobbling out of sight in the direction of Flying Squad HQ, Davidsmeadow.

Two minutes later the squad was in the air, with helmets leaning slightly forward and badges gleaming in the sunshine.

The constables fought hard to keep their minds on their work, but they couldn't resist one last look down as they sped away. The sweethearts they were leaving behind had given them a new sense of purpose, and a reason for doing what was right – and a reason to come back.

14

Inside the stable behind the inn Punch was still thinking. The dawn light crept across the moorland and slithered in through the gaps in the walls casting parallel lines across the dust and straw. Punch had been thinking all night, but no matter how hard he tried he could find no place in his mind for a plan. He always acted on instinct driven by what he felt in his heart not his head. To think and act in a premeditated manner would be to presume too much; so he thought about it some more.

While he was thinking, the stable-keeper brought him a bucket of fresh water.

'Here y'are old fella, some nice cool water.' The mallard took care not to get too close, he was still unsure of the horse's intentions. 'Now you jus' take it easy, I don't mean you no 'arm, see.'

Sensing the duck's nervousness, Punch let him put the bucket down and waited for him to step away before moving forward to take a sup.

The mallard then set about his daily tasks, the first of which was to shovel the manure from the corner into a wheelbarrow. As soon as the barrow was full he began waddling towards the stable doors to open them.

A deep voice from behind stopped him in his tracks. 'Leave the doors closed for now if you would be so kind.'

'Who, what?' The mallard's eyes whirled around in his head trying to see where the voice had come from. He looked at

Punch; Punch shook his head and huffed quietly.

The mallard called out timidly. 'Ooever you are, I don't want no trouble, see.'

From behind the partition in the corner the voice spoke again, gruff, yet well spoken, 'It is not the horse you hear.'

'What the – who?' The mallard trembled. 'But there ain't no one in the corner except…except the thing under the cloak, but 'e ain't said a word since e got 'ere.'

'Well, I am talking now,' the voice replied.

Punch listened calmly while the mallard continued muttering to himself.

'It sounds like a Bog right enough, but softer.'

By now the dawn had filled the stable with grey-blue light, finally relieving the mysterious corner of its shadow.

The mallard couldn't bear to think of what might be about to reveal itself, so he did the only thing he could think of. In a moment of panic he turned and rushed for the doors to make his escape.

The voice responded swiftly and firmly. 'Wait, I asked you nicely. Please don't open the doors, there's a good duck.'

The mallard stopped and turned. *Oh no!* He cringed. His worst fears were coming true. He couldn't believe how tall the Bog was. Until now he had only seen it sitting in the shadow, hunched beneath its cloak.

The Bog emerged from behind the partition with only its beak sticking out awkwardly beyond the black void within the hood. He looked briefly at the duck, and then he turned his attention to Punch and moved towards him with an uneasy gait.

The mallard gawped, and then looked at the doors from the corner of his eye; he desperately wanted to reach them. The Bog read his mind, his gaze fixing the mallard to the ground like a skewer; a slight tilt of the head convinced the desperate bird to stay where he was.

Satisfied that the mallard would stay put, the Bog turned once again to Punch who had so far been content to stand and watch events unfold about him.

Still cloaked, the Bog cautiously moved forward, stopping with the tip of his beak only inches from Punch's muzzle. Punch didn't flinch, nor did he blink, but held his head high, and waited.

The Bog slowly extended a clawed hand from beneath his cloak. Punch remained steadfast looking into the mysterious hood and then at the curved claws moving ever closer to his throat.

The hood slipped from the Bog's head, revealing his jet black orbs which lingered about Punch's soft hazel eyes, seeking a way in. Punch returned the stare. The quivering mallard covered his eyes with his wing, not wanting to see what might happen next.

The Bog and the horse held the stand-off for many minutes. The mallard kept very still, waiting for the sound of mortal combat to begin.

The chesnut horse stood firm with his hind legs splayed slightly to brace himself. He tucked his tail up against his rump and adopted a slight forward lean to present his massive chest with head held high, showing he was prepared to stand his ground. His heart pumped strong; his nostrils flexed, smelling the Bog and the aura about him. He knew the creature standing before him with the sharp beak and the long claws was stronger than anything he had ever encountered. A thousand hands held his heart. He studied the strange light dancing across the eyes of the Bog, turning them from dull black to a bright inky blue; so clear were they that the mallard's reflection could be seen in them, still with one wing over his face.

The Bog and the horse continued staring into each other, searching and probing. The clawed hand straightened before reaching out and touching Punch on the cheek. The points of the claws probed the dense hairs on Punch's face, and then with a tender touch they delicately explored the changing textures of the hair and the firm muscles of the magnificent horse.

The Bog eventually drew a long breath. 'Friend,' he said, 'strong, kind, and beautiful.'

Punch replied with a short neigh and one of his fluffy huffs.

The Bog carried on in his deep and refined voice. 'My dear horse, I know you are troubled. You wish to find your friend, and you wish to help those who are held in this land against their will, but most of all you wish to end the suffering of the donkeys.' His claws were still gently combing Punch's neck. 'I must tell you, if you travel through this land without a rider you will attract more attention than is good for you.'

The mallard also listened to every word the Bog spoke. He had never heard a Bog speak so kindly, and was sure it was a trick of some sort. Standing behind the Bog, he gestured with his wings and shook his head at Punch, trying to tell him not to believe anything the Bog said.

Sensing the mallard's antics, the Bog turned suddenly, causing the forlorn bird to freeze.

'Do you have something to say, Mr Stable-keeper?'

'No, sir, nothing,' replied the mallard. He was certain he was about to meet his end. Shaking uncontrollably, he forced himself to raise his eyes and look into the creature's face. He couldn't believe what he saw. The eyes were now sparkling blue, and the face bright red with deep furrows around the cheeks as if to channel the age of the world into its eyes.

'Oh, come now,' said the Bog. 'I'm sure you have a lot to say. Please speak, so that the horse and I may listen to what is on your mind.'

The mallard was surprised he hadn't already felt the wrath of the Bog's fist for daring to look so intensely into his face. *One word out of place and 'twill be my last,* he thought.

'Well, we are waiting,' repeated the Bog, 'we really don't have all day.'

Unable to contain himself a moment longer, the duck gave vent to all the emotions and frustrations he had suppressed for much of his captive life. 'You lie,' he shouted, 'you terrorize, you hurt, and you kidnap…you, you, you…and you're ugly.' He took a sharp intake of breath. 'And all your kind are cruel to everyone and everything, and you're ugly, that's my say, so there you are…and in case I 'aven't already said it, your ugly!' He fluffed up his grubby chest and waited in anticipation of the fatal blow from the Bog's hand.

The Bog shuffled forward. The duck screamed at Punch. 'Run for it, run for it, don't believe him, don't—'

The Bog reached out.

The duck screamed with tears pouring down his face. 'Go on, kill me, I don't care anymore, just do it.'

Strong hard fingers cupped themselves around the mallard's head. But they didn't crush him, or throw him to one side. Instead, the hand caressed and stroked him, taking care to stroke with the run of his feathers so as not to harm them.

'There now, calm yourself,' said the Bog in a soft whisper.

'What?' The duck sniffed loudly and stifled any crying he hadn't yet done. Again he looked into the eyes of the Bog. 'They're bright they are, I can see myself in 'em, but how? An' yer face, 'tis red not grey, but you are a Bog?'

'Well,' replied the pterosaur. 'If I look like a Bog, and talk like a Bog, and walk like a Bog, then I probably am a Bog – but who knows?' He continued stroking the mallard's head, saying, 'As in all walks of life, there is good and bad in all things, but never ugly; nothing was made ugly. Just because you find something unattractive doesn't make it ugly. Some might look at your bill and think it comical, but somewhere in this world there is a female duck who would love to stroke it for you. The secret is to recognize the good from the bad, and to work with the good to help the bad get better. Wouldn't you agree?'

The mallard wiped away the remains of his tears, and then he replied, 'How can you help a Bog when all they do is hurt and ruin everythin'?'

'Oh, come now, they don't ruin everything, just look at the horse. They made sure he was well looked after didn't they?'

'Well, I s'pose so.'

'Well at least that shows they have some compassion, and that is what you must find in others, and then nurture it and help it to grow.'

As much as the duck didn't like to admit it, the touch of the Bog felt wonderfully soothing, beyond anything he had ever known.

The Bog went on, 'If you only look with your eyes things are seldom the way they seem. You must see with your heart, let the world in through your eyes all the way to your heart. That is what the horse does.' The hypnotic tones paused briefly while the Bog sat the duck down on an upturned bucket. 'Your eyes saw my face and you called me ugly, yet you don't even know me, so how can you know if I am ugly or beautiful? Some might look at the horse and only see a huge hairy creature that walks about leaving piles of dung everywhere. Is that what you see?'

'Well, erm, no I s'pose not. 'e's, 'ansome 'e is.'

'You saw my clawed hand coming towards you and you prepared to die, but did I not caress and soothe you?'

'Well…yes you did.'

'Do you not think I might also have feelings, and perhaps I would like someone to touch **my** face gently, and ask how **I** am?'

The bewildered mallard couldn't believe what he was hearing.

Should I touch him? Is that what he wants? He nervously raised his wing, but then he stopped; he couldn't bring himself to do it. The Bog waited silently – hopefully. Then came the hefty clump, clomp of Punch making his way towards the two of them.

The mallard stared transfixed into the eyes of the clearest blue, but he still couldn't quite bring himself to touch the deeply contoured face in front of him.

Punch stopped next to the Bog and huffed calmly while holding the mallard's attention. He then turned his head and pressed his plump lips and nostrils against the Bog's bright red cheek. The Bog was taken aback, his first instinct was to back away, but he remembered what he had just told the mallard, so he stood there while Punch gave him a big, horsey kiss.

The mallard gawped, dumbfounded. He would never have believed it had he not seen it with his own eyes.

'You see,' said the Bog with wetted eyes, 'it doesn't hurt to be nice, even if you **do** think I'm ugly.'

The mallard held out his wing. The Bog carefully took it in his hand, a handshake of friendship. Such was the tension within the mallard, that he held his breath, and not until the grip was released did he breathe a long, long sigh of relief. 'Do you 'ave a name?' he asked nervously.

'Thank you for asking, yes I do, it's Abel Nogg,' came the reply. The Bog then turned towards the doors saying, 'I'm just going outside for some fresh air; while I'm gone would you be so kind as to get the horse ready for a ride, I shan't be long.'

'Yes, sir, right away, sir.' The duck picked up Punch's saddle while watching Abel take his leave. When he was sure the Bog had gone, he put the saddle back down; his curiosity got the better of him and he made his way to the far corner and began looking around behind the partition where the Bog had been hiding. Taking care not to disturb anything, he looked high and low. He was about to turn about when a feather lying on a ledge caught his attention. 'What's this,' he whispered to himself. 'A solitary feather, it can't be the Bog's on account of he don't have feathers.' He studied the feather closely without actually touching it. 'Tis a broken half, probably a coot's…or perhaps a moor'en's, yes, 'tis a moor'ens.' Having seen all he needed to he made his way back to Punch, muttering as he went. 'I don't know where that Bogs gone, but I bet he's up to no good. I bet that feather was from a poor defenceless bird what he ruffed up.'

With a head full of contradictions, the baffled mallard set about saddling Punch as instructed, feeling very confused by what had just gone on, and more than a little uncertain about his own future – or if he even had one.

Outside, the donkeys stood harnessed to the cart where they had been waiting all night. A clawed hand placed a bucket of water and some fresh roughage in front of them. 'There you are, my friends. Be strong and keep your faith in all that is good for there is one coming who will set you free.'

Both donkeys quietly brayed and gratefully took to supping and chewing, taking the words to their hearts.

15

Meanwhile, out across the moorland, seven Bogs maintained their vigil in the sky, keeping a watchful eye on the heavy wagon below. They knew of the unfinished turrets ahead and the little bridge over the stream.

Alone at the front of the wagon sat a teenaged Bog, the reins resting loosely in his clawed hands while the countryside slowly passed by. The wagon wheels of solid oak wobbled loosely on their spindles, crunching their way along the gravel track while a team of four donkeys worked hard to keep the wagon moving. They pulled together with heads low, oblivious to all about them; no ambition – no hope – this was all they knew. To slack or fail in any way would meet with dire consequences; they would work all day, with a little water at dawn and dusk, and the minimum of food, most of which they would scavenge or beg for with pleading eyes as they went along.

Moira peered out from her hiding place inside the turret. She couldn't see the cart yet, but could guess its position by the Bogs circling in the sky, assuredly getting closer. She huddled into as small a space as she could, gathering the rocks around her to disguise her shape from above. She hoped Lucky was able to do the same, but doubted it being as he was a donkey. *At least his dirty grey colour will help camouflage him*, she thought, trying to convince herself that things weren't as bad as they really were.

Peering over the top of the rocks, she could now see the wagon with the young Bog sitting up front, about half a mile away. She fretted aloud. 'Oh dear, what on Earth can they be carrying?' Her heart pounded so hard she was sure others would hear it, but she had no more time to look, lest the Bogs should spot her from their vantage point.

'Quiet and still, quiet and still, mustn't fret, mustn't fret – oh dear.' Once again she made herself as small as she could, and pulled a few more rocks around her for extra cover.

The Bogs were soon overhead, their shadows serenely sweeping over the turrets. Moira listened nervously to the constant whoosh of air passing beneath their wings. It wasn't long before the exhaustive footsteps of the donkeys also came into earshot, along with the wagon wheels gathering grit on their rims.

Please keep going, please keep going.

One of the Bogs in the air called out, 'There's a stream further along, we'll stop there for a rest and to water the prisoners.'

Prisoners? Moira's memory conjured up images of a journey she had taken a year ago. A journey with her and her friends crammed into the back of a wagon just like the one approaching now. *Oh dear me.* She cowered ever deeper into the turret.

The huge pterosaurs passed overhead with their gaze fixed on the far horizon where the stream would water them, they didn't notice her. Next came the donkeys passing close with no hope in their eyes, just blank stares down at the ground, they didn't notice her either. Then the young Bog with the reins in his hands concentrating hard on keeping the wagon in the centre of the track, he didn't notice her either. Then the wagon scrunched past. She peeped up to see the mallards and their children squeezed into the back, peering out between the bars. They saw her. Not a sound from their bills, but their eyes pleaded for help as they went by. Moira returned their gaze and gave a barely perceptible nod.

Soon the wagon was gone and with it the Bogs who had mercifully not noticed her or Lucky.

***

In the meantime, many miles away at an altitude of six trees high, the Flying Squad proceeded in regulation patrol mode, each duck having a specific task according to his flying position. The inspector was always at the point, while the duck to either side of him would act as a steadier to ensure he kept a smooth course. Positions two and five would scour the land below while one and six kept an eye on the sky above. They were at least travelling in the right direction and gaining on all those ahead of them. Every so often their minds would wander among thoughts of their new lady friends back at Smallbeef. They had never experienced such feelings of warmth and yearning before, and would be glad to get this particular mission over and done with. They could then return once again to that lovely little caravan park beneath the sunshine of southern England.

Armed with the map he had discovered, Inspector Hooter led his squad further into ever darkening skies. He kept a mental picture of the long straight road in his head, and every now and then would look down to confirm its presence. *Good, we're on the right track; we're sure to catch them soon.*

First and foremost in the inspector's mind was his duty to locate the kidnappers and young Dick Waters-Edge; second was his desire to return to the loving embrace of Marion; third was his unsatisfied yearning to use his binoculars, he had carried with him for many years but as yet had never used them. Onward he cruised while mulling the subject over, relying on his squad to steer him through the sky. *How could I hold them to my face while I'm flying? With only one wing working I'm sure to go into a spin…that would never do.*

After a few minutes of deep thought, he called out, 'I think I have a solution to my binocular problem.'

The constables listened with more than a little apprehension.

'I shall sit on the back of one of you, piggyback style, while you continue to fly. That way when I stop flapping my wings I won't go into a dive – marvellous.'

The constables understood what he'd said, but they weren't convinced of the science involved in one of them flying with the inspector on their back, but orders were orders.

'Okay, FS3 Roberts, break formation and position yourself beneath me.'

Regardless of any doubts as to his own safety, PC Robert Roberts carefully fell away from the others and turned inward until he was immediately beneath the inspector. His flight became very erratic when the downdraught from Hooter's wings conflicted with his own. Hooter immediately stilled his wings, landing with a hefty thump on Roberts' shoulders. The rest of the squad looked on with admiration for their comrade, who was now having to work considerably harder to maintain a level flight.

Both Hooter and Roberts felt more than a little embarrassed at such closeness, but neither of them said a word. Hooter was determined to look through his binoculars if it was the last thing he did. 'That's it, steady, steady,' he called. Feelings of great anticipation and excitement grew within him. He had now got himself comfortable on Roberts' shoulders with his legs dangling each side of the constable's neck. At last he was ready; now he would finally see through his prized binoculars. 'Right, this is it.' He brought them slowly up to his face. 'Steady, steady – well done, Constable,' he said, quietly encouraging Roberts to maintain his effort.

He drew the binoculars to his eyes, full of great expectations. 'Let's just have a little look shall we? This is so exciting.' He placed the binoculars against his face where he expected his eyes to be, only to find they weren't there. Utter dismay filled his head. Realization dawned. Binoculars are made for heads with eyes at the front; unfortunately, his eyes were on each side of his head, as with all ducks. His vision remained normal; he felt so foolish, so saddened. For years he'd carried them everywhere he went, waiting for a day such as this. Upon realizing his error his prime concern was that of saving face.

'Erm,' he said loudly, trying to sound as if everything was fine, 'that's absolutely marvellous; we're right on course. Well done FS3, you may resume normal flying now, thank you.'

Hooter let the binoculars fall against his chest, his bill quivering with disappointment. His wings resumed their natural duty and his legs slowly lifted from around Roberts' neck. Roberts breathed a sigh of relief and promptly took up his normal flying position, as did the inspector.

Onward flew the Flying Squad, the inspector hoping his constables hadn't noticed his absurd mistake, and his constables hoping he hadn't noticed they had.

***

In the stable by the inn, the stable-keeper sat back down on the upturned bucket with his head in his wings. 'Can't trust no one, yuh can't.' He pictured the broken moorhen feather. 'For one moment, just one moment I thought that red-faced Bog, Abel Nogg or whatever 'e called 'imself, was okay – pah! 'E's jus' like the rest of 'em 'e 'is. Can't trust 'em an inch.' His rebuttal was cut short when one of the stable doors opened unexpectedly.

Abel Nogg shuffled his way in, leaving the door open. The mallard jumped to his feet, hoping his remarks hadn't been heard.

Abel cast a knowing eye in the mallard's direction. 'I've told the pterosaurs outside that I'm going to take the horse for a ride to exercise him. I also told them that you, my dear mallard, had done a good job of serving me, and I suggested they reward you with a good bath, if that suits you?'

Keen to keep on the right side of the Bog and show his appreciation, the mallard replied, 'Why yes, sir, thanking you, sir, I can't remember the last time I 'ad a bath.'

'That's what I thought,' said Abel Nogg. 'Now listen, it's important that you stay hereabouts so I know where you are if I should need you, so please don't go divagating, do you hear?'

'Yes, sir,' said the mallard, unsure of what divagating meant. 'I means no, sir, you can count on me, sir.'

'I'm sure I can,' Abel replied. He then led Punch by the reins through the door to the yard outside where he stood close to the horse's ear and whispered, 'Are you ready my friend, this is where your adventure begins.'

Punch felt in his heart that something was waiting ahead of him; something that would give meaning and value to his very existence. Invisible hands cradled his girth while he waited for Abel Nogg to climb up into the saddle.

Abel took hold of Punch's abundant mane with one hand and held the front of the saddle with the other. He then sprang upward in slow motion, landing in the saddle with such gentleness as to cause Punch no strain whatsoever. Punch was impressed. The Bog took a few moments to sort the stirrups and gather the reins before leaning forward to talk into Punch's ear once again. 'I hope I may address you as your rider did yesterday; I believe he called you "Punch".'

Punch liked the voice; it was good and honest despite its rough edge. *But what of Dick?* He tramped his hind legs in frustration. His whispers quickly consoled him. *Be strong – take comfort, your heart has an equal – he sits atop you.* With his doubts settled, Punch turned his head and rested his eye in the face of his new rider.

'Thank you, my friend,' said Abel, gently squeezing his legs against the horse's girth. They moved off, slowly passing the two donkeys who were still enjoying the food and water mysteriously put before them. An abundant tarpaulin covered the wagon's load, cube shaped, probably a chest of some sort.

And so the unlikely spectacle of a brightly coloured Bog sitting in the saddle of a Suffolk Punch walked away from the inn, the two of them providing the only source of colour for as far as the eye could see. After a minute or two, having settled into each other's rhythm, they broke into a trot in the direction of Fort Bog, and Punch's destiny.

***

Flying straight and level and making good speed, Inspector Hooter still had his binoculars on his mind. 'They've obviously been made wrong,' he muttered, 'I mean, who has eyes in the front of their head? Ducks don't, geese don't, and even pterosaurs don't. It makes no sense.'

'Cats and dogs, sir,' PC Howard shouted.

'Where?' replied Hooter, wondering what the constable had seen.

'No, sir – that's the answer to your question.' Howard expanded his statement. 'Cats and dogs have eyes in the front of their heads, sir. I can't think of any other animal around here that does.'

'I see what you mean, Constable, but they're animals – my binoculars can't have been made for them.'

All was silent for a few moments, until the entire squad burst into laughter at the thought of a labrador looking through a pair of binoculars.

'That's quite enough, Constables, let's concentrate on what we're doing shall we?'

'What about human beings, sir?' PC Russell added to the debate.

'Hmm, human beings eh?' The inspector pondered a while.

'They certainly have eyes in the front of their heads, but I've always thought of humans as some kind of evolutionary throwback, and anyway, they're too small to use binoculars. One thing's for sure though, they'll never get on in this world with their attitude, all they ever do is fight and swear – dreadful behaviour. Perhaps one day they'll learn to behave like animals.'

Onward they flew, ever vigilant and ever thoughtful. Every so often Hooter would cast an inquisitive eye in PC Roberts' direction. He would study the position of the eyes in the duck's head, and think of ways to attach one half of his binoculars to one eye, and the other half to the other eye. *Yes, that would do it. I'll take them apart and make a frame to hold them in place over my head – marvellous.*

The inspector's thoughts were interrupted when PC James let out a shout. 'Sir, there's a moorhen in the air straight ahead, slightly below us…and a donkey on the ground.'

'So there is. What on Earth are they doing out here alone? Squad, follow my lead and descend.'

The squad promptly landed and lined up smartly.

Upon seeing the wonderful spectre ahead, the donkey quickened his pace as much as he could while Moira raced away, hardly believing her eyes. Such was her eagerness that she stumbled over her own legs upon landing and ended up sprawled on the ground in front of the constables.

Inspector Hooter helped her to her feet, by which time Lucky had clattered to a halt next to them.

'He-haw, hee, he-haw,' he brayed uncontrollably, 'he-haw, he-haw.'

The inspector took his brass hooter and held it beneath Lucky's chin, raising it slowly until the braying stopped. 'That's better,' he said, turning to the moorhen. 'Now then my dear, you must tell me what you are doing so far from home…I presume you are far from home?'

'Oh yes,' replied the moorhen with tears welling up in her eyes. 'We've been held captive at Fort Bog by the awful pterosaurs.'

'What?' Hooter exclaimed. 'Captive? That's dreadful. Please tell me all about it, madam.'

'My name is Moira Maywell and this is my donkey, Lucky...' Moira spent the next ten minutes explaining how she came to be there, and of the treatment of those she had left behind, and of the wagon she had seen loaded with more mallards.

'This is absolutely appalling.' Hooter could hardly believe what he had heard, but it all made sense. 'I don't suppose you've seen a large horse with a young mallard on it have you?'

'Why yes, they helped us when my donkey collapsed by the bridge further along. He pointed me towards Smallbeef while he went on to Fort Bog to put things right.'

'Oh dear,' said Hooter, 'I don't think that was a very good idea.' This was an unexpected development requiring quick decisions; Hooter couldn't afford to lose any more time than was absolutely necessary. 'Hmm,' he thought out loud while stroking his bill with his wing. 'We need to get your donkey back to Smallbeef where he can be tended to, but he can't possibly continue in his condition, he can barely walk.' He rubbed his bill some more while his constables rubbed theirs, as if this pooling of bill rubbing would somehow magnify their thought process.

16

A few miles ahead of the Flying Squad, Abel Nogg and Punch had settled into an easy canter. Both creatures were formidable in their own right, but together they struck a unique countenance of strength, truth and mutual respect. Abel would have made faster progress if he had flown to the fort alone, but the whole point of his presence was to get the measure of the horse, and to set certain things in motion. He had to be sure the horse's mind was in the right place for what lay ahead.

Abel found the interaction between him and the horse truly invigorating. Not for a long time had he experienced such physical strength as exhibited by the horse's massive thighs forging the pair onward. Not as fast as a Bog in flight perhaps, but surely nothing in the world could stop this creature of such immense torque and weight.

With a childlike twinkle in his eye, Abel leaned forward and gave Punch a gentle squeeze with his feet. He wasn't too sure how Punch would react to this; he soon found out. Needing no more encouragement, Punch instantly stretched his body from nose to tail. His forelegs pounded the beat while his hind legs dug in and pushed harder than ever. He galloped like he had never galloped before, accelerating with such force as to compel the Bog to grab a handful of mane to avoid being left behind.

Abel found himself up in the stirrups balancing with Punch's rhythmic motion, his cloak billowing behind like the sail of a tall-ship at full tilt. Not for a millennium had he enjoyed the intercourse of another creature so intensely. His rigid beak couldn't smile, but his eyes laughed with absolute joy and exhilaration as the horse thundered across the naked land, four hooves pounding the sound of life and vitality on the petrified ground.

Abel's adrenaline built rapidly to a crescendo until he could contain his delight no longer. 'Go, my boy, go like the wind,' he shouted. 'No mistral shall match you, no heart shall catch you – you are truly magnificent!'

Onward Punch raced. Faster and faster, nostrils flared, ears forward, eyes wide and smiling. He was stopping for no one.

***

Half a mile ahead of the horse, a working party of mallards and moorhens were busy repairing potholes in the road. They laboured beneath morbid skies while two Bogs kept guard to ensure no one slacked or wandered off.

The mallards' grunts and groans of physical exertion stopped abruptly. 'What's that noise?' said one to another. The sound of distant drumming grew in volume. 'What can it be?' They looked at each other, bewildered.

The guards also looked at each other, puzzled, and then they looked along the road. They had no time to gather their thoughts before the ground shuddered beneath them. 'Get off the road! Get off the road!' they shouted. No sooner had the words left their long beaks when the Suffolk Punch thundered through between them at incredible speed. The birds and the Bogs dived into the roadside ditch for cover, but not before being showered with gravel and grit. When they eventually scrambled back onto the road, the horse and rider had all but disappeared, leaving only a faint trail of dust hanging in the air in their wake.

The two Bogs paused vacantly, unsure of what to do next.

They drew nothing from each other's eyes, and so turned to the mallards and moorhens. 'Come on you lot, back to work, you didn't see nothing, d'you hear, nothing.'

The birds picked up their shovels, muttering among themselves as they did so.

'That wasn't nothing, I'm sure of that,' said one.

'That's right, that wasn't nothing, that was something right enough,' said another.

'What d'you reckon it was then?'

'Dunno.'

***

A long way back from all the hubbub the Flying Squad were still rubbing their bills, hoping for a thought to germinate collectively among them. Moira sat with Lucky while he in turn stared vacantly at the ground. His blank expression changed when one of his ears pricked up; his whispers roused him, whispers which only he could hear. His other ear soon followed suit. The police ducks noticed his alert demeanour. *Has he heard something we haven't?* They turned as one and stared into the distance, secretly hoping to see nothing.

'There, sir, about a mile back, just below the cloud,' reported PC James.

All eyes followed James' report. Tension raced through their veins, the adrenaline leaving a taste in the back of their throats such was their sense of impending doom. Heading straight for them in V formation were five large flyers.

Moira fretted aloud. 'Oh no, not again.'

'Defence formation,' ordered Hooter. 'Quickly now.'

The police ducks instantly formed a circle, all facing outwards, with the moorhen and the donkey protected in the centre.

'Stand firm, Constables, brave and strong, brave and strong,' commanded Hooter, holding his head high to inspire his young squad.

And so once again the seven mallards stood with their chests puffed out and heads held high to appear as big as they possibly could. With their badges shining in the dishwater light they stood out like seven beacons of hope in an otherwise hopeless situation.

***

Punch and Abel had seen no one since scattering the working party some distance behind them. The road remained as straight as ever, but the landscape had changed almost unnoticed. There were signs of grass again, albeit thin and wispy and struggling to add colour to the otherwise lacklustre canvas. Punch slowed his pace to an easy canter, and then down to a trot. He panted heavily while his lungs fired oxygen around his body, reviving his muscles after the exertion of the gallop.

'Steady, my boy.' For the first time since getting into the saddle, Abel took control, gently bringing Punch to a steady walk.

'Let's give ourselves time to look about as we go, my stout hearted friend.'

It wasn't long before they noticed chimney smoke rising into the air in the far distance. Abel's dulcet tones comforted Punch. 'That will be Fort Bog up ahead. From within those walls your heart must prove its measure. Only then will your quest be won.'

Punch champed at his bit in eagerness, huffing and jettisoning steam into the air from his nostrils.

'Nice and easy does it,' said Abel, gathering his composure after the thrill of the journey. He set about adjusting his cloak and hood to ensure there was none of his red colour showing to those who might otherwise question his presence.

'Whatever happens from here on in,' he whispered, 'you must always let your heart guide you. Do not try to be what you are not, for you are absolutely as you were designed to be.' Abel patted the side of the horse's neck. 'But you already know that don't you, my friend.'

Punch's ears pricked up, eager to take in the words of the unlikely rider on his back.

Abel went on, 'It is fortuitous that you have so much trouble thinking with your head; heads might win the moment, but moments do not last. Minds can change like the wind. Only hearts remain true, and remember, even your most formidable foe has a heart, but you will have to find it and show it to him. Only then might he see life as you do.'

The words, although foreign to him, strengthened Punch's resolve, and another amiable huff sent his breath forward into the air as he walked onward.

Before long, the stone walls of the fort appeared on the horizon like a long silvery thread between land and sky. The line thickened and the frontage grew in stature as Punch and Abel drew nearer. A sturdy portcullis of greyed oak had pride of place half way along the front wall, barring the casual visitor from entry. The walls themselves were equally grey with a square castellated turret at each end. On top of each turret stood a Bog guard keeping watch over the approaches, their eyes of pitch giving nothing away as to their aim.

Punch's eyes widened when the two Bogs suddenly took to the air; up they went, rising vertically until high enough to hold their wings at full stretch and soar like gliders towards the interlopers.

Although well hidden by his cloak, the guards had no problem identifying Abel as a Beast of Grey; his beak protruding from the front of his hood, and the way his cloak draped like a tent from the top of his folded wings left no doubt in their minds. But they were both dumbfounded by such a strange vision. *A Bog riding a horse…why?*

The guards made several low passes with the air singing like a distant cello as it slipped across their wings. They turned in a broad circle and continued their glide. Again they sailed past the strange sight, but couldn't understand what they were looking at. They turned once more, this time rotating their wings to suspend themselves lazily in the sky. They took a few more seconds to gaze down on the bizarre sight until their clawed feet delicately touched down on the track.

Punch walked two more paces and then stopped at eye level with the welcome party now standing bow-legged before him. Wearing no cloaks, their awesome tails swayed gently from side to side behind their heads. Try as he might, Punch could draw no warmth or feeling from the matt black eyes he was looking into. Neither light nor life seemed to have a place there.

The Bog on the left opened his beak slightly. 'Word has come before you, a horse the size of ten donkeys and coloured like manure.'

Abel squeezed his legs gently against Punch's sides to comfort him. Punch remained unmoved, still searching for any sign of a soul from beyond their eyes.

'What is your business here that you would bring such a creature into our homeland?' enquired the other Bog in a stern voice.

Abel replied, 'Oh, come now, my dear fellows, surely there's no need for such ambivalence. Like you I was intrigued by the appearance of this beast, and was curious to know more of its mental and physical fortitude. After all, how often do we come face to face with a creature of such stature?' He paused while studying the guard's expressions. They were clearly struggling to understand why a Bog would wish to touch such an 'unclean' animal, let alone sit on one. Abel continued, 'So I thought I would take advantage of this poor simple horse and use him to transport me to Fort Bog, and here I am. I had some game on my way here and scattered a few mallards into the ditch where they belong – gave the guards something to think about I'll wager, hah.'

Whispers rose from Punch's soul to reassure him. *These words are not meant.*

Abel concluded, 'So if you would be so kind as to let me enter the fort, I shall dispose of this impure animal at my earliest convenience for you to do with as you wish.'

The guards looked at each other silently; their wings sprang out from their sides grasping the air beneath them, and up they went, maintaining a slow stroking motion like that of a conductor directing his orchestra through a slow and gentle movement. Together they hung in the air while one of them gave an answer. 'Enter and go about your business, but the horse will be held in the barn to await his destiny.'

Punch walked on without being told, hoping each step would take him closer to his lost friend, Dick. He knew from the Bog's tone he wasn't welcome, but he had a cause, and he was determined to see it through; if he couldn't be true to his own soul, then he had nothing. Onward he walked, head held high, ears erect, eyes wide open.

The guards spun round in mid-air and flew back to their turrets, leaving the visitors to make their own way to the entrance.

'Be strong, my Punch, be strong.' For the first time in his long life, Abel found himself questioning his own judgement in bringing this warm-hearted animal to such a place.

May this fine creature find the strength to see his quest prevail? If any soul deserves the help of the almighty it is surely his, lest I should turn him now and guide him back to his land of life and love. But would he thank me, would he let me take him back? I think not.

Punch stared straight ahead, hardly noticing his own feet on the ground or the rider on his back. He just knew what he had to do, and that was enough.

Heavy chains took up the slack, and the portcullis clanked its way up to allow the horse through. Punch expected Abel to stoop low behind his head as they passed beneath the archway. It was then that he realized his saddle was empty, his rider gone. Before he had time to gather his thoughts four Bogs surrounded him; two took hold of his reins while the other two stood either side of his hind quarters and slapped him hard. Unlike Abel, they didn't think to flatten their hands first. Punch was hurt, mentally and physically. His haunches on both sides became stained crimson with blood where the claws had pierced his hide. His eyes stared wide open taking in all that was happening around him. His hind legs stamped the ground in pain. The Bogs staggered backwards to keep clear of his hooves. The two at the front pulled harder on the reins to hold him in place. Punch stiffened his neck and wrenched his head high to resist their efforts, but they were not about to release their grip. They were no match for the horse's muscle or his weight, but they had a determination to hold his reins, no matter what.

Punch jerked his head as high as he could, tugging the Bogs sharply towards him. Their bodies slammed into his chest with an impact that was heard throughout the fort – a dull resonating thump. They both fell to the ground seriously winded. Flat on their backs and struggling to draw breath they held their hands high with the reins still in their grip. Punch lowered his gaze, and for one second his eyes met and held theirs. In that brief moment he saw through the creatures' hardened facade, their sadness and distress was plain to see. It lasted for but a second before the Bogs blinked, and the eyes once more gave nothing.

Bogs came from everywhere. Some floating in the air close above him while others formed an unbroken circle around him.

By now there were many onlookers. Mallards, moorhens, and donkeys; all had stopped their work to see what the commotion was about. Now they all looked on in horror.

Exertion and pain had Punch sweating profusely. Steam rose from his body. The Bogs grimaced at such a sight; steaming was something they never did. To them it was disgusting, as was the vapour gushing from the horse's nostrils into the cool air of the compound. The Bogs found this totally distasteful. He was indeed a dirty animal and had no place in their world.

The injured Bogs lay in the dust, struggling to draw breath but still holding the reins. Punch hadn't meant to hurt them. He lowered his head again and gently nudged one of them, pressing his soft muzzle against the creature's side.

Suddenly a voice bellowed angrily from the sky. 'Get him off!'

Beeroglad, the Bog leader, held the air beneath his wings, hovering above all in the fort. He glowered at the sight of a horse daring to touch one of his own kind.

Punch looked up at him. *Dick's blue hat*!

Beeroglad screeched again, but louder. His voice echoed furiously between the fort walls. 'Don't let the horse touch them – get him off now,' he raged.

The two injured Bogs let go of the reins, and their winged arms fell to the ground. They lay still and almost lifeless, their beaks pointing skyward, open, only managing shallow breaths. Four other Bogs grabbed them, two to each one, and hauled them away. Once again for a split second Punch caught a glimpse of vulnerability in their eyes, a look of fear. Then they were gone, only drag lines left in the dust. Little did he know that in the not too distant future he too would leave such marks.

'Contain him,' came the order from Beeroglad.

Four more Bogs closed in from above, encircling him with their clawed feet ready to strike if need be. Another four Bogs surrounded him on the ground; likewise their clawed hands were perilously close to Punch's sides and rump, effectively cocooning him within a living sheath of needle-like talons pointing inwards from all directions.

Punch's instinct told him to kick out and send his captors to the ground, broken, which he knew he could do. But his whispers guided him, *That is not the way.*

The Bogs were very wary of his strength, they cautiously ushered him towards the barn, taking extra care to keep away from his broad hooves. Punch resisted their efforts at first but instantly felt the claws prick him from behind. Again his whispers comforted him and urged him to comply, for the moment at least. They approached the barn doors, and the Bogs ahead of him parted, leaving the way clear for him to enter. He hesitated again, but the claws were quicker still to prod his rump, so in he went. The few shafts of light that found their way in through the gaps in the barn walls did little to relieve the interior of its darkness. The doors were quickly shut behind him, followed by the rattling of chains to hold them fast.

Punch mumbled and huffed in frustration. He was alone in a very dismal place. He was tired and wanted to sleep. He was thirsty and wanted to drink. He was hungry and wanted to eat. But most of all he wanted to find his friend, Dick.

His hind quarters quickly turned cold as the sweat cooled and his open wounds let the air into his body. He looked about as best he could in the poor light but could see nothing to drink, not so much as a damp bucket or trough to lick. He clomped his way across the floor, following his nose towards a hay net at the back of the barn. The hay wasn't particularly fresh, but he needed to eat. He tugged at the stale roughage and chewed, staring into nowhere, hoping a thought would come to him. He stared some more, and chewed some more. Then he stared some more.

17

Back along the track, still in their defence formation, the police ducks braced themselves for yet another encounter with more fearsome beasts from the sky.

'Oh dear, oh dear,' sighed Moira Maywell, fixing her gaze on the five distant shapes closing in at quite a lick. 'I don't believe I want another brush with those dreadful creatures, they've left me for dead once already, I'm sure they won't give me a second chance.'

'Fear not, madam,' said the inspector, gallantly. 'They'll have to get past my constables and me first, and we won't make it easy for them.'

The constables couldn't help but rub the bruises while thinking of their last encounter with the Bogs, but they would stand by their leader no matter what the cost, for that was their duty. They also had another reason to stand up for what was right – they had their beautiful new loves waiting for them at Smallbeef. Their new emotion served them well, swelling their hearts with desire, giving them courage way beyond their weight.

'They're still heading this way,' said Hooter. 'Definitely five of them and definitely bigger than us…a good bit bigger than us.' He concealed a nervous gulp. 'Oh dear, they're losing height – I think they've seen us – yes, they're coming straight for us.'

Moira put a wing around Lucky's shoulder. 'Dear me, whatever will become of us?'

'Hee-haw,' said Lucky, not really knowing what else to say.

Hooter's commentary went on, 'I can see them more clearly now. They keep a good formation I'll give them that, a very good formation indeed. They're a quarter of a mile away and closing fast. Prepare yourselves, Constables, stand firm…I can make out more detail now, yes, I can see their hats as plain as day.' It took the inspector a few moments to realize what he'd just said. 'Hats? They're wearing Stetson hats, and listen…can anyone else hear hooters?'

'Yes, I believe I can, sir,' replied PC Roberts.

'So can I, sir,' said PC Russell.

The raucous honking of hooters grew louder and louder.

'They're coming straight at us now, the nerve of them, taking the mickey out of my hooter indeed. Brace yourselves for impact.'

Unlike the soft, polite monotone of the inspector's bulb hooter, these incoming hooters were coarse and two tone. The honking rapidly grew to a deafening crescendo, honk-onk, honk-onk they went, the 'onk' being a higher pitch than the 'honk'.

Determined to look his adversaries in the eye, Hooter kept his gaze on the leader of the pack who was now very low. *Probably preparing to strike.*

'Remember, Constables, this time when I say duck, I mean duck down, not "ooh look there's a duck".'

Having cleared up that misunderstanding they stood ready, one and all, as brave as always. 'Good heavens,' exclaimed Hooter, struggling to make himself heard, 'what a dreadful din!' The incoming hooters were almost on top of them, and ear piercingly loud.

Suddenly, and hardly believing his eyes, the inspector yelled almost euphorically. 'What on Earth? Well I never – it's all right, it's all right. Look everyone, look!'

With bills agog, those on the ground stared up at the airborne formation.

'What a sight,' shouted one constable.

'They're wonderful,' added Moira. 'They're not pterosaurs at all, they're Canada geese.'

'It's the Mounties,' shouted another.

Having ceased honking their hooters, the five geese whistled past low and fast before turning in a broad arc to make their return. They displayed none of the bright colours of the mallards, but were none the less very smart looking birds. Their feathers of black, beige, and white afforded crisply defined patterns about their bodies and wings. Especially smart were their black necks and heads shown off with a pure white band from cheek to cheek beneath their chins. *Superb artwork.*

The constables breathed a sigh of relief. Moira released Lucky from her grasp and clapped her wings in joyous excitement. 'Oh, how handsome they are,' she cried, as tears of joy ran down her cheeks. Lucky brayed uncontrollably as usual. 'Hee-haw, hee-haw.'

Maintaining their formation throughout, the geese prepared to land at the side of the track. With their wings held high and wide they slowed in the air as much as they could without stalling before completing their landing with half a dozen strides on the ground.

'Impressive!' Hooter muttered, just loud enough for everyone to hear. His constables too were impressed. They eyed the newcomers up and down, comparing the Mounties appearance to their own.

Four of the geese remained at attention, heads up, chests out, with the wide brims of their Stetson hats perfectly parallel to the ground – absolutely immaculate.

The lead bird cleared his throat with a 'honk' and then waddled smartly towards Hooter. He stopped two paces short and raised a wing in salute. 'I'm Sergeant Bob Uppendown of the

Royal Canadian Mounted Police, at yer service, sir.'

Hooter gladly returned the salute and replied with an obvious note of relief in his voice. 'I'm Inspector Hooter of the Flying Squad, we're very pleased to see you, Sergeant. For one moment we thought we had a fight on our hands.'

'How's that, sir?' queried the sergeant.

Hooter explained, 'I'm afraid we're all somewhat paranoid at the moment. When we saw you in the distance we thought the worst, and assumed you were more pterosaurs coming to sort us out. Bogs – they're nasty bits of work, and ugly too, not a bit like you and your officers. I must commend you on your appearance, Sergeant, very smart, very smart indeed.'

'Why thank you, sir,' the sergeant replied in a kindly North American accent. 'I guess you've been through a hard time lately. May we offer you some refreshment?'

'We could certainly do with a drink,' replied Hooter, 'but what supplies do you have?' He scanned the other four Mounties who were still standing to attention, a good bit taller than him and with no obvious supplies among them; or any horses for that matter. *How can a Mountie be a Mountie without a horse to mount?*

'Well, sir, my other two officers will be here any time now,' explained the sergeant. 'The five of us were flying ahead to scout fer any trouble when we spotted yer group here.'

The sound of distant hooves on the track interrupted the conversation. Sergeant Uppendown looked over his shoulder and gestured. 'Here they come now, right on cue.'

The approaching spectacle lifted the mallards' hearts enormously, and once again Moira couldn't contain her emotions. 'Oh my, look at them, oh, how wonderful, look, Lucky, look, we're saved!' She wiped the tears from her eyes as into view came two fine dark brown horses pulling an open wagon with a single Canada goose sitting at the front. To the left of the wagon was another horse complete with rider, lance and red pennant – so grand.

The wagon came to a halt ten paces short of the waiting group so as not to bring the rising dust too close. Behind the wagon five more horses were tethered, all dark coloured and in fine physical shape, most likely of Hanoverian descent. The entire ensemble drew immense admiration from the inspector and his constables. 'So smart, so smart,' they all muttered.

'You made good time,' said Sergeant Uppendown to the two new arrivals.

'Fer sure, Sergeant,' replied the Mountie on the horse.

Uppendown continued, 'Let's not waste time. Break out the food and water fer our English friends. I guess this is as good a place as any to rest up.'

Everyone gathered round the wagon while the geese set down water barrels and buckets of food pellets for all to share. Using planks and boxes to create makeshift benches, they were soon all seated and enjoying the food and the company.

All were quick to engage in conversation. The constables were keen to know all about the Royal Canadian Mounted Police, and likewise the Mounties were fascinated by the Flying Squad.

'How did you come to be all the way out here?' asked Hooter while mixing the pellets with water, and fashioning the whole into a pellet cake.

Sergeant Uppendown replied, 'Well it wus a curious thing, sir; my constables and I were returning from a supplies run with our wagon. We were about halfway between Smallbeef and Davidsmeadow when we came across one of yer police constables. I have to say he wus in quite a state, he had this bicycle—'

Hooter interrupted. 'Ah, that would be the village bobby; he's not actually one of my squad, but I sent him with an urgent message to HQ asking for reinforcements. He wasn't on a bend in the road was he?'

'Well, as a matter of fact, yes he wus. And the truth is he wusn't on the bicycle so much as the bicycle wus on him; it took quite a while to untangle him from it. When I asked what wus in the message he wus holding, he refused to say, insisting that his instructions were to deliver it to HQ and no one else.'

The inspector nodded. 'That sounds like the village bobby, right enough.'

The sergeant went on, 'He wus a tough little character fer sure – it took all seven of us standing over him and a direct order from me to persuade him to relinquish the note. However, once I'd read the message which I now know came from you, I assured the constable that we would divert and try to locate you. Then we sat him back on his bicycle with the note, put his helmet on as straight as we could and bade him good luck, and that wus the last we saw of him. I sure hope he gets through okay.'

'I'm sure he will, Sergeant; he's nothing if not persistent.'

Likewise, the constables had engaged in enthusiastic conversation with each other while tucking into the food laid out around them.

'I'm PC Robert Roberts, so you're Canadian then, what's your name?'

'Kintooit, Constable Lou Kintooit,' replied the Mountie. 'None of us are really Canadian anymore. Our forebears were; they migrated to this country many generations ago. They must have liked it so much that they ended up staying here. We're all from West Sussex, about a hundred of us altogether. We moved inland fer better grazing and to stock up on supplies before moving on. That's when we bumped into yer village bobby.'

'Fortunate for us you did.' Roberts couldn't help but gaze at the perfectly flat rim and the four identical dimples around the dome of the Mountie's hat which sat precisely upon the goose's head. The buff colour and the brown leather strap completed the understated look.

'You wanna try it on?' said Lou.

'Okay, I'll try yours and you try mine,' replied Roberts, eagerly swapping hats, much to the amusement of the others.

Roberts carefully placed the Stetson on his head taking great care not to misshape it. Despite the difference in size of the two birds, their heads were of similar girth, and the buff coloured hat contrasted exquisitely with the bright green-blue of the mallard's head.

'Wow,' exclaimed the others. They had to admit he looked strikingly handsome in his borrowed headgear.

Roberts couldn't help himself from indulging in a little light humour. He carefully tipped the hat to the back of his head and performed a rather dubious impersonation of a Canadian accent.

'Well hi there, stranger, how yer doin'; an' a rootin' tootin' yawl, fer sure.'

In response to this comic assault, Lou Kintooit placed the PC's helmet on his own head, and then proceeded to prove that he too was capable of a poor impersonation of another breed.

With his wings behind his back, he bent his legs up and down, saying in a very dodgy English accent, 'Ello 'ello 'ello, what 'ave we 'ere then? I hinsist you stop in the name of the law, sonny, or helse I shall 'ave to harrest you for bein' a duck-filled flatter puss.'

Such a distraction was very welcome for the Flying Squad and their charges, and for the next half an hour they enjoyed the mutual aspirations and respect which they so happily shared.

Eventually, Hooter brought things back down to Earth. 'I'm afraid we'll have to bring this joviality to an end for the time being, Sergeant. We really need to think about getting the donkey back to Smallbeef for treatment, he's very unwell.'

'I guess yer right, sir, we'll be glad to be of assistance.'

'Splendid,' said Hooter. 'In that case I suggest the moorhen and the donkey both travel in the back of your wagon, how does that sound?'

'That sounds fine, Sir. I think we'll have to leave some of the supplies here to make room fer them?'

Hooter agreed. 'A good idea, the supplies can be picked up later when the reinforcements pass this way.'

'Fer sure, sir,' said the sergeant.

The wagon was soon emptied of all but a few essentials. It was then turned round and positioned with a plank leading up into the rear. Lucky was first up, being steadied by Moira from behind and a Mountie on each side, but he needed considerable coaxing. Walking up the ramp didn't seem natural to him. His head had never been that high off the ground before. *If my head was supposed to be that high off the ground, I would be a giraffe...whatever that is.* He nervously put his front feet on the plank, and then looked down and hee-hawed at it. Nothing happened. *Nice plank*, he thought. He figured he would try his back feet next. Once they were also on the plank he looked down and hee-hawed at it again. Still nothing happened. This went on for several minutes, with Lucky moving one foot at a time and hee-hawing at the plank between each step. The Mounties looked on, patiently standing each side of the plank in case he should become unsteady.

Having fluttered and leapt up into the wagon, Moira now stood at the top of the ramp beckoning him with words of encouragement and her wings held out waiting to embrace him. He eventually made it to the cheers of all around him, this causing another outburst of braying. 'Hee-haw, hee-haw, hee-haw.' Moira put her wing beneath his chin and he stopped. The back of the wagon was promptly closed.

The Mounties' horses looked truly splendid with their

immaculate leather-ware and deep blue and gold numnahs contrasting with their glorious dark glossy coats.

All the geese mounted their steeds and took up position in readiness to leave. Sergeant Uppendown rode point with two pairs behind him, followed by the wagon with a lone driver, and one rider following up at the rear.

'I'll report yer situation to my field officer as soon as I can, sir,' said Uppendown.

'Thank you, Sergeant, until we meet again then,' replied Hooter.

'Until we meet again, sir.'

Uppendown and Hooter then exchanged salutes as the wagon with its unlikely cargo of one donkey and one moorhen moved off at a steady walking pace in the safe hands of the Royal Canadian Mounted Police.

'Okay, Constables, form up for take off,' ordered Hooter, eager to show the Mounties that his squad could also put on a decent flying display. He was about to give the order to take off when he noticed the lid on one of the boxes left behind by the Mounties was slightly open. He waddled across to put it right; something glinted inside. He removed the lid to take a closer look.

'Hello, what have we here?' Inside the box was a helmet, similar in shape to the ones worn by his own constables, but this helmet was pure white with a highly polished spike on top and a guilt chain chin strap.

'How odd.' The inspector noticed there were six other boxes just the same. *Obviously one for each Mountie.* He replaced the lid and put the matter to the back of his mind for the time being, and returned to his constables who were still waiting at attention for his next order. 'Okay squad, prepare for take off… Take off!' They were quickly into the air at a height of five trees.

The Mounties looked up to see them in a perfect V, helmets

tilted forward at exactly the correct angle, badges gleaming and their iridescent greens and blues sparkling.

'Impressive, fer sure,' shouted the sergeant to Hooter.

They then parted company, going in opposite directions; the RCMP back to Smallbeef, and the Flying Squad onward into the land of the Bogs and whatever fate awaited them.

18

It had been a hard day for Punch. Thinking had proved fruitless. His heart lamented the loss of his red-faced friend with whom he had struck a heartening rapport. The slithers of light between the planks died as night fell. Once again thoughts of forcing his way out of the barn entered his head, but his whispers bade him not to do anything rash, and so in the absence of any other plan, he settled uneasily where he was – and tried to think some more.

The poor light couldn't conceal the look of sadness in his eyes as he lay down on the straw-covered floor. He stared into the strengthening darkness and listened to the sounds of the fading day while the incoming night elbowed its way into the fort, bestowing the surroundings with a fake peacefulness. He eventually closed his eyes and drifted into a light uneasy sleep; a sleep which afforded him scant rest while still filtering the occasional sounds from outside.

His ears pricked up when the portcullis clattered its way up, and a wagon could be heard approaching. He got to his feet and listened to the goings-on outside. The wagon stopped close by.

A deep gargled voice spoke just above a whisper, only intending to be heard by those who needed to hear it. 'Up you go, and keep quiet.'

The sound of someone climbing a ladder against the outside of the barn was plain to hear. Punch listened acutely, building a picture in his head.

The hushed voice spoke again. 'Okay, haul it up, nice and

steady.'

Above where Punch stood was a broad ledge, a mezzanine floor; he could hear someone shuffling around. Someone was up there.

'That's it, careful now, ease him in.'

Fine particles of dust floated down from between the floorboards above, dancing to the sound of something being dragged across them.

'Right, that's our job done; down you come.'

Peering through a gap in the barn wall, Punch observed the shadowy figures descend the ladder before making their way across the yard and disappearing into the night. He knew he wasn't alone; someone had remained upstairs. He couldn't see or hear anyone, but his whispers dispatched a thousand unseen hands to comfort him while he waited for more clues.

A rustling sound tickled the silence. *A mouse or a rat perhaps, scurrying along the rafters.* Quiet, then he heard it again. *Feathers? Yes it sounds like feathers.* His ears stood firmly to attention; wherever the noise was coming from he would soon find its source. A more prolonged shuffling filled the air with scent. *A familiar smell, a mallard smell.* The aroma filled his head. His heart cheered within him and he tramped his front feet on the ground in celebration.

A voice groaned from above. 'Oh, my aching head.'

Punch replied by way of a quiet huff, hoping his friend would hear without raising the attention of those outside.

'Oh, this doesn't feel like my head,' said the voice.

Punch huffed more loudly, and then again, followed by much scraping of his front hooves on the floor. He reared up on his hind legs to see a wooden crate with a caged front sitting on the ledge above him. Through the bars he recognized the shape of a mallard, not just any mallard – it was Dick looking out at him.

'Where am I?' Dick sighed. Dazed and bent double in the cage, he struggled to change his position. 'Blimey, my legs are so stiff, and my neck aches like mad.' He looked around at his surroundings as best he could in the poor light. Nothing looked familiar until his eyes fell upon his trusty companion. He raised his voice excitedly. 'Punch, my old mate, am I glad to see you, how did I get up here?' He rubbed his head again. 'Oh – I remember now, the Bogs in the inn, and the sack with the strange smell, it must have been some sort of sleeping potion.'

His talking was cut short by the rattling of chains. The barn doors opened just enough to allow a single duck to enter, pushing a wheelbarrow. The duck, a gadwall, was of similar size and shape to Dick; his plumage however, was more mottled brown and white, but he had a pleasingly friendly face nonetheless.

The gadwall pulled the doors shut behind him, and with an aching sigh he pushed the wheelbarrow nearer to Punch and set it down. In the barrow was a bucket full of clean water and a mound of fresh hay. The duck was about to lift the bucket out of the barrow when Punch buried his head in it and proceeded to drink his fill.

'I guess you wus thirsty then,' said the duck in a robust country accent.

Punch huffed a loud wet huff, letting the water trickle from his lips.

'Now then, oi've gotta make sure you two are fed and watered proper, that's what oi 'ave t'do. An' oi s'pose oi'll 'ave to go an' git some more water now, on account of you just drunk it all yerself, you nawty 'orse.'

The duck disappeared briefly outside to return a few moments later with the bucket replenished. This time Punch let him put it down on the floor.

'Roight then, oi'll fetch this 'ere mug of water up the ladder fer you ter drink, young un, but you mus' promise me there'll be no tricking goin' on, 'cos oi don' want no trouble.' The gadwall carefully carried the tin mug up the ladder and handed it through the bars.

Dick eagerly took it from him and downed the lot in two gulps. 'Aw, that's good,' he said. 'You're not the same keeper that was here earlier.'

'No, oi don't reckon oi am, but that's 'cos 'taint the same barn as you wus in earlier. You bin asleep fer a noight an' a day you 'ave.'

'A night and a day? Oh dear, where am I now then?'

The gadwall explained, 'You be in a barn in Fort Bog, that's where you be. You wus brought 'ere in the middle of the noight in a wagon, an' wus put straight up 'ere.'

'But I don't understand,' said Dick, 'why have I been locked up?'

The gadwall took the empty mug from Dick. 'Well now, young un,' oi reckon you must 'ave annoyed someone who you didn't ought ter annoy, that's what oi reckon.'

He descended the ladder and sat himself down on a hay bale, and continued chatting. 'The 'orse on t'uther 'and rode in 'ere as proud as yer loike yesdy af'ernoon – on 'is own 'e wus. Oi don't know whoy the two of you come to this land when you didn't 'ad ter. But oi got ter tell yer now, oi don't think yer goin' t' get out as easy as what yer got in, cos no one gets out, if yer see what oi mean.'

Punch steadily munched his way through the hay in the wheelbarrow while listening to the differing tones in the duck's voice. He wasn't sure if things had just got better or worse, but at least he was eating, so things were a bit better at least.

***

Inspector Hooter and his squad were approaching the humped

bridge over the narrow river. They decided to land there and make camp for the night, taking advantage of the shelter afforded by the bridge and the fresh water to drink and wash in.

Having landed, the constables lined up as smart as ever, heads up and chests out. 'Squad, fall out,' called Hooter, sniffing the air inquisitively. *Hmm, that's an odd smell.* The constables gladly relaxed, removing their helmets and stretching their legs and wings.

'Phew, that was a long day and no mistake,' said PC Roberts for all to hear.

'You're telling me,' replied Russell, his nostrils drawing the aroma of something familiar.

'At least the Mounties will get the moorhen and the donkey back to Smallbeef safe and sound, that's one good thing,' added James.

'That's right,' said Howard, 'I just hope we get some help out here before we meet any more trouble.'

'Those Canadians had a certain something about them didn't you think, Tom?' said James to Thomas while taking a welcome drink from the side of the river.

'I know what you mean. Not very colourful, but they were certainly smart.'

Russell came back into the conversation. 'And they can certainly fly all right, not an inch out of line I reckon, not an inch.'

'One thing puzzles me though,' remarked James. 'Where did they keep their hooters?'

'That's just one of the things I was wondering about,' said the inspector, joining in the discussion. 'There was something odd about those Mounties.' He paused and waved his bill in the air, sampling the scent once again. 'Horse smell, can anyone else smell it?'

'Here, sir.' Russell pointed to a dropping of dung on the grass verge.

'And look here, sir,' added Thomas. 'Hoof prints, large ones at that.'

'Marvellous,' replied the inspector, 'Dick and his horse can't be far ahead. With any luck we'll catch up with them tomorrow.'

Buoyed by their progress, the squad washed and drank, each recalling the strange events of the day, and wondering what tomorrow might bring.

***

In the barn at Fort Bog, Dick continued to quiz the duck. 'My name's Dick, what's yours?'

'Well now, moi name's Gordon – Gordon Gadwall, on account of oim a gadwall duck yer see'.

'I'm pleased to meet you, Gordon, can you open this cage so I can get down?'

Gordon looked down at his feet and shook his head. 'Well yer see, oi don't know as oi should do that on account of if oi do, then oi shall be in all sorts of trouble.'

'What do you mean, trouble?'

'Well, yer see, there's a simple rule in this place what says if yer behaves yerself yer won't get 'urt. But if yer don' behave yerself yer will get 'urt, an' so will a few others too.'

'But surely that's not right,' protested Dick.

'Well, it moight not be roight, but that's 'ow 'tis see, on account of the rules.'

Amazed at the Gadwall's attitude of resignation, Dick asked, 'How long have you been here?'

'Well, let's see now, oi've bin 'ere fer, oo, erm, well now, erm, ooh, fer as long as oi can remember, not that oi remembers much moind you.'

'But surely you'd rather live somewhere where you can do

whatever you want without getting punished for doing it.'

'Well now, that's what we do 'ere. Yes, we do whatever we loikes.'

'In that case then, you can let me out of this cage.'

'Ah, no oi can't do that, see.'

'Why not?'

'Cos oi 'aint allowed ter, that's whoi.'

'But just now you said you could do anything you want to.'

'Yes, that's roight. Anythin' we wan' ter…as long as we has bin told ter do it, that's what oi meant ter say.'

'What! Oh, this is too bad; do you mean you can't actually do anything unless you've been told to?'

'Yes, that's what oi mean, we can do anythin' as long as we has been told ter.'

'But that's ridiculous and very unfair,' Dick protested.

'Well, 'tis loike oi said, 'taint roight but we gets fed and sheltered roight enough.'

'But wouldn't you like to just go down to the river whenever you like and dabble with your bottom in the air, or even have a nap beneath a shady tree, or just wander about aimlessly?'

'Well oi dare say oi would loike ter do that, now as yer mentions it.'

'That's great then, let me down and we can get going.'

'Well, oi can't do that, yer see.'

'Why not?' said Dick, getting rather irritated by the gadwall's single mindedness.

'Cos 'tis loike oi said, 'tis against the rules, an' someone will get 'urt… In any case, you only got ter look outside in the mornin' ter see what oi mean.'

'Why, what's going to happen?' asked Dick, suddenly worried by the change of tone on the part of the gadwall.

'Well now, it seems that t'uther day, one moor'en an' a donkey went out with a load of rocks, and they hasn't come back, and a Bog scout says he saw 'em both not far from the towers what are being built, an' the moor'en wus troying ter floy. That wus until the scout caught 'er a good un in mid-air.'

Dick interrupted. 'Do you mean she was caught?'

'No,' Gordon went on, 'she wus hit, an' she wus fallin' roight enough, but then she jus' slowed roight down and made a soft landing – sort of mystical. So the scout floys back here and reports it to the leader. Any'ow, 'er 'usband and young un will pay fer it, you mark moy words.'

***

The constables huddled beneath the little bridge for warmth. The night had wiped the land and sky into one canvas with no joins. No visible horizon, no sparkling ripples on the water, no sound or shadow anywhere.

'Sir, what did you mean about there being something odd about the Mounties?' asked Russell.

Hooter explained, 'Well, it was quite strange really, there are some thoughts in my head of which I don't know the origins. But they're there sure enough, and some of those thoughts are to do with the Royal Canadian Mounted Police, the RCMP.'

'But they didn't look strange to us, sir, just like Mounties should look,' added James.

'Oh, they looked the part, and I have no doubt they are real Mounties, but I'm not quite sure where they came from. They seemed to be from different times in history, a sort of admixture.'

'Eh?' said the constables in one of their delightful moments of not understanding.

'Let me explain. You see, they were wearing Stetson hats which are part of their normal uniform, but then, when I looked in those boxes from the wagon, there were white pith helmets, presumably one for each of them.'

'Don't they wear them for posh occasions, sir?' asked Thomas, hopefully.

'Hmm, maybe PC6, maybe. But pith helmets went out of fashion way before Stetsons came in. I also noticed the outrider who arrived with the wagon, he was carrying a lance and pennant; that was the pennant of a lancer regiment, and I'm sure they were about when the North West Mounties were formed, long before they were renamed "Royal Canadian".'

The inspector looked into the blackness, puzzled and tested. The constables did likewise.

'To be honest, sir,' said PC James, 'none of this makes much sense to any of us. It's as if there's something not quite right with everything we do.'

The inspector continued, 'And then there was the sergeant's terminology. He referred to his superior as a field officer, but I'm sure these days they're called inspector, the same as me.' He paused a while, and then nodded wearily. 'You're right, Constable, this is too confusing, and it's getting late. I think we should all get a good night's sleep, and perhaps things will make more sense in the morning.'

Beneath moody clouds of inky cream the police ducks collectively sighed. They each looked down at where they knew their feet were in the darkness and wiggled them, and wondered, *Why are they webbed?*

Soon, they were all asleep.

19

Next morning the constables woke within a few minutes of each other. It felt good to shake the stilled slumber from their feathers and have a long stretch. An unfamiliar light greeted them when they emerged from beneath the bridge. The heavy dew had bestowed a silver plating upon the moor, holding all component parts of the land in place; nothing moved, no sound, the cold stillness awaiting the ingredients of life to stir it into action once more.

The constables were soon washed and watered, checking their helmets to ensure they were fit for morning parade. By this time Inspector Hooter had also readied himself. With his binoculars and hooter in place and his cap smart and sharp, he called out keenly, 'Right, Constables, fall in for muster.'

The constables lined up perfectly straight, heads up, chests out, helmets inch perfect.

Hooter walked the line, inspecting each constable in turn, speaking as he went. 'Today, we will probably make contact with the Bogs. I don't need to tell you things might get a bit tricky, but I know I can count on each and every one of you to do your duty. With due diligence I'm sure we shall prevail and bring about the safe return of the captives from the stagecoach.' He stepped back and viewed his squad as a whole. 'Well done, Constables, well done.' He then turned his attention to the ever darkening clouds in the direction they were headed. 'We have no time to lose – prepare for take off.'

The constables spread a little apart and braced themselves, waiting for the command.

'Take off!'

Into the air they rose, disciplined as one and quickly into formation with the inspector at the point. At a height of just three trees they continued to follow the track hoping it would lead them to their goal. The truth was, they didn't really know where it would lead them, but they had their faith, and sometimes that is all a duck has.

***

Travelling in the opposite direction and facing an ever brightening sky, Sergeant Bob Uppendown rode alongside the wagon whenever the width of the track permitted. 'Another few hours and we'll have you back in Smallbeef where you can get yerselves fixed up.'

'Thank you so much,' said Moira. Visions of her husband and young son soon filled her mind while tears filled her eyes.

'Hey now, ma'am, please don't upset yerself, everything will be fine,' said the sergeant. 'The Flying Squad will soon be at Fort Bog, and I am sure they won't let any harm come to yer family.'

Moira knew he was just trying to make her feel better. She knew that the seven police ducks would be no match for the dozens of Bogs waiting for them at the end of the road.

A call from the front of the group interrupted their conversation. 'Sergeant, there's someone or something on the road ahead, about half a mile distant.'

The sergeant returned to the point to survey the scene. From a pouch at the side of his saddle he took a fine black telescope. He closed one eye and held the glass up to the other. 'Well, I'll be darned…it's okay, he's friendly.'

The party continued its way along the bumpy track for five or six more minutes before halting just short of the approaching figure.

'Well, we meet again, Constable,' greeted the sergeant.

'Yes, sir, oooh,' replied the village bobby, falling from his bicycle in slow motion and clattering to the ground. Two of the Mounties jumped from their horses and helped him to his feet before dusting him off.

***

Bleak morning light lurked about the barn where Dick and Punch were stirring. Punch took his time to study his surroundings; nothing had changed apart from the weak shafts of grey light sneaking in through the gaps in the barn walls, barely making it to the floor. All outside seemed quiet while the tide of life balanced on the turn; a time when the night creatures had slipped away and the day dwellers had yet to awake.

Dick yawned and stretched his wings through the bars of the cage. 'Ahem,' he said, hoping to wake the sleeping gadwall who was blowing raspberries in his dreams. 'Ahem,' Dick called again, but louder.

'What, who, where, eh?' Gordon Gadwall bump-started into life; it took him several seconds to remember where he was, and that he had guests. 'Oh, roight, well now, of course,' he said, trying to avoid any long spells of silence while he composed himself. 'Yes, roight you are then, first things first. Oi'll go an' git some more water an' hay afore we do anythin' else.'

He opened the barn door slightly, and pushed the wheelbarrow outside with a tired sigh as if it was already the other end of the day. A few moments later he returned with fresh supplies. Punch set about devouring the hay with great gusto while Gordon took a mug of water up the ladder and handed it through the bars to Dick. 'Don't you drink that all at once, young un; oi'll be back up in a tick with some pellets, so you moind you saves a drop of water to soak 'em in.'

Gordon promptly returned with the pellets. Dick was unsure about eating them at first, not knowing what was in them, but eventually his hunger got the better of him and he set about gobbling them up to the sound of a crowd gathering outside.

'That'll be the judgin' about ter start,' said the gadwall. He turned towards the door to take his leave but his exit was blocked by Punch standing in his way. 'Oi, what's goin' on 'ere?' he asked.

Dick spoke up, 'My horse isn't moving until you let me out of this cage.'

Gordon tried to side step Punch. 'Now you be a good 'orse an' let me out, see.'

Punch side stepped with him, his unshod hooves asserting his position with a soft but heavy thud. To the right they went, then to the left. Punch's width was such that he didn't have to move much in order to block the duck's exit, either way.

'Now don't be daft, an' let me pass roight now, you nawty 'orse.' A hint of deference had entered Gordon's voice. 'Oi'm in charge 'ere don't forget, so let me out will yer, please?'

Punch gently raised and lowered his huge feet on the spot, confirming his thoughts. *I'm not moving.*

Dick called down with an air of confidence. 'My horse weighs nearly one ton, and he doesn't like seeing me locked up, if you know what I mean. So I suggest you let me out of here before he does something you might regret.'

'Well, this is a foin state of affairs this is.' Gordon scratched his head, most perplexed. 'Well, you don' give me no choice does yer. No good'll come o' this, you mark moy words, young un.' He made his way back up the ladder and released the chains from the cage door.

'Thank you,' said Dick, stepping out from the cage and taking a long stretch. The pair of them then made their way down the ladder, Gordon mumbling disconsolately as he went.

On reaching the ground, Dick had another stretch before turning to give Punch a big hug. It was then that he noticed the bloodied wounds on the horse's rump and sides. 'What the—? How did this happen?' he cried, clearly distressed.

'Ah, well now, that would be the Bogs what done that,' replied Gordon.

'Why would anyone want to hurt Punch?' Dick pushed the gadwall aside and made his way to the doors. 'Where are these Bogs?' he shouted, 'I'll show them.'

'No, young 'un, don' go out there. No good'll come of it, please,' Gordon pleaded.

Punch huffed loudly to endorse Gordon's concerns.

Dick stopped and turned. 'But how did they manage to hurt him like this?' he sniffled, holding back the tears of anger and sadness in equal measure.

'Well, there wus a lot of 'em – surroundin' 'im they wus,' replied Gordon.

'But surely Punch could have sorted them out.'

'Well, oi dare say 'e could 'ave. But oi reckon 'e wus confused cos 'e didn't know where you wus, an' 'e didn't wan' ter make things worse fer you – if yer see what oi mean'. Punch nodded his head while the gadwall continued, 'So in the end they put 'im in'ere. 'E's bin roight deep in thought ever since, oi can tell yer'.

Dick gave Punch a long hug. 'Don't worry, mate, we'll soon make you better,' he said. He then took the bucket of water and began cleaning the wounds, ably helped by Gordon.

The horse peered through eyes of soft hazel and his heart warmed to be in such amiable company once again.

Before long, the noise from outside had swelled to a level that Dick could no longer ignore. 'What **is** going on out there?'

'Well now,' replied Gordon, 'tis loike oi wus sayin'. Tis the judgin' an' the juryin' of the moor'en's husband – y'know – the moor'en what went missing with 'er donkey.'

'Do you mean they're putting the moorhen's husband on trial for something his wife did?'

'Yes, sir, that's zackly what oi mean, an' what's more, they'll probbly put the young 'un on trial too.'

'What, the baby moorhen?' Dick said in disbelief.

'That's roight. That's what oi bin troying ter tell yer. If we behaves ourselves we gets treated okay, but if we misbehaves, then someone 'as ter pay fer it, see.'

'But they can't punish the dad and the baby for something someone else did.'

'Ah, well see, they can do just about whatever they wants t' do, cos they makes the rules…an' they're big an' mean.'

Dick paced up and down, visibly shocked. 'This is dreadful.' He was beginning to think he should never have interfered. 'Should I have let Moira and Lucky come back here like she wanted? She tried to tell me what would happen if she didn't return on time, oh dear me.' He made his way to the door again, and put an eye up to the gap to get a view of the yard outside. Punch joined him and put his huge head up to the next gap along.

Gordon Gadwall didn't bother to look, he already knew what was going to happen. ''Tas 'appened so many toimes afore,' he said, forlornly.

The captive mallards and moorhens had been released from their huts, and had congregated on the far side of the yard. Like Gordon Gadwall, they knew what was coming, and gossiped anxiously among themselves while waiting for what was to be a gruesome spectacle.

The crowd parted when a team of four donkeys entered the yard pulling a sturdy four-wheeled trolley; on the trolley was fixed a large crude catapult rather like the ones used in Roman times. The weapon was already tensioned and had a large rock loaded onto it.

'I don't understand,' said Dick, 'who are they going to fire that rock at?'

'No one,' answered Gordon, 'no one.' Tears pooled in his eyes. 'They use the boulder to test the aim an' range of the catapult afore they puts it to its proper use.'

The donkeys halted when the front wheels of the trolley came to rest against two pegs standing slightly proud of the ground. This was the firing position.

Dick and Punch were puzzled by such goings-on. Again they put their eyes up to the gaps and continued to peer through.

Two artillery-bogs unharnessed the donkeys and led them away; they then returned to the side of the catapult and eyed an imaginary line along the side of the trolley, casting their gaze way beyond the walls of the fort into the far distance.

'What on Earth…?' Dick whispered to himself.

Beyond the rear wall of the fort the landscape was altogether more rugged. Sharp craggy pinnacles of razor-like rocks projected upwards from the mists far below. The rocks drew the eye to a place where the murky sky descended upon the hazy horizon many miles distant.

On the rear wall of the fort stood three Bogs, one at each end and one in the middle. Their job would be to observe the boulder as it passed overhead and confirm the distance it travelled.

The muted hubbub from the crowd was silenced instantly when a voice boomed across the fort. 'Artillery-bogs, are you ready?'

The voice sent shivers through Dick and Punch; they knew that voice. There was no mistaking the rasping chords of Beeroglad the leader.

'Ready, sir,' came the reply.

'Eeland Ross, are you ready?'

'Aye, ready, sir,' replied a young voice on the rear wall. This was the voice of the young Bog who had driven the prisoners' wagon previously. He was the son of Beeroglad, and as such was learning all aspects of Bog work in preparation to take his father's place when the time came.

Beeroglad took up position in the centre of the yard from where all could see and hear him. 'Very well,' he shouted, 'bring on the accused so that they may learn their fate.'

The crowd stood silently while a solitary donkey pulled a small open cart onto the yard. As with all donkeys in Fort Bog, he held his head low. To the Bogs, donkeys were the lowest of the low; dirty, smelly, and lacking any intelligence whatsoever, and certainly not worthy of any consideration.

On the back of the cart stood Moira's husband, William Maywell, his wings tied firmly by his sides. Next to him stood his young son, barely knee high and still mostly covered in grey fluffy down. He cheeped repeatedly while looking up at his father. This was Moira's family – the family she had fretted so anxiously over – the family she had entrusted to Dick to keep safe.

'Look well upon this boulder, moorhen,' proclaimed Beeroglad. 'If you are found guilty, you will soon follow in its wake.' With that, he turned to the two artillery-bogs who were waiting by the catapult for their orders, one of whom was armed with a hefty wooden mallet. Beeroglad gave the slightest nod. The artillery-bog struck the safety pin with the mallet; the pin shot out to the side and the arm of the catapult sprang upward with tremendous power. The trolley recoiled and juddered backwards, hurling the huge boulder with such force that it cleared the walls of the fort with ease, still rising as it passed over the head of young Eeland Ross.

The boulder flew through the chilled air for at least two hundred yards before losing height, finally crashing back to Earth a quarter of a mile away. Shards of rock flew high into the air as the boulder ploughed a cutting fifty yards long before disappearing into the mists from which the landscape stemmed.

Eeland Ross turned and called out, 'Trajectory good…range good.'

Beeroglad ordered the catapult to be re-tensioned to await its final load. He then raised his voice again, and when he was sure that everyone was listening he turned to the father moorhen. 'You, William Maywell, are charged with being the husband of the moorhen who took it upon herself to abscond with one donkey not belonging to her.' Still speaking to the father, he lowered his gaze to the baby moorhen. 'Can you confirm that this pathetic little bird is of your descent?'

'No, he's not mine, I've never seen him before,' said William, deliberately not looking down at his son for fear of his emotions giving him away. But his son looked up, cheeping expectantly, innocent of the evil workings of some grown up minds.

'I think you are lying, moorhen. It is clear that this little one is yours. Has he not followed you since his birth? Have you not fed him every minute of the day? Do you not sleep with him under your wing by night?' Beeroglad paused, keeping his stare straight at the eyes of the father. 'Well, I'm waiting for an answer. Yes or no? If you deny him, he shall be treated as an unwanted urchin and disposed of here and now, so is he yours or not?'

William knew the leader meant every word. He had no option but to tell the truth to avoid the baby being slayed on the spot. He replied quietly while looking down at the fluffy head next to him. 'He is my son.'

'Louder please, so that everyone can hear,' insisted the leader, cynically.

William shouted with tears pouring down his face. 'Yes. He **is** my son.' He struggled and twisted in an effort to release his bondage, desperately wanting to hold his little baby, but the ropes around him clung ever tighter, preventing him from doing so.

His son looked up at him – and cheeped. *My Daddy.*

20

Many miles away from the fort, Inspector Hooter and his constables were diligently following the track below them. Once again the boring landscape gave them the opportunity to let their minds wander, mostly back to the loving caresses of the beautiful lady ducks who they hoped were waiting for their safe return.

Hooter's thoughts settled on his recent encounter with the Mounties. Where did those Canadian chaps keep their hooters? And why did they have one each? My one is perfectly adequate for the entire squad. Perhaps it's in case they get separated from each other, so they can call from a distance…hmm, there might be something in that. Satisfied with his reasoning, he continued to lead his squad ever further away from home.

'Smoke on the horizon, sir, dead ahead,' called PC James.

'I see it, Constable, stay alert everyone.' Onward they flew, providing the only sparkling dash of colour in an otherwise colourless world. Their iridescent blues and greens infused the dull air with goodness and life for the briefest of moments while they passed through it.

'Upward, Constables, upward,' called the inspector.

Up they went, levelling out at a height of ten trees.

'Now we can see better,' said Hooter, concentrating on the building coming into view. 'Can anyone see anything suspicious?'

'No, sir, just someone on the veranda, sitting down I think.'

Directly over the inn, Hooter called out. 'Spiral down, follow my lead.'

Turning in a broad arc, the squad viewed the building from all sides. The figure seated on the veranda kept his head beneath his cloak, but his lifeless black eyes were measuring their advance.

After making several passes, the inspector called out again. 'Prepare to land.'

They landed immediately in front of the inn, heads up, helmets at precisely the correct angle and chests out.

'Stay alert, Constables, stay alert.' Hooter took a few moments to peruse the lacklustre building of grey timber, *Hmm, no colour whatsoever, how sad.*

The lone figure rocked back and forth in the rocking chair, concealed by his heavy cloak. With his head down, his long beak lay on his chest unnoticed, and the cloak draped on the floor, covering his clawed feet entirely. Despite it being almost midday the light was still poor, worsened by the dim shadow cast by the porch above the veranda. Such conditions served to transform the shape of the cloak as it hung from high above the Bog's head concealing its folded wings and its lethal tail.

The inspector waddled slowly but surefootedly towards the entrance, sharing his gaze between the seated figure and the door. He observed no movement at either and stepped up onto the veranda and began reading the sign above the door.

'B...of, er, something or other, are welcome to stay, all the...erm. Oh, it's no use. I can't make out the rest of it.' He turned in blissful ignorance of what was lurking beneath the cloak. 'Excuse me, sir,' he said.

The figure did nothing to acknowledge the inspector's address.

'Ahem.' Hooter raised his voice, almost sounding impertinent. 'Excuse me, sir, can you tell me where my constables and I might find some refreshment and a place to rest for a while?'

The figure raised one arm beneath the cloak and gestured towards the door. Hooter followed the aim. The door slowly opened. From within came the sound of jollity and much conversation punctuated by the frequent chinking of glasses.

'Ah, that's wonderful,' said Hooter, beckoning his squad in the direction of the door. 'We'll take a drink or two in here and see what we can find out from the locals.'

The six constables followed their inspector onto the veranda and in through the doorway, passing within inches of the Bog. Inside there was no one to be seen; no chairs, no drinks, no one; only the sound of a room full of souls enjoying themselves; a shady empty room devoid of life.

***

At the fort, the two artillery-bogs had repositioned the catapult and were busy cranking the ratchet to re-tension the arm. The crowd waited in silence with heads low, desperately sad. The baby moorhen chirped at his father, unaware of what was going on. Again the father writhed and wriggled in an attempt to release the ropes holding him, but to no avail; they remained as tight as ever.

Beeroglad raised his head to declare the fate of the father and son. He pointed his beak to the sky and held his wings at full stretch, but his address was abruptly interrupted when an ear-piercing crack echoed throughout the fort. All eyes were on the centre of the yard where the two artillery-bogs were now lying on the ground with the arm of the catapult split in two.

The Bogs scrambled to their feet in an undignified fashion. One called out with an air of trepidation, hoping desperately not to receive any blame for the misfortune. 'Broken tension lever, sir.'

'Then pull it out of the way and bring on another unit, quickly,' retorted Beeroglad, angry at having his flow interrupted.

'Aye, aye, sir.' The two Bogs, relieved at not being chastised further, quickly harnessed the donkeys to the trolley and began hauling the broken catapult away.

'Make way, make way,' they shouted at the crowd. 'Out of the way there.'

The donkeys dug their hooves into the dust and heaved for all their worth to drag the wagon round in a tight turn. They hee-hawed and champed as they inched their way forward, overcoming the pain from their backs and feet. Like Lucky, they were uncared for, but this was their life; it would get no better as far as they could see, so they just got on with it, sharing each other's whispers for comfort.

Behind the scenes, ten Bogs armed with levers and ropes hurriedly loaded a test boulder onto the replacement catapult. At the same time, four more donkeys were harnessed up and immediately whipped into action. Two Bogs tried to re-tension the ratchet as the wagon was being hauled onto the yard, but in the interests of safety they decided to wait until the weapon was at rest in its final firing position before completing their task.

Beeroglad tapped his clawed fingers on the ground, frustrated by the delay. He quickly grew tired of waiting, and turned to William Maywell.

'Worry not, moorhen; this minor failing will not prolong your agony or your existence for too long.' He continued to deliver his verdict while the catapults were being exchanged. 'I find you guilty by association with the felonious Moira Maywell with whom you are partnered, of the theft of one donkey, and guilty by association with the same moorhen, of desertion.'

William kept his head low throughout the address. He knew his fate was sealed, but he was still hopeful of his son being spared to live with another family who would gladly take him in.

Beeroglad dashed such hopes. 'Equally, as you are in association with your partner, so indeed is your son, therefore he shall endure the same punishment as you.'

Everyone knew what that punishment would be…it had been dealt many times before.

William heaved within his bondage. 'No!' He looked straight into the dark eyes of the Bog. 'Let my son live, he—'

'Shut up!' The leader's abrasive chords stopped the moorhen's protestations dead. 'You know the rules, you all know the rules.' He shouted at the grief stricken crowd. 'As soon as the catapult is ready, William Maywell and his son shall be placed in it and fired into oblivion as the rock was before them.'

'Please, not my son, you know he is innocent,' William pleaded. But his words meant nothing to a soul as black as the eyes through which it saw the world.

'You have been judged and found guilty,' Beeroglad growled, 'that is an end to it. If you break the rules you pay the price – dearly.'

'Says who?' A youthful voice called from the far side of the yard.

A hundred breaths drew sharply, followed by an eager expectant silence; a silence which knew there was no way back. Time had inexorably brought this moment about, a moment which might not allow passage for all, but for whom remained to be seen.

Beeroglad flinched. *Someone has dared to interrupt me, dared to question me. No one does that…not if they value their lives.* He very slowly turned his unforgiving gaze in the direction of the voice until his long beak halted like a pointer aimed at its target.

There on the other side of the yard stood the beautifully muscled chesnut Suffolk Punch, his broad head with bright eyes looking straight at Beeroglad. No fear, no trepidation, just faith and honesty. On his back sat his immaculate young mallard friend, with no hat. Two pairs of eyes with one cause, one hope, and of one heart, dared to stare into the eyes of a loveless tyrant.

The horse and rider presented a vivid spectacle set against the drab greys of the fort walls and the monotone grey of the Bogs. Even the mallards in this place took on a dusty grey hue concealing their once vibrant colours.

Dick and Punch maintained their resolute stance. *No turning back now.*

Beeroglad lashed out in a sharp fit of rage striking the nearest bird to him, a mother mallard. His arm with clenched fist dealt a heavy blow to her chest, sending her hurtling backwards completely off her feet. She was out cold before she landed in the bosom of the mallards standing behind her.

Ignoring the bird he had just struck, Beeroglad took two steps forward to clear himself from the crowd. He wanted everyone to see him deal with the bolshie mallard and the do-gooder horse. Until now he had been undecided as to what to do with them, but now he had no choice. If he was to maintain his credibility he had to deal with them swiftly and permanently. That was all he knew.

Punch exhaled loudly; his nostrils flexed in anticipation, feeling the air. The whites of his eyes contrasted boldly with the rich brown of his pupils, such was his concentration. He stood firm with every muscle poised; his huge thighs, his chest and neck flushed with powerful blood. He could smell the mind of the Bog facing him; he didn't need to hear his words. His whispers painted pictures in his head, warming and guiding him. He felt the thousand hands from previous times of hardship cupped around him, comforting him.

Dick's legs very gently squeezed Punch's girth. Punch moved forward slowly, each hoof softly but firmly pressing the dust into the ground as he went.

Beeroglad remained where he was, content for the horse to come to him. He stared heartlessly into the horse's eyes. He knew it was from here that the reckoning would come, not from the mallard whose hat he was still wearing in arrogant defiance.

Ten paces apart, Punch walked onward, slowly closing the gap. No one dared make a sound; not one bird nor a single Bog cast so much as a solitary breath into the air.

21

Somewhere out on the moor the squeak squeak of bicycle pedals tickled the silence. The village bobby pedalled for all his worth, trying to catch up with the Flying Squad. He had a written message to deliver from HQ. He had passed the Canadian Mounties earlier that day and read the communication aloud to them. *'To Inspector Hooter from HQ – stop – Reinforcements unable to get to you for two days – stop – Suggest you make camp and wait for their arrival before engaging the pterosaurs also known as Bogs – message ends.'*

***

Inside the inn, the Flying Squad stood in puzzlement at their surroundings. The sounds of jollity were coming from somewhere, but there was no one to be seen.

'Hmm, something's not quite right here, Constables,' said Hooter, stating the obvious. He suspected someone might be listening in on him, so he continued in a whisper, 'Spread out and search the room very carefully.'

The constables searched every nook and cranny in the dim and musty room. The anticipation of discovering something unpleasant was tangible, but wherever they looked there was nothing there. They looked under the tables, *nothing*; they looked under the chairs, *nothing*. They searched the shadowy corners, *nothing there either*. This was a room held prisoner by its own confines, depriving itself of the company of others. A sad room within a sad building.

PC Russell had reached the bar; he stretched and peered over, half expecting to see a staircase leading down to a secret basement from where the voices were coming. There were no stairs and no basement, but something disturbed him. 'Oh dear, oh dear,' he said, 'this doesn't look good.'

'What is it?' asked Hooter.

'I think you should look at this, sir – I think we're all in danger.'

'Why would you think that?' said Hooter, making his way across the dusty floor with the rest of his constables following behind.

Russell pointed silently with his bill, drawing the inspector's gaze over the bar to where the old wind-up gramophone whirred round, busily generating the voices and merriment which had drawn the mallards like flies into a spider's web.

'What the devil?' murmured Hooter. 'It's some kind of voice machine…but why?'

All seven mallards stared over the bar, side by side. They watched the record going round and round, gradually slowing as it unwound, until finally the ever lowering tones ground to a halt and the record lay still and silent, resting, waiting.

Not knowing how such a contraption worked, the mallards gazed at it, puzzled and unsure if it might start up again of its own accord. They watched and waited a few moments more. Nothing happened. Nothing, until a lump of wood slid across the floor from the doorway, stopping at the inspector's feet.

They all turned round expecting to see someone. No one was there. They looked down at the floor and quickly realized the piece of wood was in fact the sign from above the door outside. Now it was Hooter's turn to read it aloud just as Dick had done when he passed this way previously.

'Beasts of Grey are welcome to stay, all the rest shall become our prey.'

No sooner had the inspector finished reading it when a figure shuffled into the doorway. The mallards looked up to see a cloaked Bog holding back the light and silhouetting himself against the laboured day behind him. He stepped over the threshold and paused. His cloak which had previously aided his concealment fell heavily to the floor. Dust rose lazily from the boards then quickly fell to where it had lain for ages past.

Memories of their last meeting with the Bogs were only too clear. This one remained quite still before them, seemingly happy to let the birds study him in detail.

As far as the mallards were concerned, he was identical in every way to Beeroglad, perhaps an inch or two shorter but his build, claws, and folded wings all looked the same. The eyes as black as tar couldn't be seen in the shadows, but the mallards knew they were there, looking at them, thinking, waiting and plotting. The Bog's tail continued to sway slowly back and forth behind his head, as if to remind them of what might be to come.

The constables gleaned little of the reptile's intentions, such was his inanimate posture. Hooter finally decided he would have to make the first move. He waddled forward to separate himself from his squad. The Bog's eyes gave no sign of movement.

'Now look here, my friend,' began Hooter in his dependable and proper police-duck voice, 'we are on official police business and at this moment we have no quarrel with you, so let's have no trouble, shall we?'

The Bog remained unmoved. All he could see was a group of strangers, all very smart and clean with very posh hats upon their brilliantly coloured heads. He instinctively felt he shouldn't let them pass, but he didn't know why. If he'd had a companion whose eyes he could stare into he might have come to a conclusion. He felt alone and empty. He couldn't let them go on their way, for that was not the way of Bogs, and yet he didn't feel he should commit an act of aggression without some good reason. He continued staring, giving nothing away, but looked menacing all the same.

'Erm, right, Constables,' said Hooter, with a slight hesitancy in his voice, 'follow me – nice and slow.'

PC Roberts anxiously offered a suggestion. 'Perhaps if we all blow our whistles at him, sir. That might be enough to convince him to move.'

'It's worth a try,' said Hooter. 'Prepare your whistles, Constables.'

Each constable put his whistle to his bill.

'After three. One…two…three.' They all blew furiously, but seven duck whistles 'quacking' had no effect on the monster before them. 'As I thought, this character isn't about to go quietly.'

Hooter then took a deep breath and slowly made his way to the doorway which at this time was effectively blocked by the Bog.

One by one the constables waddled in single file in the wake of their trusted inspector. Hooter hoped the Bog would move aside as he neared him, but the creature remained resolute in his bearing without so much as blinking. Hooter looked to one side of the Bog, and then to the other, but neither side afforded enough room to squeeze past.

Standing almost twice the height of the inspector, the Bog tilted his head and looked down. Hooter looked up. The Bog's eyes, devoid of the slightest fleck of light or life sent a chill down Hooter's spine. Their stares remained locked.

Hooter continued the dialogue, 'I'm asking you very nicely to move out of our way. Please don't make me use force to persuade you.' The next few words had little weight attached to them, as the entire squad recalled the comprehensive beating they'd received the last time the inspector uttered them. 'After all, there is only one of you and seven of us, so be a good chap and be on your way, thank you.'

Those words meant nothing to the Bog, and he remained as still as a statue in the doorway, giving no hint of thought or intention. Once more Hooter sized up the gap at each side. *Hmm, the right side looks the best bet.* He knew in his mind he had no hope of actually passing through the gap, but he had no other option. Ducks don't do walking backwards, and he was certainly not going to give the order to about-turn and retreat back into the room; that would be one capitulation too far. So, knowing that his next move might well provoke a reaction from the Bog, he took another deep breath and side stepped to line himself up with the very narrow gap. He moved forward until his shoulder gently came into contact with the hard bone of the Bog's wing. He then squeezed himself against the door frame and began to push gently, hoping that this would be enough to persuade the Bog to move aside.

The Bog yielded at first, allowing his body to be eased away from the frame just a little, but his feet stayed firmly where they were. The constables watched nervously as their leader pressed further into the gap. There soon came a point when Hooter was neither in nor out. The Bog then resumed his original stance, leaning firmly on the hapless inspector and bringing his passage to a halt.

'Ooh, ahh, erm, oh dear.' Hooter's words became stifled and crushed as surely as he himself was. Such was the weight of the Bog leaning against him that he could neither go out nor come back in. Mallards are very softly built creatures and don't do well when subjected such abuse. The Bog remained firmly fixed in the doorway, and was beginning to have a dire effect on the inspector who had now stopped making any sound at all.

The constables realized something had to be done quickly. PC Howard shouted with an urgency he had never employed before. 'Come on, lads, charge in the name of the law!'

Their effect was staggered as each one of them impacted against the Bog at one second intervals. The Bog stood firm, as one, then two, then three, then four mallards put their shoulders into him – then five. He began to waver, but his tail above his head took a lot of the strain against the top of the doorframe, so preventing him from being pushed through.

By now Hooter was in a serious fix, being slowly but surely crushed against the door frame, and having great difficulty in breathing. Then the last mallard, PC James, weighed in. The Bog stood firm until the frame above the doorway yielded with a dull crack. Fragments of timber fell about the birds below. With no frame to brace himself against, the Bog stumbled backwards, succumbing to the weight of six mallards pushing against him. He struggled to regain his balance as he and the constables fell blindly out onto the veranda. The Bog gave out a shrill cry when he finally lost his footing and reeled backwards down the step, landing in the dust outside the inn. The six constables haphazardly came to rest on or around him.

'Keep on him!' called one of them. 'Don't let him get up or we've had it.'

The Bog surprised them with his speed and agility. Spreading his hands and feet wide, he arched his back with such force that the two ducks sitting on his chest were thrown up into the air like big soft toys. Using their wings to direct their descent they landed clear of the others, but the Bog was now standing on his feet, and clearly not happy.

The constables quickly formed a circle, hoping to contain him.

'Don't let him open his wings,' shouted PC Thomas.

They should have known his wings weren't the problem. The Bog opened his beak wide and let out a chilling cry, calling to the sky and bringing his tail down just above the ground. The police ducks had no time to think about jumping on it before it swung round at an incredible rate. Almost a blur, it took every duck off his feet in less than a second.

All six constables were on their backs, their legs badly bruised.

Hooter lay on the veranda trying to get his breath back after being almost crushed to death. He stared helplessly at his young constables who were once again in tatters on the ground.

Intent on finishing the fight there and then, the Bog twisted his body to create more tension before delivering one final swipe at the ducks lying in the dust. He straightened his tail to gain maximum centrifugal force, and then he raised his head and sent another spine-chilling shriek into the air.

The inspector was sure he was about to witness his brave young constables being dealt a lethal blow. 'No!' he shouted at the top of his voice. 'Stop, in the name of all that is good …please!' He closed his eyes, unable to bear the conclusion of the fight. *My dear young constables, please, no! Please don't do it.* A thousand miniature ducks wept bitterly into his heart.

The next thing he heard was a clattering, followed by a muted squawk, and then the odd tinkle and squeak. He opened his eyes, as did all his constables. The Bog tried to complete his assault, but it wasn't easy; not when a bicycle frame had just been flung over his shoulders and pulled down onto his hips, and so keeping his arms strapped to his sides.

'Should I arrest him, sir, or would you like to do it?' said the village bobby standing with his helmet on crooked. 'They're better than handcuffs, these bicycles.'

The Bog struggled to ease himself from the metal bondage thrust upon him. Each twist and wriggle caused the bicycle frame to tighten around him. When the pedals and handlebars began to dig into his wings he stopped trying; such damage was to be avoided at all cost, and so he yielded to his unlikely captor and stood silently awaiting his fate, as if expecting some unimaginable award for his failure.

'Well done, my lad, well done. Brilliant bicycle work!' shouted Hooter, joyously. 'I knew that bike would come in handy one day,' he added. 'Oh yes, no doubt about it, brilliant bicycle work.'

The bobby stood proudly next to his prisoner as if about to have his photo taken with a prize catch. But there were no such things as cameras in this strange land of talking ducks in policemen's hats. Unfortunately, the jubilation was short lived.

'What's that noise, sir?' asked PC James.

They all listened curiously. There was no mistaking the sound of whooshing wings – large wings, and getting louder by the second.

'Quickly, everyone inside – leave the Bog where he is,' shouted Hooter. 'Take cover'.

The ducks quickly waddled into the relative safety of the inn. Once more their minds filled with dread as they wondered what might be about to descend upon them.

The lone Bog stood outside in the dust with the bicycle wrapped tightly around his body, preventing any movement. He looked up to the sky and once more gave a desperate cry for help.

The police ducks peered out through the grimy window panes.

Hooter's chest hurt. The constables' legs hurt.

Shadows of large wings raced across the dust-laden ground, getting larger and lower.

22

At Fort Bog, the confrontation between Beeroglad and Punch continued. Beeroglad focused intensely upon the eyes of the horse. *Come closer,* he thought, all the time trying to figure him out. *Why are you here? Why should you care about these pathetic creatures? Their future has no tie with yours; you stand to make no profit from this mission, and you shall gain no effect on your well-being. So why are you here?*

The barely audible duff, duff of unshod hooves belied the true weight of the horse that would tread so softly but stoutly upon the earth. His whispers comforted him as they always did in times of trouble. He remembered the words of the coloured Bog, warm and good. *See with your heart, not your eyes. Serve your heart, not your ego.* He hadn't understood the words at the time, but now, strangely, his mind was clear and his resolve strengthened by them. But other words from the past also came to mind, words he knew to be a portent of malevolence – these were the words of Beeroglad on their first meeting. *'Do not try to face me down, for I shall unleash a wrath the like of which even your big head can't imagine. Your muscles will fail before me.'*

The warmth of a thousand hands caressed Punch's heavily ribbed sides, he knew this was where he had to be. For his part, Dick held no tension on the reins and no pressure on the stirrups. They were now only five paces from Beeroglad, with not a sound from the onlookers. Mother Nature waited with bated breath, issuing not so much as a puff of a breeze. Beeroglad drew long streams of air from the horse, hoping to smell the smell of fear, but there was none of it. Punch searched for the smell of anything other than anger, but the Bog hid his feelings well.

At three paces, Beeroglad spoke abruptly. Punch stopped and listened.

'This is as far as you go, horse, you may turn and leave with no hindrance, but listen and pay heed; if you take one more step it will be your last, you shall neither turn nor prevail.'

The chesnut horse stayed where he was, looking into the solid eyes blocking the way to the Bog's heart.

Beeroglad had never known anyone to persevere in this way, but his patience was running out. 'Well, what is it to be? Will you turn, or will you be wiped out along with your feathered companion who sits atop you?'

Dick said nothing. He knew Punch was in the hands of his heart and soul, and no words were going to change that.

Beeroglad stooped a little more until his eyes were level with those of the horse.

Rightly or wrongly, Punch took this as an invite to come closer. He gave a soft huff and walked forward. One pace – two paces – three paces. Only a few inches separated them; the crowd waited; Mother Nature waited.

Beeroglad felt uncomfortable with the horse's eyes lingering in his, trying to lure him out. He remained unmoved, his wings firmly at his sides and his breathing barely discernible. *He will come no closer,* he thought to himself. *I cannot let him come closer.*

But Punch did come closer; he leaned forward, stopping so close that his whiskers touched the tip of Beeroglad's beak. A momentary flash of blue flickered in the Bog's eyes, the call of a soul desperately wanting Punch to reach in and hold it. In less than a second it was snuffed out from within, but not before Punch had seen it.

Beeroglad could smell and taste Punch's presence, so close

were they. At first he gagged in revulsion at such a disgusting creature being in his face, and yet the air between them was sweet, but he was having none of it. He opened his beak the tiniest amount, enough to utter on his breath for Punch alone to hear.

'I cannot let you do this – do not try me – do not take away my choice, for I shall not lose face before my people.'

Like a dam in full breach, whispers gushed between Punch's heart and soul, compelling him to complete his move. He gently pressed his nostrils against the Bog's beak, and waited, knowing a response would not be long in coming.

Beeroglad couldn't be seen to look away. 'You ask too much of me, horse.'

Warmth, softness and love trickled from the horse's big bright eyes, flying brazenly in the face of the Bog.

'Enough!' cried Beeroglad. Another flash of colour desperately sparked in his eyes.

Punch peered in, but the eyes instantly filled with blackness and shut him out again.

The Bog flexed his claws and tore at Punch's shoulder. Four lines of flesh were bared through the rich chesnut coat. Crimson freely trickled from each.

Punch's eyes widened, his nostrils tightened and his lower lip dropped. His feet stayed planted on the ground while his eyes continued their search for the light beyond the black orbs.

The dark presence within Beeroglad would have him slay the horse there and then, but he couldn't help but be drawn to the expression on the horse's face, the furry ears still upright, the big brown eyes still looking straight at him, and the soft plump lips now portraying a look of sadness and hurting.

Beeroglad's emotions pounded against the inside of his head, emotions long since buried and denied the light of life by the corrupt dark one that had made its home within him.

Why can I not cut this beast down where he stands? He mocks me, and yet his eyes encourage me. He goads me, and yet I feel a kindly warmth all about him. He seeks to humiliate me, and yet he takes nothing from me.'

Beeroglad pressed his beak against Punch's muzzle. Punch slowly tipped his head downward, and the Bog followed until their foreheads touched. Beeroglad pushed harder, trying to show that he was the stronger combatant. Punch braced his hind legs and leaned forward, their foreheads now pressing hard against each other's.

Standing on all fours, Beeroglad repositioned his feet further back to get a better purchase, and pushed harder still.

Punch stood firm, all the time keeping his eyes fixed on those of the Bog.

'Yield,' Beeroglad commanded, 'or this moment shall be your last.'

But Punch wouldn't yield. His voices welled up inside him, and his unseen hands reached out lovingly. He knew that somewhere deep within the Bog was a soul crying out to be held. Again Beeroglad's eyes succumbed briefly, acknowledging something trying to enter.

Punch held his stance. His whispers raced to the fore, calling to him, *Now, now let us loose*, they cried. His hazel eyes widened and his whispers rushed forth, overwhelming the Bog and not giving him a chance to rally his dark defences.

Beeroglad's eyes flashed back and forth from blue to black, and back to blue again, desperately trying to bar the horse's advance. 'No!' he cried, 'I shall prevail over you.' Summoning every ounce of strength in his body, his thighs swelled, as did his back and chest muscles, delivering their massive thrust against the horse. Keeping his forehead firmly against that of the horse, he grew in stature as his entire body became engorged with all the hatred and anger he could muster. Not content with pushing heads, Beeroglad lowered his stance and leaned his hard bony shoulder into Punch's chest. Now he pushed with all his might. Now he would vanquish this horse before the eyes of all present, and force him to his belly.

But Punch would not move.

The Bog redoubled his efforts and let out an ear-piercing scream while sinking his shoulder further into the horse.

Without uttering a sound, Punch fired all his strength into his hind quarters.

The Bog slid his feet further back, forcing his bony shoulder ever deeper into the huge muscles of the horse's chest. Punch kept his head low, his sheer weight and strength combining to overhaul the grey beast, who by now was becoming exhausted from his exertion.

Somewhere in heaven is the blueprint for a Suffolk Punch, on which it clearly states: *Such a creature shall be capable of pushing, and then pushing harder for longer – and then pushing some more.* Punch was a supreme example of his breed, and so he just kept pushing – pushing into the Bog, forcing him backwards until his back was against the fort wall and he could go no further. The crowd gawped in disbelief. Punch halted instantly.

Dick leaned down from the saddle. 'I'll take that,' he said, removing the blue hat from Beeroglad's head.

'If you want the hat, then go and get it,' shouted Beeroglad, snatching it back from Dick's grasp and throwing it across the yard. The hat whirled through the air straight and level until it struck one of the artillery-bogs right in the eye; he staggered and fell back against the catapult, accidently striking the firing pin and releasing it. The catapult, still not fully tensioned, half-heartedly hurled its boulder into the air. The lump of rock had barely enough energy to make it to the fort wall where Eeland Ross was posted. The crowd gasped. The observers on each end of the wall jumped for their lives, but Beeroglad's son seemed transfixed as he watched the boulder coming towards him.

'No, no!' screamed Beeroglad, watching what was certainly the last few seconds of his son's life. 'No, please no!' His eyes were now fully coloured, brilliant blue and sparkling, unashamedly giving vent to all his emotions.

Upon hearing his father's calls, Eeland Ross suddenly realized his plight. His wings shot out to the sides and he leapt outwards from the wall. The boulder crashed down on the very spot where the youngster had been standing. Lumps of rock fired in all directions, striking and shattering nearby carts and sending splinters of wood into the air. Ducks, moorhens, donkeys and Bogs all dived for any cover they could find.

When the sound of falling debris finally abated they looked up one by one. Despite many being wounded with splinters and cuts, no one was seriously injured.

Beeroglad looked into the sky hoping to see his son on the wing, but the sky was empty. He turned back and looked Punch in the eye. Punch huffed and took two paces back and allowed him to pass.

The Bog quickly made his way to the centre of the yard. 'Stand back, make room,' he roared. Those who had staggered to their feet moved quickly away to give him space; his wings sprang out from his sides, high and wide, lifting him upward in the typical upright stance of a Bog taking-off. He hastily climbed into the air through which dust and grit was still falling. 'Guards, stand fast,' he ordered, 'the rest of you, get up here now.'

Every Bog not on guard duty sprang his wings, narrowly missing the mallards and moorhens who had to duck and dive to avoid being hit. Dozens of winged reptiles taking to the skies at the same time presented an eerie sight, their bodies perfectly upright as they rose up from the ground. Not until they were three trees high did they assume a horizontal posture. The sudden mass movement and the thrashing of so many vast wings stirred the debris into swirling dust storms, filling every corner of the fort. Those on the ground squinted, trying to keep the dust and grit from their eyes while still avoiding bumping into each other. All was chaos, visibility almost nil.

'Spread out and find my son,' Beeroglad yelled. 'Don't land until he is found.'

The air slowly cleared, allowing the mallards and moorhens to tend to the injured under the watchful eyes of the guards. Punch studied the frantic activity high above him. The giant pterosaurs circled in overlapping patterns in the sky, heads down, their eyes scanning the debris, desperately hoping to spy the young Eeland Ross.

Eager to help, Punch began walking towards the broken wall to where Eeland had last stood. Three guards instantly barred his way, standing line abreast and each armed with a long wooden staff shaved to a point. They stared at no particular part of Punch, but their gaze falling somewhere about his chest.

'Let us pass,' called Dick, 'we can help.'

The Bogs didn't respond; Punch moved forward another step; the Bogs remained planted, waiting for inspiration way beyond the walls of this broken place.

23

Thoughts of painful expectations filled the inn. The police ducks peered nervously through the corners of the windows. Powder-fine soil rose from the ground outside to dance hand in hand with the winged shadows whirling flamboyantly around the building.

The bicycle-bound Bog raised his head and let out a despairing cry before the grey dust obliterated him from view.

The police held their breath. Fearing the worst, they slid down beneath the window sills and engaged in a serious bout of bill rubbing.

'How many do you think there are?' whispered PC James.

'Who knows, probably a whole squadron like when they attacked Smallbeef,' replied PC Russell.

The inspector rose boldly and straightened his cap. 'This won't do, we are the police, we shouldn't be hiding beneath this window.' He looked briefly into the eyes of each of his constables, every one of them keen to do the right thing. 'There's no point waiting any longer, smarten up, Constables, we have work to do so let's get to it.'

The constables duly straightened their helmets and lined up behind their trusty leader.

'I'll count to three,' said Hooter. 'Then we'll rush out the door and take them by surprise, understood?'

'Yes, sir,' came six replies.

Hooter drew a long breath and reluctantly started counting. 'One, two, three – charge!' He threw the door open and rushed forward with the constables following close behind. In leaps and bounds they crossed the veranda and disappeared into the dust-filled air.

After blindly fumbling their way past the Bog in the bicycle frame, the brave seven engaged the invaders in a determined effort to apprehend them.

'I've got one,' shouted PC Peters, grappling his opponent to the floor.

'I've got one too, someone give me a hand,' yelled PC Howard.

'Ouch, Aagh, crikey!' Many such expletives vented into the air as the fight got under way.

PC Thomas joined the pile on top of one of the suspects. 'I think we're in luck,' he shouted. 'There's only two of them.'

'Watch their tails, watch their tails,' Russell hollered, as if they needed reminding of the danger.

Despite not being able to see a thing through the dust, Inspector Hooter appraised the situation and satisfied himself that his squad had the upper hand. He cleared his throat and bellowed loudly while exerting his weight onto the creature beneath him. 'I arrest you in the name of the law, and I insist you stop fighting back because that's **very** naughty.'

'Fer sure, sir,' replied a Canadian voice, 'I'd be glad to stop fighting back if you and yer constables wouldn't mind getting off me.'

The dust settled and the air slowly cleared. The Bog in the bicycle frame looked on, bemused. The fighting stopped, and one by one the mallards got to their feet.

'Oh, dear me,' said Hooter, looking down.

'How yuh doin', sir?' said one of the two Mounties lying in the dust.

'Quickly, Constables, help them to their feet,' said Hooter, somewhat embarrassed.

The constables gathered round and eagerly helped the two very dusty and slightly battered geese to their feet.

'Thanks guys,' said one.

'Er, don't mention it,' replied PC James.

The two geese shook themselves vigorously to shed most of the dust from their plumage. They were in remarkably good shape considering the ordeal they had just been through. Sadly, the same couldn't be said for their hats.

'Let me get those,' said Hooter, bending down to pick up two very flat Stetsons.

He was about to fashion them back into shape when both Mounties interrupted respectfully. 'Please, sir, we would rather do that ourselves.'

'Of course, I quite understand,' replied Hooter.

The two Mounties lovingly did their best to reshape the four dimples in their hats and shake the grey dust from them. Once done, they placed them back on their heads with the brims perfectly parallel to the ground, and then they saluted the inspector.

'How do you do, sir, I'm Constable Case, first name Justin, and this is Constable Duprite, first name Stan.'

'Oh, erm,' replied Hooter, humbled by their apparent fortitude and understanding. 'We're very pleased to meet you. I must apologize for the misunderstanding. We had no idea who you were.'

'Please, sir,' said Constable Duprite, 'perhaps we were partly to blame.'

'That's right, sir,' added Constable Case. 'We should have identified ourselves before we landed, instead of just rushing in like we did, but we thought you were in some kind of trouble.'

The inspector shook wings with both of them, relieved that

the episode was over. He recognized them as two of Sergeant Uppendown's troop from the previous day.

A minute later, more fluttering from above preceded the arrival of another bird. This was a less polished landing.

'My word, it's Mrs Maywell,' exclaimed Hooter. 'What are you doing here, my dear?'

Before she could reply, Constable Stan Duprite spoke up on her behalf to lend some support to her being there. 'Well, sir, by the time we were halfway back to Smallbeef, Mrs Maywell wus fretting to the point where she wus making herself quite ill. Sergeant Uppendown realized she couldn't possibly rest until she had seen her family again. So he dispatched the two of us to escort her back this way, and to lend you a hand if you should need it.' The Mountie cast his eye over the Bog standing resolutely wrapped up in the bicycle, and concluded, 'But you seem to have everything under control here. I must say, you British police have a certain way of handling yerselves, that's fer sure.'

Standing by the side of the village bobby, Hooter replied, 'Yes, I suppose we have. It's all down to the training you know. Simple but effective, I think you'll agree.'

'Fer sure, sir,' replied Duprite.

The bobby wondered silently to himself. *What training?*

Hooter continued with an air of urgency. 'We mustn't waste any more time here.' He looked the Bog up and down. 'We must get to the land of these terrible creatures as quickly as we can.'

The bobby interrupted, 'But, sir, I have a message here from HQ.'

'A message, eh, well let's see what it says, shall we?' Hooter took the note and mumbled the message to himself. The others could just about make out the odd word as he made his way through it. 'Mumble, mumble two days, mumble, mumble reinforcements, mumble, wait mumble before engaging.' He pondered for a moment. 'Hmm, this puts a different complexion on things. We shall make camp here until reinforcements arrive.' He turned to the two Mounties. 'We would be glad of your company while we wait.'

'That's no problem, sir, we're glad to be of service.'

'Excellent,' said Hooter.

Before long, eight mallards, two geese and one moorhen were sitting on the edge of the veranda with the lone Bog standing before them, securely fastened with the bobby's bicycle around him.

They chatted awhile between themselves, ever interested in each other's culture. While they conversed with one another they couldn't help but look at the Bog. He cut a sad figure, clearly distressed at his incarceration and not daring to move for fear of damaging his wings. Every so often he would raise his head and utter a soft cry to the heavens, hopeful that he might be heard, but his cries were in vain and getting quieter as time went on.

'If we are to stay here for a while we shall need to secure more water,' said Hooter. 'It will be dark in about an hour, so we should make the most of what light is left and search the area to see what we can find.'

PC Thomas asked, 'What about the prisoner, sir?'

'Hmm, we can't leave him standing there,' Hooter replied. 'Two of you carefully take one side of the bicycle each, and walk him over here and help him sit down on the veranda, but take care not to damage his wings.'

The confines of the bicycle frame limited the Bog to very small steps at a time. As he walked he gave the odd quiet squawk, almost like that of a budgie, not at all what the police expected from a creature of his size. At the veranda they slowly turned about, the Bog making dolly steps on the spot while the constables revolved around him. They gently lowered the frame, and the Bog sat down on the dusty boards with his feet over the edge. Never had either of the mallards seen a more desolate or forlorn looking creature. PC Thomas stayed with the prisoner while James joined the others in the search for water and anything else that might prove useful during their stay.

Their search was most fruitful. By nightfall the constables had discovered a well by the side of the stable with a good supply of clean water. Inside the stable was a cart full of clean hay and, strangely, two sacks of food pellets which to all intents and purposes smelt and tasted the same as those they were used to back home. These were looked on with suspicion at first until Moira Maywell reassured them that the Bogs always kept some food at the inn for the work parties that passed that way from time to time.

'In that case,' called Hooter, 'we'll use the stable as our base for tonight – there's plenty of hay for bedding, so we should be quite comfortable.'

'What about the prisoner, sir?' asked PC Russell.

'A good question.' The inspector rubbed his bill while a solution formed in his head. 'He'll have to join us in here for the night. Three of you go and help PC Thomas to bring him in.'

Russell, James, and Roberts promptly set off. A few minutes later they appeared at the stable door with the Bog still wrapped in the bicycle. Despite their previous encounters with Bogs, the mallards felt a sense of humility and remorse on his behalf as they ushered him in to the centre of the stable. His steps grew smaller than ever as the bicycle slipped further down his body, restricting his movement all the more.

Hooter walked up to him and asked, 'Do you have a name?' The Bog lowered his head and uttered a solitary chirp.

'You won't fool me you know,' said Hooter. 'If you think you can lure me into a false sense of security so that I'll release your bondage, you must think me mad.'

The Bog resumed his statuesque stance as if he had accepted a fate beyond the understanding of the birds in whose company he now found himself.

'Perhaps we should offer him some water,' said Constable Stan Duprite, 'it's only fair after all.' With that, he made his way towards the Bog under the watchful eyes of the others.

The ancient looking creature stooped as the Mountie approached him. *A sign of deference perhaps?* Duprite held the bowl up in front of the Bog's face and slowly tipped it. The water trickled into the Bog's open beak and down his throat. He gulped it eagerly, his eyes showing the slightest hint of colour. For the merest fraction of a second the tiniest spark of something from inside tried to make its way into the world, and then it was gone. Stan Duprite noticed it, and so did the others. They sat quietly thinking on it, but said nothing to each other in case they had just imagined it.

'Help him to sit on that bale of hay over there.' Hooter pointed to the base of the upright support in the middle of the stable. 'He should be comfortable enough there for the night.'

The fading light soon made a timely withdrawal from the stable, leaving the birds to settle down in the hope of reinforcements reaching them some time tomorrow.

24

At Fort Bog, the prisoners had been shepherded into their huts for the night, and the hurricane lamps lit. William Maywell and his son found themselves back in the relative safety of their hut under the close watch of the guards; they had won a reprieve while the search for Beeroglad's son went on.

Many Bogs roamed the sky, some high and some low. Beeroglad had been in the air since the boulder crashed into the wall over an hour earlier. 'Keep looking, he must be here somewhere,' he shouted, hoping that by saying it loud enough would somehow make it happen. 'Change shift, new scouts up here now,' he hollered. A fresh crew of Bogs took to the air, raising the dust as they did so. The off-going watch moved away to make room for them before they themselves came to rest on the ground, obscuring the dim light of the hurricane lamps and casting the fort into a temporary dusty darkness.

When the air cleared and the light returned, the three Bogs who had been guarding Punch found themselves with no horse or rider before them. Punch had quietly moved around them and now stood at the gap in the wall where the boulder had crashed.

The Bogs in the sky ventured as close to the cliff face as they dared, aware that they could easily slice a wing on a sharp edge, and thus plummet into the mists covering the land far below. They bravely swooped and hovered within inches of the craggy edifice which beckoned them closer, hungry for any soul that might take one chance too many.

To spot the young grey Bog among a jigsaw of grey rock wasn't easy, the poor light making it all the more difficult for the Bogs to see among the nooks and crannies. Every so often the searchers would call out and then listen in silence, but so far nothing had come back.

Punch stared into the darkness. *There is hope*, his whispers told him, but he didn't know where or how – not yet. So he stared and thought some more.

Dick slid from the saddle and gathered up three lamps and some rope. Upon seeing him, two Bogs quickly moved to bar his way. Dick stopped where he was, but rather than abandon the lamps, he hurriedly lashed them together. 'If we lower these over the edge, we can see – look,' he said. The light from the swinging lamps danced about the ground, illuminating the Bogs' legs. The Bogs paused for a second, and then moved aside, keeping a suspicious eye on his every move.

Punch remained quite still; voices stirred within him, whispering and painting more pictures in his head. He knew the young Bog was somewhere below among the rocks, and alive – just. He huffed loudly. At first Dick ignored him; he huffed again. Dick stopped what he was doing. Punch scraped a hoof on the ground to keep the duck's attention, and then, huffing louder than ever, he patted the ground again before letting out a long fluffy raspberry of a neigh. *Here, here!*

'Well done, mate,' cried Dick, realizing what the horse was telling him.

Punch's verbal outburst hadn't gone unnoticed. Beeroglad dropped from the sky on narrowed wings, spreading them at the last minute to land on the cliff edge.

'I do not have time to waste on you now,' he growled sharply. 'Guards, move them back and keep them away from here.'

The guards moved in, their claws making straight for Punch's rear end.

Dick shouted to Beeroglad, 'Wait, he knows where your son is, don't you see? He's marking the ground.'

The guards moved closer to Punch's rump; they knew better than to hesitate in the execution of Beeroglad's command. They raised their clawed hands. Punch knew what was coming, but he stood firm, neighing loudly into the darkening sky and shaking his head up and down to protest. His eyes widened as the claws came down on his flank.

'Stop,' shouted Beeroglad. The claws halted, their points not quite breaking Punch's skin. 'Move back and give the horse room.'

The Bogs promptly stepped back a few paces.

'What do you know, horse? What can you see that I cannot?' quizzed Beeroglad. 'And why would you concern yourself with my son? After all he is a Bog in the making – you should be glad of one less of us, one less ugly creature to deal with.'

Dick replied on Punch's behalf. 'Your son is young, about the same age as me. He only knows what you've taught him. If he's suffering somewhere among the rocks, then he deserves another chance.'

Beeroglad peered deeply into Dick's eyes, trying to fathom him. *He's only a duck, a stupid young mallard. How can he philosophize with me – a Bog?* He stared for as long as he dared, ever anxious of his son's time running out, and then he sprang his wings and took to the air, quickly taking up a hovering position level with the top of the cliff. He cast a brief eye towards Punch. Their gaze met and held for no more than a couple of seconds, time enough for a mutual understanding to pass between them.

Dick carefully let the rope out, the lanterns jostled their way down the cliff face. Shadows came and went among the rocks while fifty Bogs maintained a motionless pose in the air, their eyes seeking the slightest hint of life.

Dick had let a good deal of rope over the edge when the lamps became caught in a crag, their light being confined to the hollow in which they had become trapped. Dick tugged carefully, but the rocks refused to release their catch.

'Wait,' came a shout from somewhere in the dark sky above the cliff face. 'There he is, where the lamp is caught, I can see his face – but he's buried.'

Beeroglad steered his way through the darkness. 'Move aside and let me see.' His son was in a real fix with only his head visible and his beak protruding through a gap in the rocks. His wings were pinned down, and his body completely obscured by an array of boulders precariously lodged against each other.

Beeroglad called out. 'Talk to me, son, show me you have air.'

To Dick this seemed a strange thing for a father to say at such a time. *What does he mean, show me you have air?*

'Please talk, son, talk,' Beeroglad pleaded. Everyone waited in silence for a reply.

A few seconds later a sound came from the rocks. 'Cheep, cheep.'

'Hoorah,' shouted Dick, 'he's okay.'

Beeroglad landed back on the cliff top with tears welling up in his eyes, reflecting the yellow light of the lamps. Dick assumed they were tears of joy at finding his son alive, but Beeroglad stared silently into the far distance; blackness seemed to engulf him as if he had just lost everything.

'What's the matter?' asked Dick. 'If we take our time we can get him safely up from there, we just need—'

'You don't understand.' An air of despondency tainted Beeroglad's voice. 'Bogs are strong creatures as you have witnessed, but as with most beings, we have our Achilles heel.' He let out a long sigh. Tears fell from his cheeks and slid off his chest into the dust.

'Achilles heel?' Dick rubbed his bill. 'What do you mean, Achilles heel?'

Beeroglad went on, 'We are a mutation from a time long since passed. We can fly almost endlessly. Our chests host massive lungs which energize us at great heights and over long distances, but they rely on the movement of our wings to create space and stimulation.' He paused, his voice quivering, and more tears falling. 'Even when we sleep, our wings spread and retract autonomously, just a little, but if they are constricted for more than three hours—we slowly suffocate – and die.'

***

In the stable by the inn, the constables were having a restless night, each of them drifting in and out of sleep, never quite floating away before landing with a start in the unfamiliar darkness. It was darker than usual with not the slightest hint of moonlight which might have otherwise seeped through the walls. Tonight there was nothing coming through, just more blackness to darken the room beyond the limit of the single hurricane lamp.

While waiting to drift back to sleep, the inspector looked around at his companions, at the rise and fall of plump feathered chests and the occasional chunter or shuffle of a dream. The Bog in the bicycle frame had a different appearance; the position of the lamp casting its yellow glow across the contours of the grey beast made him seem motionless. *He's almost lifeless*, thought Hooter. He allowed his gaze to dwell on the creature while he himself dozed, sleepily studying the ancient form. *He's so still – really still.* 'Oh no,' he called out loud, waking everyone.

'What is it, sir?' enquired Constable Duprite. 'What's the matter?'

'Oh my, oh my.' Hooter's voice carried a distinct note of

distress. 'It's the Bog, I don't think he's breathing.'

'What?' said the constables, all now awake. They jumped to their feet, donned their helmets, and gathered round the Bog. The bicycle frame still had its unforgiving grip on him.

His head hung low and his beak rested on his chest, quite still.

'Oh no, no,' said Hooter, now very worried. 'Give him a prod, perhaps they sleep deeper than us, but be careful, you never know, it might be a trick.'

They prodded gently – nothing, and then another prod – the faintest squeak vented from the long grey beak, barely audible.

'Quickly, get the bloomin' bicycle off him, I don't think he's very well.'

Four of the mallards carefully raised the bicycle up and over the Bog's head while the two Mounties steadied him by his shoulders, lest he should fall from his seat.

***

At Fort Bog, Punch grew more anxious, scuffing the ground and huffing louder. *No time to lose.*

Beeroglad shouted to those circling in the sky. 'Two of you land by my son and try to move the rocks away.'

Two Bogs immediately made a very slow and precise descent onto the cliff face, each one landing a couple of paces either side of the trapped youngster. Dick quickly lowered an additional lamp to each of them.

Using their claws to gain the most tenuous handholds, the two Bogs proceeded with extreme care, their long tails aiding their balance.

The young Bog was soundly encased by rocks all around him. One particular boulder, equal to Punch's mass, sat precariously on top of the others. This was the boulder that had been fired from the catapult and had done all the damage. Until it had been removed no attempt could be made to move any of the others for fear of it falling in on its victim.

Another ten minutes had passed and no progress made. If anything, matters had been made worse by the movement of the Bogs among the rocks. The large boulder refused to budge.

'It's no use,' called Beeroglad, dismayed. 'Move away before you cause the whole thing to collapse.'

'Get me more ropes,' shouted Dick, making his way to the donkeys who were still harnessed to the catapult trolley.

Beeroglad, realizing Dick's intentions, muscled his way in and grabbed the reins. 'Quickly, move back you stupid donkeys, or so help me this will be your last—'

'No,' called Dick, 'let me talk to them.'

'We have no time for pleasantries,' Beeroglad retorted, throwing the reins to the young mallard.

Dick rested a wing against the chest of one of the donkeys. 'Come on, boys, back we go. Please, be good lads.' The trolley slowly wheeled its way backwards and stopped close to the edge of the cliff, by which time more ropes had been gathered.

'Mind out, we're quicker at this than you,' said Beeroglad, beckoning four of his troops to tie the ropes to the axles of the trolley. As soon as this was done the other end of each rope was thrown over the edge of the cliff. 'Stand from under!' went the call before the ropes unfurled down the rock face. The two Bogs waiting among the rocks closed in again, and hurriedly tied the ropes around the offending boulder. One hour and a half had elapsed. Time was running out if the leader's son was to be saved.

'Haul aloft!' the Bogs called to those above.

Dick took the reins once again and whispered to the donkeys. 'You can do this – pull together, lads – ready?' He gave a gentle pull on the reins. The donkeys took up the strain on the ropes and Dick encouraged them again. 'Come on, boys, pull, pull!'

The donkeys pushed hard into the harness, trying for all their worth to haul the boulder up. The unforgiving ground did nothing to help them, affording little grip for their crippled feet. The boulder teased the rescuers by moving a fraction, but not enough to allow access beneath. The donkeys continued to work together, one holding his stance firm while the other repositioned his feet to exert more weight into the harness, but their combined effort barely tested the ropes strength, let alone the boulder's determination to hold fast.

'More, more!' Beeroglad screeched impatiently. 'Try harder!'

'Come on, lads, you can do it!' shouted Dick.

Both donkeys were almost bellies on the ground, pushing every ounce of strength they could find into their abused bodies. Their hearts and souls so wanted to move, but their hooves, distorted from neglect and misuse on the part of their masters, struggled to find grip, slipping painfully and causing the trolley to lose ground. They strained and heaved, and slipped and slid, their cries of anguish painfully distorting their faces. *Hee-aaw.* With all their might they forced their chests into the harness, their exertion denying them the breath to bray in agony.

Lower and lower to the ground the donkeys went, their faces almost in the dirt, and their hind legs quivering beyond their limit. They were spent. The boulder hadn't moved.

'It's no use, stop! Stop!' ordered Beeroglad. 'We're wasting time. Put every donkey we have into the harness – hurry.' His air of desperation grew ever more apparent with each order he gave.

'That's no use,' called Dick. 'They can't do it because their hooves and feet are so bad, they can't grip properly.' He led Beeroglad's gaze to the pathetic sight on each and every donkey in the fort. 'Look, they're **all** lame – it's a miracle they can walk at all with those feet.'

Not one hoof was shod, none trimmed, all curling and

splaying outwards hideously; every donkey in pain, never complaining, just crying in their hearts for care which cost nothing.

Punch neighed long and hard, high into the air.

'Punch can do it, I know he can,' shouted Dick. 'Untie the ropes from the cart and get it out of the way, quickly.'

As soon as the cart was freed from the boulder, the donkeys hauled it out of the way, glad that their ordeal was over. Helped by the dexterous hands of the Bogs, Dick set about lashing a makeshift harness together from whatever ropes and tack he could find.

Beeroglad called from the cliff edge. 'Son, Eeland Ross, call to me.'

There was no reply.

One of the Bogs below moved in and addressed the youngster. 'How are you doing, sir?' He looked into the young eyes, now pale blue.

'Chirp,' was all the heir to the throne could muster.

'He is alive, sir, but he's only chirping.'

25

In the stable by the inn, the Mounties gently laid the Bog on the floor beneath the full light of the hurricane lamp.

'What can we do for him?' asked Hooter, hoping one of his protégés would cast him a line of hope. The constables rubbed their bills thoughtfully, to no avail. It was a strange creature lying on the ground before them, wings still by his sides, beak on his chest.

Constable Case extended a wing and gave the Bog a gentle shake. No response. He then put his cheek to the creature's neck. *Cool to the touch.* 'He isn't well at all, sir.'

'Quickly, get some water,' said Duprite. 'This isn't supposed to happen.'

Roberts applied a damp cloth to the Bog's brow. If the look of hope on the ducks' faces could bring about a miracle the Bog would have risen there and then, but he remained quite still. They waited for a moment or two, wishing something would happen. The silence was tangible, painful, and wanting to be over. Menacing clouds added to the dire atmosphere by bringing thunder to the distant hills.

Constable Case carefully put his head to the Bog's chest. He listened, and then he listened some more. 'His heart and breathing are very faint, sir, hardly noticeable.'

The thunder paced to and fro beyond the horizon, growing tired of waiting.

'We must keep him warm,' said the inspector.

'But there are no blankets or anything in here,' said Roberts, casting an eye as far as the lamp would allow.

'Then we shall have to keep him warm ourselves,' Hooter replied.

The Bog's wings began to move out from his sides to aid his breathing.

'Quickly, tuck his wings back in and form a circle round him to keep him warm,' said Hooter, trying to do the right thing. The birds quickly closed in on the wilting Bog; at first they tried not to actually touch the reptile, but they soon realized the futility of their action and jostled in tighter, sharing the warmth of their bodies – and hoping for the best.

The thunder rumbled closer, sending lightning across the sky to light up the slits in the timber walls; sharp silver lines flashed across the stable floor within, scaling the hay bales and the birds for a split second before leaving them alone with their thoughts once again.

***

The same thunder echoed throughout the landscape beyond Fort Bog. The heavy clouds jostled for position above the fort, keen to have the best seats for the contest.

Punch was now harnessed up. Four rope lines tied to the leather straps about his chest were wound together to form one thick line behind him. This was then thrown over the edge of the cliff and tied around the boulder with no trolley in between, only the rock pulling down and the Suffolk Punch pulling up. The stage was set.

Punch braced himself. Beeroglad stood next to him, eye to eye, cheek to cheek and whispered gruffly. 'Hear me now, horse, if you should fail in this effort, then as of this night no duck shall walk this world in peace; no duck, no goose, no feathered bird of any kind. But if my son is saved, then you may leave this land with all your wards free of our tyranny for evermore.' He paused for a few seconds, allowing Punch to look into his eyes. The colours danced about; the soft brown lights of the horse and the pale blue of the Bog touched and held, and trusted. Then they broke away. The Bog's eyes reverted to black, the horse's stayed bright and beautiful.

'I know you understand,' Beeroglad concluded.

Punch knew from deep in his belly what he had to do; no threats or bargains would affect his motives or beliefs. He huffed, and then tramped his hind feet to let the boulder know he was ready – ready to relieve him of the young Bog whose life was slowly but surely fading with every shallow breath.

Beeroglad hobbled to the edge to maintain a watch on the situation below.

Dick stood next to Punch to offer encouragement. 'Okay, mate, this is a tall order, and you really don't have to do it you know – there would be no shame—'

Punch snorted before Dick could finish. There was no question of him not fulfilling his heart's wishes. Dick patted him on the shoulder and took a step back to give him room.

Punch leaned forward to take up the slack of the rope. The makeshift web of leather tightened across his chest as he eased his weight into it, gently at first to let the tension travel the full length of the rope and tighten its grip around the boulder.

Keeping his weight into the harness, Punch brought one hind leg slightly forward of the other and crouched a little to exert more forward thrust. He then brought the other hind leg into line. He could feel the weight of the boulder compounded by the friction of the cliff edge, all conspiring to dash his hopes. A long deep neigh poured from his mouth, sending the dust away in all directions.

He filled his lungs again, air flowed in through his wide open mouth and nostrils. His chest expanded with every breath, testing the harness to its limit by the expanse of muscle beneath. He pushed forward keeping his feet firmly in place. The boulder pulled back in equal measure. Again Punch forced his chest into the harness, but the boulder sat resolute. All eyes were on the Suffolk as he wrestled with the forces of nature. Every Bog in the air watched, every Bog on the ground watched, the mallards that had spilled out from their huts watched, willing him on, but not making a sound.

The clouds above the fort hammered into each other like drunkards turning up late to a party, making no attempt to be discreet. The thunder sent a flash of green lightning across the sky, illuminating all below.

***

The same light struck across the constables while they maintained their vigil in the stable by the inn. They waited, watched and hoped, unaware of the battle being waged at the fort beyond the horizon.

***

Punch would not be swayed. His whispers called him on, drowning out all other sound. He lowered his hind quarters and then crept each rear foot a little further forward, his belly was now closer to the ground giving him excellent forward thrust; this is where Suffolks excel. The whispers called again. His heart responded, powering every muscle in his back and legs, his massive thighs, his huge second thighs, every joint winding his torque into the ground and taunting the rock below.

He heaved into the advantage, but the sky roared like a tormented audience, rounding on the side of the boulder. Lamps rattled and the buildings shivered as the heavens thundered once again. Sheets of brilliant violet lit the sky from one side of the world to the other.

***

Again the lightning lit the skies above the stable, ricocheting off the police badges, and firing violet coloured spears of light in all directions, but the ailing Bog didn't notice.

***

Punch was beginning to hurt. He daren't give an ounce of let, for he knew the boulder would quickly retake the ground from under him. *Forward, I must move forward.* That was the extent of the horse's plan. He struggled to fill his lungs, his breaths became short and laboured, and his energy slipped into deficit. *I mustn't go backwards.*

Again he bent his hind legs to bring his body closer to the ground. This would be his last attempt before he was spent. His whispers sang to him, rallying his soul. Louder and louder they chorused, filling his heart with determination. He dropped his head almost to the ground, and then he pushed into the harness. The rock pulled back. The horse pushed more, and the rock pulled back. The horse's muscles swelled, engorged with oxygen, and painfully, slowly, his hind legs straightened, levering him forward. The leather harness creaked and groaned around his chest.

Nature heckled again, and this time the air lit up indigo among the deafening skies.

***

Blue and violet rods of brilliant light rebounded off everything within the stable, enriching the constables' iridescent colours. But the dying Bog still didn't notice.

***

'It's moving,' an excited shout rose from the cliff face. Beeroglad took to the wing and hung in the air from where he could see both protagonists. Time was almost up for his son. The horse had to win the battle for there would be no return match.

Punch panted heavily, dust flew from beneath his muzzle. He gathered every ounce of strength he could find and pumped it into his hind quarters. At all costs he had to keep his belly off the ground. To collapse now would silence his voices, and his fight would be over.

Nature grew impatient, the boulder unrelenting, pulling constantly with immense weight, giving no respite for the horse. Another thunderous round from the skies sent a sheet of electric blue searing into the earth.

***

The old stable shuddered, letting many a plank fall away to be swallowed by the dust. The constables remained unmoved, as did the Bog.

***

Unable to lift his chin from the ground, Punch cast his gaze across the yard in desperate need of inspiration. His heart lifted when he saw Abel Nogg standing among the crowd, towering head and shoulders above those around him.

Drawing strength from Abel's eyes of crystal blue, Punch's whispers numbered thousands in perfect harmony, flooding his heart with vigour beyond his wildest dreams. He pushed his chest into the harness again, every muscle in his body supporting the next. The boulder raged back at him, desperately trying to stay put. Punch felt it move, only a fraction, but enough for him to reset his stance.

The heavens angrily compressed the air beneath the clouds with another thunderous roar, this time spitting an arc of brilliant yellow light across the fort, illuminating the horse, highlighting his musculature, and holding him for one second in time for all to behold.

***

The spit of lightning lit up the stable like a torch. The constables huddled around the Bog, hoping for a miracle. The Bog remained still, his beak resting on his chest while yellow lights reflected from the constables' badges, and sympathetically fell upon him, warming him and willing him to breathe. But he couldn't see them.

***

Punch desperately needed to rest awhile, but the boulder was waiting for just such a moment when it would surely haul the horse back to his start.

A myriad of miniature horses responded to Punch's plea, holding every muscle at full tension. His heart pounded painfully, his eyes remained fixed on his friend, Abel Nogg, who willingly let the eyes of the Suffolk into his own to give whatever succour the horse might draw.

Beeroglad continued hovering in front of the cliff. 'Just a bit higher!' he called. 'Remember my words, horse,' he shouted in Punch's direction. 'I am a creature of my word. If you fail now, then you fail all around you.'

Punch's solitude was total. No one could help him now. His fortune and that of all the birds and donkeys in the fort rested on him. He felt truly as if he was battling against the world for all that was good. Seeds of doubt entered his mind. He couldn't understand why Mother Nature hadn't sided with him. Again he sought the eyes of Abel Nogg, longing for his touch and his comforting words. But this was the horse's fight and his fight alone.

Pain screamed within every ounce of muscle as if being torn alive from him. His voices rallied and sang louder in response, ready for the next push. His mind was now far beyond what he thought his body could endure. His determination had carried him into an unknown place where defeat was inconceivable regardless of the cost to himself.

His head rested heavily on the ground. All his energy now powered his legs and body forward in defiance of the boulder which was hanging its full weight on the ropes. Hard into the harness Punch forced his chest, his hooves struggling for grip. Again the boulder laughed back.

Punch had no more to give. His strength was spent; he could do no more than hold his position, going neither forward nor letting back. He couldn't stay where he was for more than a few more seconds without letting go altogether. Tears gathered in his beautiful hazel eyes as he looked to Abel Nogg for help, but all the coloured Bog could do was return his own tears to the magnificent horse, while the entire world hung on the ends of the ropes.

Punch's legs trembled with exhaustion. He fought to keep his belly off the ground. If he collapsed now he would never get back up, he knew that much. Scrambling his front legs forward, he lifted his head to keep his face out of the dust. One inch – his hind legs slid under his belly just one inch.

One more inch was enough. His voices sang as they had never sung before. His chest expanded, letting his lungs fill to bursting point. A million miniature horses raced through his veins, carrying oxygen-enriched blood to every muscle in his body. The hands which had guided him before were there once more, holding him and squeezing each side of his girth, lifting him and carrying him forward.

Nature responded with a thunderous volley like the guns of a thousand warships. Bang! Bang! Bang! Every impact sent a blaze of orange flashing violently across the sky, forcing all on the ground to cower and shield their eyes from the fiery light.

***

In the stable the constables huddled close to the Bog, unaware of his inner workings. His time too was running out.

***

'Keep it there,' shouted one of the Bogs from below the cliff edge. 'We can reach one of his wings; whatever you do, don't let the boulder drop.'

Punch panted desperately, his ribs flexing painfully with each rapid inhalation. Almost on the floor, he couldn't imagine how he would retrieve himself from this position, but that didn't matter to him; all he wanted was for young Eeland Ross to be saved.

The Bogs were now able to reach into the space beneath the boulder and touch the youngster. 'Just a bit more,' one of them shouted, 'just a bit more.'

Punch remained locked in his stance, oblivious to all but his own voices and the thousand unseen hands that held him. His lungs had been tested beyond their limit, leaving his muscles crying in pain once again.

The young Bog chirped at the touch of a clawed hand on his wing. A few small rocks were carefully removed from around him, and his wings eased out from their confines. The youngster's chest instantly expanded allowing the cold night air to rush to the rescue, filling his lungs to capacity.

'He has air, sir, he has air!' the jubilant cry rang throughout the fort. All the Bogs, whether in the air or on the ground gave vent with a raucous cheer. The mallards and moorhens added to the applause which was further expanded by the cacophony of many donkeys braying at random.

'Silence!' Beeroglad brought their jubilation to an abrupt halt. 'He can breathe, but he is not yet free,' he shouted from his airborne vantage. 'Hurry – move the other rocks – don't stop until my son is freed.' He then turned his gaze towards the horse, trying to catch the brown eyes in his, but the horse stared blankly into the dust, his voices fading.

Steam rose from his flanks. He had overcome the boulder and withstood the testing onslaught from the thunder and lightning, but he had no strength left to retrieve himself from the ground. He dared not relax so much as one muscle until the young Bog was released. Now he knew what it was to feel alone – his voices were leaving, and the hands were slipping from his sides. Abel was nowhere to be seen.

Dick cried in the horse's ear, 'No, Punch, please don't go, please.'

Tears welled up in the young duck's eyes and quickly overflowed. Punch breathed shallow and fast; the air from his nostrils barely moved the dust which his nose now rested in. His head lay full weight on the ground.

'He is saved!' Beeroglad rose up above the cliff with his son firmly in his grasp.

The sound of the fort in full cheer briefly lifted Punch's spirits until an urgent call came from the cliff face. 'Stop, don't let the horse lower the boulder, there's nowhere for it to rest, it will pull him over the edge.'

With his ear to the ground, Punch could hear the grey earth talking to him, calling and beckoning him to lie down.

'Cut the ropes! Cut the ropes!' shouted Dick.

The boulder had not surrendered.

Punch remained rigid in his pose, but he was slowly being

dragged backwards towards the cliff edge, his belly and hooves leaving drag marks in the dust. With nothing beneath the boulder to arrest its descent, the horse's future seemed grim. The land from beyond the abyss called out to him, willing him to come closer, willing him to let go. Dick frantically tried to untie the ropes from the harness, but the boulder had tightened the knots during the fight. This was his end game.

26

The harness had tightened around Punch's body, hugging him in an insane lover's embrace, making it hard for him to breath.

'Quickly, someone help me untie these knots.' Dick desperately fumbled as a duck would, tugging uselessly at the ropes. Several Bogs responded to his call, but despite their superior dexterity their efforts to loosen the knots were in vain. The ropes clung ever tighter; like a mob of boa constrictors they were determined not to release their quarry.

The horse could see only the lines in the dust as his front hooves followed him backwards, his bottom lip also leaving a solitary line scuffing along in his wake.

They're coming, his whispers softly confided in him. *They're coming.* Punch huffed at the ground, no longer understanding his own thoughts, *Who's coming?*

Many Bogs joined Dick in putting their weight against the horse's rump in an effort to slow his journey to the cliff edge, but the boulder was having none of it; it had the motion in its favour and intended to keep it that way.

Punch huffed again, and his whispers comforted him in response. *Here they come – coming to help you.* Such honest words that only exist in a horse's heart. *Can you hear them now?* Something – something in the distance, a sound he couldn't recall and yet it brought a sense of familiarity with it. He was now only three body lengths from the abyss, from where his opponent was assuredly pulling and waiting for him.

***

Meanwhile, back at the inn, Nature paused for breath. The old stable rested in darkness with many planks missing from its sides. The dispirited air hung from the underside of the clouds, causing no draught. Inside the stable the Bog lay quite still with his wings by his sides and his beak resting languidly on his chest. Every now and then one wing would flinch, trying to move outwards, but the closeness of the birds prevented it from doing so. So he lay some more under the hopeful eyes of the ducks, the geese and the moorhen.

The heavens waited impatiently for the clouds to reload their guns. Slow abstract curves of thick black treacle swirled silently among the skies. The silence was soon brought to an end when more rumbling came into earshot, but not from Fort Bog; this time it was coming from the direction of Smallbeef, a continuous roar in the far distance, gaining strength and momentum by the second.

'Not again,' murmured Hooter disconsolately, 'will it never end?'

The constables had never heard the inspector sound so disheartened, they too grew more concerned as yet another storm chased them down.

Louder and louder, darker and darker grew the night. The new storm brought no lightning with it, nor any clouds, but a solid blackness through which no mortal eyes could see. The turmoil was almost upon the stable now. The police tightened their circle around the Bog, drawing strength from each other's closeness.

The ground beneath their feet became tremulous. The water in the bucket rippled uneasily while dust and hay fell from the mezzanine above their heads. The Earth grumbled and the sky roared above them while the air howled all around the stable. The police knew their fate was in the hands of their creator. They could do nothing but hold each other tight and wait; vulnerable and afraid of whatever was going on outside, but never losing hope. One by one they lowered their heads into the centre of the circle like a rugby scrum, in search of refuge from the unbelievable roar all around them.

Anything not firmly rooted danced about the ground and took to the air in the mayhem that followed in the wake of the raging wind. Sand, grit and debris blasted against the walls of the stable like a thousand storm troopers vandalizing everything within their reach and trying to force their way in, testing the birds resolve to the limit.

Tighter held the ducks, the geese and the moorhen. Quieter lay the Bog.

The deafening storm raced onward with no time to spare, leaving the stable quivering in sudden silence. As quick as it had come, it was gone.

'Phew, I think it's over!' exclaimed Hooter.

The light from the hurricane lamp continued to softly colour their surroundings, highlighting small particles of hay and dust floating slowly to the ground. Russell and Roberts waddled over to the wall and cautiously peered out through the gaps.

'It's so dark,' said Russell. 'I can't see a thing.'

'Perhaps we're not supposed to,' said Roberts, warily.

'Did you notice there was no lightning?' added Russell, 'A storm that loud with no lightning, that's weird.'

Quietness carefully took its place once more. The Bog remained motionless, unaware of anything around him.

***

At Fort Bog, the boulder was having its way with the horse, dragging him unrelentingly to the edge of the cliff. Inch by inch Punch was losing the battle. With little energy left to put up a fight he watched the ground pass slowly under his muzzle, abrading his soft furry chin as he went.

Oblivious to the pain, he huffed in an attempt to keep his whispers awake. His whispers called back. *Listen,* they said, *can you hear them? They're almost here.*

One by one those in the fort looked down, puzzled by the ground vibrating beneath them. The dust about their feet became animated in anticipation of the tempest racing headlong towards them. Having left the police in the stable, the storm was now aiming directly at Fort Bog.

Punch was now only two body lengths from the edge. Beeroglad looked down at him through eyes now crystal blue. Still clutching his son, he maintained his height above the cliff from where he was able to see the dust and sand rising from the ground in the far distance.

What nature of storm is this? Why does it bring its anger to level my land?

The storm was assuredly travelling over the moor at an alarming speed, straight towards him and his fort. A sentry called from one of the turrets. 'Sir, there's something coming this way, something huge and fast.'

'I see it,' replied Beeroglad. I see it, but I don't know what it is.

Louder and stronger grew the roar. Buildings began to shake. Shingles fell from the rooftops, glass cracked in the windows.

From within their confines the mallards and moorhens couldn't see the approaching wave of destruction, but they began to panic all the same, especially the moorhens. 'Oh my! Oh my!' they cried to each other, running first this way then that way. 'Oh my! Oh my!'

Beeroglad boomed from above. 'Take to the air, everyone take to the air as high as you can. Hurry, while you still have time.'

The mallards and moorhens looked up at him, and then at

each other. 'Does he mean us?'

'No, he can't mean us. You know what happens to us if we're caught flying.'

Again Beeroglad yelled with an air of impatient desperation, this time looking straight at the hapless birds. 'Hurry, all of you, before it's too late – mallards – moorhens – everyone as high as you can. Get above the storm before it takes you with it!'

The fort erupted into total pandemonium when all the birds within tried to take to the air at the same time. Many collided with each other while others simply ran out of room on take off, crashing into buildings and carts. Feathers filled the air, but no ducks, moorhens or coots with them.

During all this chaos, Punch lay in the dust despairing at the sight of the birds foundering on the ground, helplessly flapping and crashing about. *Have I suffered for nothing?*

The boulder pulled selfishly, with victory in its sight. *Yes you have.*

They'll soon be here, assured Punch's whispers. But there seemed to be no time left. The storm would surely lay the fort to waste within minutes.

The birds grew tired very quickly, their prohibition from flying had left them too unfit to get off the ground, and so they stood in their own family groups, despondent, resigned to their fate. Mothers, fathers and children huddled together waiting for the raging beast to gather them up for their final flight into extinction.

Strangely, the donkeys showed no sign of stress; they gathered together in groups, taking shelter against the sides of whatever building they happened to be nearest to. They too had their whispers. *They are coming.*

In all the commotion William Maywell found himself freed from his bondage. He wrapped his wings caringly around his young son. At least they would be together at the end. The fluffy youngster looked up at his father and chirped, 'Cheep, cheep,' blissfully unaware that his new life might soon be over. He cheeped even louder when two clawed feet descended upon his body; the claws closed around him and lifted him from his father's embrace.

'No, don't take him from me, please don't take him!' cried William. But before his pleading was done he felt the grip of clawed feet about his own body as he too was lifted straight up into the air. He looked around to see one hundred and thirty Bogs rising up from the fort, each one carrying a helpless bird in its grasp. Higher and higher they went until they disappeared through the syrupy cloud above.

'What cruel trick is this?' shouted one mallard, fully expecting to be dropped to his death at any moment.

The Bogs said nothing in reply, but held their position in the clear night air above the cloud. Even when carrying the extra weight of a large mallard they assumed an air of proficient grace, keeping a firm but gentle grip on the bird in their care.

Here they come, said Punch's whispers, *do you hear them?* Punch could hear them clearly now. But the boulder pulled ever harder. It had been robbed of the young Bog, but would settle for the horse as restitution.

'Not so fast, horse,' said a voice close to Punch's ear.

Having seen his son safely into the air, Beeroglad had returned to Punch's side. At the same moment another two Bogs clambered up and over the edge of the cliff. Beeroglad called to them. 'Quickly, both of you, find an axe and bring it here.'

They both hobbled as fast as they could to the tool shed, some twenty paces away.

'Sir,' came a cry from a Bog in the sky, 'the storm is closing – it will be here in a couple of minutes.'

Struggling to make himself heard above the raging roar, Dick shouted to Beeroglad. 'Save yourself, quickly, while there's still time.'

'I live by my word, young duck,' was the Bog's sharp reply. 'The horse has fulfilled his part of the bargain, I'll not leave him now.'

The two Bogs returned, one of them holding a crude flint axe strung to a stout timber handle.

Beeroglad bellowed at the top of his voice. 'Use it to cut the ropes, quickly!'

The ground shuddered violently under their feet, sending the dust rising and dancing in Punch's face. Punch blew from his nostrils to keep it from choking him.

If the boulder could keep hold of Punch until the storm joined forces with him, victory would be his, as would be the horse.

'One minute, sir, one minute and the storm will be here!'

The axe was raised. Nature questioned such an action with a rumble from within the clouds. The axe was brought down, but only a few strands were severed. The boulder was still in the game.

'Sir, sir!' called another Bog in the sky.

'What is it? Can't you see we are rather busy down here?'

'Yes, sir, but it's the storm, sir, it's…it's…'

'It's what?' replied Beeroglad impatiently.

'It's got horses' heads sticking out of it.'

Beeroglad looked up incredulously, and then shouted to the Bog with the axe. 'Keep cutting the ropes, I'll be right back.' He ascended hurriedly into the air. As he climbed, the axe fell once more, and the sky retorted angrily with another thunderous thump into the ground. The rope was still intact.

Beeroglad gazed out over the wall. A quarter of a mile away a wave as high as a house and a mile wide was racing his way; a wave which could carry a hundred surfers a hundred miles. But this was not a wave of water – this was a wave of the land. The very moor was rising up and careering towards him, hurling dust, grass and bushes into the air as it went.

'What on Earth?' He had no time to count, but there were innumerable horses' heads reaching out from the dust storm roaring over the land. Heads reaching as far forward as possible, all dark brown with a white flash, their bodies engulfed in the earth racing them to the finishing post.

Beeroglad rose as high as he dared to improve his view, mindful of the urgency of matters on the ground, but he needed to know more of what was about to overrun his fort. He still couldn't believe his eyes. Riding the wave were one hundred horses, line abreast, each being ridden by a Canada goose sitting perfectly upright. Some wearing white pith helmets, others wearing Stetsons; majestically eerie.

They soared surreally over the uneven ground at an impossible speed, each rider managing at all times to sit as one with his horse. The wind howled about them at an unforgiving rate, and yet their hats and helmets remained at precisely the correct angle in defiance of all that this world could hurl at them. Four hundred hooves thundered at the charge, raising the earth like a bow wave ahead of them to leave it airborne in their wake.

Beeroglad returned hastily to Punch's side. 'Give me the axe!' he hollered. 'I don't know if they are friend or foe, but at the speed they are running they will never stop before the edge, and will surely take us all with them.'

The clouds rumbled again as he swung the axe into the stubborn rope. But still it resisted; a few more strands yielded, but the rope held firm.

The ground juddered with such violence that the fort walls shook to their foundations. First one stone fell from its place, then another and another. The destruction rapidly spread to the turrets at each end. They leaned, and then became dislocated from the walls on each side as one turret and then the other fell like a drunkard into the dust. The portcullis joined in the melee; it shook, then wavered and came to earth with a clatter which was quickly stifled when the towers on each side fell upon it.

Beeroglad held the axe above his head once more, and once more the sky raged in anger at him, hammering the clouds into each other. The axe fell true and swift. Of the four ropes which formed the line, one was now almost severed, but that was not enough. The boulder still heaved at Punch with heartless determination. Soon the horse would be gone.

Beeroglad stood alarmingly close to the cliff edge, ready to strike at the rope again. Dust, grit and all manner of debris served to obscure his sight as the air in the fort rose up in riotous disorder. The raging horses were only seconds away, the noise painfully deafening. Words were no longer of any use. The entire length of the front wall crashed to the ground, raising an impenetrable barrier of fine airborne earth in its place. But nothing of this world would hold back the intruders seeking to make an entry.

Beeroglad raised his axe for what would be the last time if the horse was to be saved. He took a deep breath and tightened his grip on the handle, but the raging wind, the thunder and the pounding of hooves was upon them, about to overwhelm and devour them all.

In an instant, Mother Nature's soundtrack was silenced, even she had been caught unaware and held in abeyance. The roaring wind muted, the thunderous clouds hushed. The thick grey dust hung stubbornly like a curtain where only a few moments earlier the fort wall had stood. Out of sight of everyone, the boulder continued to bring its full weight to bear on the rope.

27

The dawn light crept up on the stable by the inn, whereupon it peered through the many gaps between the planks and roused the birds within. The constables got to their feet and had a good stretch, relieved to still be in one piece. The inspector wound the hurricane lamp down, the flame gladly taking its leave and giving a farewell whiff of black smoke as it did so.

The silvered light of day soon filled the interior of the stable, but the Bog on the floor couldn't see it.

Inspector Hooter stood over the dormant body. It had an air of peace about it which only comes with death; a certain stillness that cannot be mimicked.

'Sir…do you think he's…?' PC Thomas paused sympathetically.

'Yes, Constable, I'm afraid our prisoner has died,' replied Hooter.

Seven mallards, two geese and a moorhen stood with heads down in respect of the ugly creature which they had fought against, and yet still felt a sense of loss for.

'Should we take his body with us to the fort, sir?' asked PC James.

'No, that would be too difficult, we have no way of carrying him,' said Hooter rubbing his bill. 'We shall bury him here with a prayer.'

The squad hastily set about digging a grave behind the stable, assisted by Constables Justin Case and Stan Duprite.

After considerable effort, the grave was dug, and the body of the pterosaur laid at the edge of the hole. 'We can't just put him down there and shovel dirt on top of him,' said PC James. 'It wouldn't seem right.'

'I saw a roll of sack cloth inside the stable,' Duprite replied. 'I'll go and get it.'

With the cloth laid out on the ground the birds rolled the deceased one way and then the other until he was fully wrapped.

'That's better,' said James, 'I wouldn't want dirt thrown all over me when I go.'

They all nodded in agreement and continued with their task.

Meanwhile, Hooter sat inside the stable recounting the events of yesterday while being comforted by Moira Maywell.

Eventually PC Duprite peered in from the doorway. 'We're ready, sir.'

By this time the constables had dug the grave, put the wrapped Bog in, and back-filled the hole. The inspector and Moira joined them at the graveside. Again they stood with heads down while Hooter said a few kindly words and wished the Bog a peaceful rest. He then turned to his colleagues and said, 'Well, there's no point staying here any longer. Take five minutes to gather your thoughts and then be back here ready for take off.' He couldn't help but feel a sense of responsibility for the death of the Bog, but was at a loss as to what more he could have done for him. He collected his belongings from the stable and made his way outside. *I'm supposed to make things better for others, not worse. How did this happen?*

His six constables were lined up in front of the inn with a Canada goose at each end and Moira standing to one side next to the village bobby.

'Constable,' said Hooter, looking directly at the village bobby.

'Yes, sir?'

'Where is your bicycle?'

'I don't know, sir, I can't see it anywhere,' he replied, nervously.

'Well it can't just disappear, can it?'

'No, sir,' replied the bobby. 'Perhaps the storm took it during the night, sir.'

Hooter studied the faces of his constables, who in turn fixed their gaze straight ahead, not wishing to expose their guilty look. Hooter knew they were hiding something, but this wasn't the time to dwell on such things; he had to move on to Fort Bog without delay.

'We shall talk more of this later,' he said to the bobby. 'In the meantime we have to think of a way to get you to Fort Bog without transport.'

The bobby asked, timidly. 'Could I possibly fly, sir, with the rest of you?'

'But you haven't had any flying lessons, Constable.'

Constables Case and Duprite raised a puzzled eyebrow at Hooter's remark.

The bobby thought he was really pushing his luck, but he took a gulp and said in as bold a voice as he could. 'I'm a duck, sir…ducks fly, sir.'

'He's right, sir,' said Constable Duprite in his most respectful Canadian accent.

'Yes, but does he know his left from his right, or his up from his down? We can't risk a mid-air collision just because he's lost his bicycle and wants to fly with us.'

'Test me, sir,' said the bobby.

'Very well,' said Hooter, keen to maintain control of the situation. 'Let's see what you can do. Put your left wing out.'

The bobby put his left wing out.

'Now put that wing down and put your right wing out,' said

Hooter, quite sure that the bobby would get it wrong.

The bobby put his left wing down, and his right wing out.

'Hmm, you seem to be gifted,' said Hooter. 'Now keep both wings down, and look up first, then down.'

The bobby kept both wings down and looked up, then down.

Hooter moved forward and shook the bobby's wing vigorously. 'Well done!' he said. 'Most impressive, you've obviously been studying in your own time, most commendable.'

The Mounties raised an eyebrow once again – Hooter's constables didn't.

'That's settled then,' said Hooter. 'You will fly at the rear along with Mrs Maywell, but you mustn't slow us down, do you hear?'

'Yes, sir, thank you, sir.' The bobby's eyes smiled excitedly.

Within a few minutes the whole group was airborne and flying in the direction of Fort Bog. From a height of six trees the constables looked down with a knowing glance at the grave. It seemed a little wider than it need have been for just a Bog.

***

At the fort the silence had brought with it a stillness. Punch lay perilously close to the cliff edge. Everything and everyone within the fort had slowed to an imperceptible pace, each being held by an invisible hand. The swirling clouds had become stuck in the sky. No air moved. Every living creature, bird or beast remained fixed in a moment in time, all facing the incoming storm; whether in the air or on the ground, time held them firmly in place. Mother Nature had been overruled, stilled by a force that had not visited this world since the beginning of time.

All eyes stared at the huge wave of unmoving dust which had halted abruptly where the front wall once stood.

Here they come, the whispers in his heart told Punch, but his eyes were tired and heavy, and his heart exhausted, all he could do was wait – and keep his faith.

Every eye in the fort widened when without warning, and in total silence, one hundred horses leapt into view, line abreast. Through the dust in slow motion came the hooves and the legs at full stretch, and then the handsome heads each with a white flash on its beautiful face. Ears forward, and eyes bright. Then came the riders in classic upright pose, sitting uncannily still in the saddle with heads, helmets or hats at precisely the same angle as each other. All immaculate, with not a speck of dust daring to spoil their colours.

The horses' hooves landed in wraithlike silence without disturbing a grain of sand. Standing side by side and each with the same willing expression, their line stretched from one side of the fort to the other, their brightness contrasting vividly with the grey of their surroundings. These were special creatures, beautiful and strong.

A second later, as though a switch had been thrown, the world started up again. The skies mixed and folded heavily, and the Bogs' wings simultaneously continued sweeping the air as they kept safe hold of their charges in the sky.

Here they are, said the whispers. At last Punch knew his quest was won. One hundred hearts stood before him, each one as true and bold as his own. His soul sang and warmed the backs of his eyes which let go the tears they had been holding for just such a moment. These were tears of happiness and relief in equal measure. It didn't matter what happened to him now. *Let your mind rest*, his whispers said. *You have prevailed. Your strength and trust has secured the freedom of all these creatures.*

Punch mustered the energy to turn his head to see all the Bogs gently placing the birds down on the ground; they were free at last.

And you have seen and opened the hearts of the Bogs by

showing them your own.

Suddenly from the sky came another familiar sound.

'Honk honk!' Seven mallards of the Flying Squad circled above; to each side of them a Canada goose wearing a Stetson hat, and of course Moira and the bobby following close behind. As soon as they had landed, Moira ran excitedly to her husband and baby. 'Oh, my dears, you're alive,' she cried.

Punch watched as the baby 'cheeped' in her embrace. But he could still hear the ground calling him. The boulder taunted and tugged, and the heavens writhed in turmoil filling their lungs for another thunderous outburst.

Beeroglad brought the axe down with all his might; it sliced into the rope, severing it cleanly and finally.

The heavens roared and screamed in protest. The boulder relinquished its hold and was sent plummeting into the unseen depths, alone.

The straps about Punch's chest relaxed their grip. At last he could breathe and let his muscles loose. He lay with his face in the dust, his lips rubbed raw, with Dick and Beeroglad by his side. The dour atmosphere of the land around them began to lighten. Beeroglad looked into Punch's eyes and gladly let himself be drawn in; the sparkling blue of his, and the soft brown of the horse's caressed each other warmly and deeply. A thousand unseen hands reached out, holding the pterosaur captive while the horse's whispers flowed gaily between the two.

Beeroglad's senses reeled, freeing his heart to colour him brilliantly, he too had been freed. Tears flowed from his crystal eyes as they had never flowed before. 'No, please, no,' he sobbed.

Yes, replied the whispers. You have a mind of your own, you have a choice – the horse has nought but his hearts will, like all creatures but one. And that creature waits at the threshold of this world – and like you, he will have a choice. Choose wisely.

Punch huffed into the ground. Now all around him was coloured. Every Bog was the image of his red-faced friend, Abel Nogg. Their arms and legs of pale blue, soft vibrant grey chests, and crimson faces set alight by the most sparkling yellow or blue eyes with glistening black pupils. *All the colours of the world*, his whispers echoed quietly.

The grass became lush. The sand, shades of yellow; even the dowdy grey covering had been cast away from the birds and the donkeys. All was as it should be. Punch was ready for whatever was to come. His head was heavy. He settled his cheek on the ground, still able to see his hundred horses.

One hundred souls sang to him through two hundred eyes of hazel.

'Oh my…' Moira's voice quivered, and all eyes fell longingly upon the golden Suffolk Punch.

The thunderous clouds volleyed a billion gun salute that shook the world; the sky lit in crimson and vermillion travelling around the globe and back again in seconds.

It was dawn, a new day.

28

Pink underbellies of the dawn clouds also heralded the new day in the world of humans – your world. Smallbeef had an air of recovery and restfulness about it. This world had also had a turbulent night, one filled with the colours and energy of a violent storm. Mother Nature now stroked the air with a calming breeze, sweeping away the last of the clouds and leaving an empty azure sky.

Professor 'Digger' Hole mopped his brow nervously. Despite it only being nine thirty in the morning and rather cool, beads of sweat formed on his forehead. A sense of unease washed over him. His two assistants, Jim and Clive, both students in palaeontology, had spent the previous hour carefully removing the final layer of soil in the bottom of the pit that they had been excavating all week. To date they had only found the odd coin or broken saucer, nothing more than a few decades old. The professor's speciality was the prehistoric era, a time when this part of the world was almost certainly inhabited by dinosaurs of one type or another. Broken crockery and old coins did little to excite him. This was to be their last day at the dig before packing up and heading home – empty handed. But one of his helpers, Jim, had unearthed something in the bottom of the hole, which was now as deep as he was tall. The professor looked on in anticipation.

Jim tugged gently at what seemed to be a piece of cloth showing through the soil right in the centre of the pit.

'Be careful,' called Digger, 'wait a minute while I climb down.'

With that he made his way down the wooden ladder, carrying his rucksack over his shoulder. At the bottom he turned and Jim and Clive moved aside to let him have a better look. 'Hmm,' he felt the piece of cloth between his fingers and gave it a gentle tug, just as Jim had done. The cloth remained firmly in the ground. With a stiff hand brush taken from his rucksack, Digger carefully swept the earth away to reveal a little more of the cloth. 'It seems to be some sort of hessian, sacking perhaps, strange though, at this depth.'

Both students began scraping more soil from the centre of the pit to expose more of the cloth in the hope that it would come free. 'It should come up quite easily,' one said. 'It can't be too big, I wouldn't have thought.'

'Here we go,' said Clive as he slowly pulled a continuous edge of the cloth away from the soil, almost from one side of the pit to the other. 'Ooer?' he said. 'This doesn't make sense, Professor. This cloth looks too clean, like it was only put here recently, hardly ancient.'

'Mind out, lad,' said Digger, more than a little puzzled. He continued to lift the cloth away, exposing a second layer beneath. 'It seems to be wrapped around something, but you're quite right, it doesn't look very old.'

The three of them spent the next hour gingerly shovelling the soil into buckets and hauling them up to be emptied on the substantial pile topside. They then stood back as far as the confines of the pit would allow and stared down at the bizarre contours of the exposed cloth. Peaks and troughs abounded, making it impossible to surmise what lay beneath.

'Whatever it is, it's quite a size,' said the professor. He took a stick and tapped it randomly over the cloth. Most parts issued a dull 'duff' sound while the more pronounced parts sticking up sounded almost metallic. 'I can't imagine…'

'That's really weird, sir.' said Jim.

The professor replied, 'It certainly is. But when you think about it, this entire dig has been a bit odd.'

'In what way, Professor?'

'Well, the soil seems to have come up too easily, almost as if it had been dug recently, not thousands of years ago.'

They pondered a while longer, trying to conjure up images of what could be causing the weird shapes in the covering. They all knew that cloth such as they had discovered would not have lasted more than a year or two in this soil, and yet it was barely aged at all.

'There's no point putting it off any longer,' said the professor. 'You two pull that side away and I'll pull this side; after three. One...two...three...'

Together they pulled the cloth away along its entire length.

Their hearts jolted, eyes popping out of their heads, mouths agog. *What the...??*

Clive turned and vomited in the corner of the pit. Jim managed to hold himself together, the professor remained totally still, his head reeling on the inside. They'd had no idea of what to expect, but they hadn't expected this. What they had unearthed was indeed utterly unearthly, at least, not the Earth they had come to know.

Digger felt he should say something, but the words just wouldn't come, sounding gibberish between his ears.

Jim managed a few words to break the silence. 'What on Earth is it?'

Digger forced a reply in a voice just above a whisper. 'It's some sort of pterosaur.' He struggled to calm his breathing, balancing precariously on the edge of hysteria. 'It's a prehistoric reptile, millions of years old, wrapped in sack cloth and in perfect condition as if it were buried only yesterday.' He began chuckling nervously, not believing what he was about to say.

'And he's got a bicycle with him.'

The early morning Sun gently warmed the group while they stared long and hard at their unbelievable discovery. None of them could believe what they were looking at.

'Surely it must be some sort of prank,' Jim proclaimed.

'Of course it is,' said Clive. 'Something like that just isn't possible…is it?'

'I bet it's made of rubber,' Jim added. 'Brilliantly done though. It certainly had us going for a minute, eh?'

Digger began talking aloud to reckon things in his head. 'This patch of soil looked undisturbed before we started, and yet it was almost too easy to dig, as if someone had only recently filled it in. I just don't understand it.' His eyes fell upon the dormant find for a few moments more. 'Throw me my gloves, please; we'll soon see if this thing is real or not.'

He donned the thick leather gauntlets and took a deep breath before proceeding.

His assistants hardly dared breath, not wanting to risk waking the thing up.

The thing lay on its back, wings tight by its sides and long beak lying on its chest.

Using a short stick to extend his reach, Digger calmed himself and gave the unlikely find a gentle prod. Nothing happened. He took a deep breath and gave the creature a firmer poke in the side. The flesh deferred an inch or two, resuming its shape as soon as the stick was withdrawn. 'It's pliable.'

Jim and Clive looked on in silence.

Digger threw the stick up onto the side of the pit, and then he reached forward resting his gloved palm on the creature's stomach. Not knowing what to expect, he slowly pressed and squeezed; again the grey flesh gave way to the pressure. 'Oh, merciful heavens,' he whispered. 'It feels right, it feels right.'

Nervous sweat now trickled down his forehead. 'Hand me my magnifying glass please.'

'Right, of course,' replied Jim, hastily rummaging through Digger's shabby rucksack. 'Here it is.' Digger's complexion was now redder than ever. He removed his gloves and tossed them aside before shuffling along the side of the pit towards the lifeless but nonetheless incredible head. He gazed in awe, still thinking aloud, 'Such a pronounced domed skull, and such a long beak,' he shook his head slowly. 'But it can't be real; it just isn't possible.' His eyes travelled the length of the body from head to foot while his oration continued. 'It must have stood over eight feet tall, with a wingspan of over twenty-five feet…amazing, just amazing, but what is it doing with a bicycle…a metal bicycle with pneumatic tyres?'

His attention returned to the creature's face. The eyes were shut, the heavy eyelids showing no sign of stress. 'He must have been very carefully placed here,' said Digger, mopping his brow. Everything he had learned and experienced in his long career told him that this could not be real, and yet everything, every detail, the pigment, the pores, the claws and the scars were there before his eyes, defying logic.

His underlings looked on in stunned silence, unsure if they wanted it to be real or just an elaborate prank. Either way, none of them was able to add anything to the professor's reasoning.

Digger held the magnifying glass over the creature's face, and then he very gently pressed the closed eyelid with his finger. 'It feels firm to the touch.' He slowly moved his finger round and round. The eyelid slid fluidly over whatever lay beneath. 'Oh, dear Lord.' Digger shivered, and his stomach churned. 'What on Earth have we uncovered?'

Clive could hold his patience no longer. 'Tell me, what does it feel like, what does it feel like?'

'It feels just like an eyelid with an eye beneath it,' replied Digger, unable to raise his voice above a whisper, so dry was his throat. He gulped nervously; his finger visibly trembled in readiness to draw the eyelid open. 'It's soft and supple,' he mumbled, 'but it must be millions of years old, so how can it be?' With his breath steadied, he raised the eyelid fully.

Poor Clive turned and vomitted again, yelling, 'Oh crikes, its…grooo'

A spine-chilling eye, totally black and offering no reflection, stared out into a world it had never seen before. Digger quaked in his stout leather boots, and took a few moments to study the eye through his magnifying glass before forcing his voice to break above a croaky whisper.

'It's wet…I believe the eye is still wet.'

***

Meanwhile, back in the world of giant ducks and living pterosaurs…the exhausted body of Punch lay in the centre of the bailey. His ordeal with the boulder had taken its toll, and now the early morning Sun cast its warmth over him while Mother Nature caressed his soiled coat with her loving hands of gold.

Dick Waters-Edge had spent the night beside him, yearning to see him open his eyes and give one of his hefty snorts, but the horse had remained silent and still all night long. The coots, moorhens, mallards and donkeys gathered round in the brightening morning light, their gaze fixed on the faint movement of Punch's ribs as he breathed. So tenuous was his hold on life that the breath from his nostrils raised no dust from the ground on which his head lay.

Dick's unbound tears fell onto the horse's cheek, thoroughly wetting the dusty fur. 'Please open your eyes, mate, please,' pleaded the young duck. The crowd of fur and feather looked on, offering their hearts full of hope and wishing they could do more.

The fort's compliment of donkeys, numbering thirty in total, eased their way to the front of the crowd and gathered round their fallen hero. Without exception they stood on grotesquely deformed hooves, and their shabby coats displayed deep sores across their backs caused by the perpetual loads previously inflicted upon them by the Bogs. Seeking the way to Punch's soul, and caring little of their own suffering, the donkeys lovingly swept their eyes of midnight blue across the Suffolk's face as he slept – but try as they might, they could find no way in. There was no reply to their whispers, just the smallest rise and fall of his ribs as Mother Nature sustained his heart and lungs, but nothing more.

'Please don't die,' Dick whimpered.

Punch's eyes remained closed, adorned with eyelashes so long and delicately curved as to surely be a mistake on such a stout animal, but not so; such natural beauty is no accident, simply the finishing touches by a supreme artist to a lovingly crafted masterpiece.

Upon seeing the efforts of the donkeys come to nought, the eerie Mounties released their horses to lend their support. Their steeds, all Hanoverians, moved as one to encircle the donkeys and augment their efforts. Tall, dark and handsome, all one hundred of them rested their unearthly gaze upon Punch's face, hoping for a reaction.

The birds and the Bogs looked on in silence, acknowledging something far beyond their understanding.

One hundred and thirty equine souls now combined to caress the mind of the fallen horse. Their unseen hands reached out, stroking his sides – but deeper he slept, slowly he slipped.

'Young duck,' a bold voice from above interrupted the silence. Dick looked up to see the biggest pterosaur ever to fly over these parts. 'Move away, trust the horses…give them room.'

The pterosaur's gaze of startling blue struck deep into Dick's eyes, reassuring him and moving him to one side as surely as if he had gripped him with his unassailable hands. The donkeys too, stepped back to make room.

The Hanoverians' whispers were now free to dance about Punch's body with nothing in the way. His eyelids twitched, acknowledging the compassionate callers. His eyes slowly opened. The Hanoverians had been granted rite of passage; one hundred whispers flooded in, racing each other towards the soul that gladly welcomed them.

Punch huffed and snorted, sending a flurry of dust up from the ground while Mother Nature filled his lungs with oxygen. The secret whispers of the magnificent Hanoverians danced hand in hand with those of the Suffolk, bolstering his heart and helping him raise his head from the ground.

'Oh, how wonderful,' the onlookers gushed with relief.

The Suffolk horse widened his eyes letting the world reflect in them once more, and then, with a grunt from deep within his chest, he exerted one powerful surge and rose to his feet. His legs quivered under the weight but quickly gathered their set.

After several robust shakes to loosen the dust from his coat, he vented a skyward neigh. The Hanoverians joined him in his song while the donkeys brayed uncontrollably. The birds had never witnessed such an awesome spectacle; the air about them shimmered and reverberated in response.

'Hoorah, hoorah!' The birds rejoiced in loud echoes while the Bogs squawked and crowed at the tops of their voices. Punch was back in the land of the living, heralded by all around him.

The huge pterosaur called again from above the crowd, 'Please give me room to land next to my friend.' The air gathered beneath his wings and lowered him as gently as a mother would place her baby in a cot. His powerful clawed feet delicately touched down on the ground and he swiftly folded his wings against his sides. His eyes soaked up the gentle aura that cloaked the Suffolk, and as soon as he was close enough he reached out with a flattened hand. 'Friend, beautiful and strong,' he whispered, gently combing Punch's cheek. Punch's eyes smiled back at him, recalling their first encounter some days ago.

Inspector Hooter took it upon himself to enquire who this new arrival was. He knew it wasn't Beeroglad, and until now his encounters with any Bog had shown them to be aggressive and certainly not to be trusted.

'Ahem. Excuse me, sir,' he said, 'would you mind telling us who you are, in case I have to arrest you?'

'Of course,' replied the huge pterosaur. 'My name is Abel Nogg, as you can see I am a pterosaur, a Beast of Grey – a Bog.'

'And what is your purpose here?' Hooter quickly turned to his constables and whispered, 'Be ready to jump him if he tries anything.'

The constables understood Hooter's concern, but somehow they couldn't imagine this giant with amazing sparkling eyes doing anything untoward, and quite frankly they didn't fancy their chances against such a formidable creature if he did. However, just to appease their inspector, they leaned forward a little and employed as mean a look as they could manage, which wasn't very mean, being as they were mallards, albeit very large mallards at five feet eight inches tall, but mallards all the same.

The moorhen, Moira Maywell, thought this a good time to lend some support to Abel Nogg. 'It's quite all right, Inspector,' she said with a spring in her voice. 'He's the coloured Bog I told you about. He saved me from falling to my death when I was attacked by a Bog scout. Do you remember?'

'Ah, yes, I see,' replied Hooter with that delightful look of understanding which seldom graced his head. He turned and looked up to the pterosaur, but before he could enquire further the hubbub of the crowd subsided abruptly when the voice of a juvenile Bog squawked, 'Thank you; please let me through.' This was Eeland Ross, the heir to the throne of Fort Bog, he jostled his way to the front of the assembly with his father, Beeroglad, close behind. The youngster stopped warily in front of the Suffolk Punch, unsure of how he would be received.

Beeroglad rested a hand on his son's shoulder and eased him forward, saying quietly, 'It's all right, son, the horse understands us without knowing our words.'

Eeland blinked a long slow blink. His young eyes, now of pure blue, splashed into Punch's. The youngster extended his hand, flattening it first to make safe the claws, and then he nervously combed the horse's coat. It felt so good to offer friendship rather than hostility to another breed; something his kind hadn't done for a long time.

'Yours I believe,' said Beeroglad, proffering Dick's blue tricorn hat.

'My hat!' exclaimed Dick. He reached out to take it, still not entirely sure of the Bog's intentions. Beeroglad released his grip willingly, saying, 'I am grateful to you, and to your horse for his strength of body and caring heart to which my son owes his life.'

While spiritual accounts were being settled between the former protagonists, Abel Nogg studied those among the crowd. *I have no time to lose. There are too many to talk to here*, he thought. *I must single out a few individuals for my cause.*

Noticing the nearby hut, he raised his voice above the crowd and pointed with a winged arm. 'Please listen carefully. Will the following individuals accompany me so that I may address them on a matter of utmost urgency?' He briefly cast an eye over the crowd to identify the select few before calling their names: 'Inspector Hooter and his six constables of the Flying Squad –

Sergeant Bob Uppendown of the Royal Canadian Mounted Police – Dick Waters-Edge, and...' he paused for a moment while his eyes lingered in those of the Bog leader. '...and Beeroglad.'

The crowd looked on while those whose names had been called followed Abel obediently into the hut. Inspector Hooter and Beeroglad were the last to enter. Their previous encounters with each other had been aggressive in the extreme, and the inspector still had the bruises to prove it. They both paused at the doorway, Hooter looked up, and Beeroglad looked down; this time their eyes exchanged a mutual respect, but Hooter was still not sure if the massive pterosaur could be trusted.

'Please, after you,' said Beeroglad, gesturing with his folded wing.

'No, I insist, after you,' replied Hooter, not wishing to show his back to his former enemy.

Beeroglad tried to smile, but his beak wouldn't allow such expression, so he nodded and went through the doorway ahead of the inspector as a sign of deference.

'Please close the door behind you, Inspector,' said Abel with smiling eyes.

'Yes Mr Nogg,' replied Hooter politely.

The six constables stood smartly to attention with Sergeant Uppendown at one end of the line and Dick at the other. Beeroglad peered over their heads from behind, his height being of good advantage.

Inspector Hooter called out from the front. 'Squad, stand at ease.' The birds promptly relaxed their posture, eager to hear what Abel Nogg had to say.

'You must all listen very carefully to what I am about to tell you,' said Abel in his uniquely reassuring tones. 'My words will make no sense to any of you at the moment, but you must believe and trust that they are true.'

29

Abel's gruff voice filled the storm battered hut. 'My words will seem incredible, but you must act upon them if you wish to avoid a disaster besetting your world.'

Inspector Hooter immediately interrupted Abel's flow. 'Rest assured, you have our undivided attention, Mr Nogg.'

'Thank you,' replied Abel, purposely settling his eye on the inspector. 'Please look around you and tell me what you see.'

Hooter rubbed his bill, unsure of what the pterosaur meant. 'Oh right, well, let me see now,' he said, hoping to get the answer correct. 'I can see you standing in front of us.' He turned his head slowly. 'Then there are my constables, and Sergeant Uppendown, and young Dick Waters-Edge.' His gaze finally came to rest on the long beak of Beeroglad. 'And of course, there is Mr Beeroglad.'

'Thank you, Inspector,' said Abel, 'you can relax now.'

The puzzled look remained on Hooter's face. 'Have I missed something?' he asked.

'No, Inspector, I asked you to tell what you see, and that is what you did…' Abel paused briefly before continuing, 'What would you think if I was to say that you and your friends are not the only creatures living on this planet?'

'I would say you are quite right, Mr Nogg.' Hooter replied confidently. 'There are many other creatures living here…' He pondered while the rest of the answer gathered in his head. 'There are the tiny birds such as blackbirds, robins, and sparrows, and then there are all the animals such as the horses, we mustn't forget the horses. Oh, and then there are the little humans—'

Abel forced his way back into the conversation with a sigh. 'I know you can see all the creatures with whom you share your world, but there are other worlds sharing this planet; they are the ones you cannot see, but they are here none the less.'

'Eh,' said Hooter, his brain suddenly struggling to keep up.

Sergeant Uppendown took up the conversation on Hooter's behalf. 'You seem to be saying that this world of ours and this planet are two separate things, sir.'

'In a manner of speaking, that is correct, Sergeant. There are many worlds occupying this planet at any one time; each world is separated from the next by Nature's ether, a veil so fine and yet impossible to see through.'

'Do you mean there are other creatures standing right here, where we are standing right now, and we can't see them?' said Uppendown.

'Well done, Sergeant; that is exactly what I mean.' Abel was heartened by the goose's grasp of what he was saying. 'You can't see them and they can't see you, but the ether can sometimes wear a little thin, and if you happen to be in the right place at the right time you might peer through and glimpse another world for the briefest of moments, until the ether restores itself.'

'Eh?' said Hooter, trying to make sense of what he had just heard.

Uppendown asked, 'Would that be when someone thinks they have seen a ghost, perhaps?'

'Right again, Sergeant,' said Abel.

'But what has this got to do with us?' Dick piped up.

Abel replied, 'Ordinarily, everything stays in its own world without any problems, but a few nights ago a storm of immense strength came to rest in a world close to this one. Mother Nature had her hands full and lost control for less than the blink of an eye, but that was all it took for things to get misplaced.'

Abel pointedly looked at Dick and held his gaze for a few moments. Dick sensed he was about to be told something he didn't want to hear.

'Young duck, I think you know of what I speak.'

Dick replied with a worried look on his face. 'Yes, sir, I think I do. I must admit I can't really remember when Punch came into my life, or how he got here. I think I just woke up one morning and he was in my shed with all his tack, hay, straw and everything. It felt as if he'd always been there, and like I'd always known him. I knew something wasn't quite right though, but it felt so right him being here.'

'He was not born here,' Abel replied. 'Mother Nature misplaced him a while ago. No doubt he has thoughts which do not always make sense to him, just as you do.'

Inspector Hooter finally caught up. 'Does that mean he will have to be sent back to where he came from?'

'He can stay for a while longer,' Abel replied, 'but a soul must be laid to rest in its own world, therefore, the day will come when he will have to return to his own land. However, Punch is not the issue at the moment.' Abel paused deliberately.

Those in the room were getting used to Abel's mannerisms. They expected such a pause to be followed by a profound statement of some sort, and so they hung on to his last word, waiting to be picked up by the next.

Abel studied each of the constables and gathered up their aura to get the measure of them. A feeling of guilt washed over the young ducks while Abel's eyes swept along their line. He took less than a second to peer into the conscience of each bird before moving on to the next while they waited innocently for him to expound on his issue.

'Do you remember the night before last, Inspector?' asked Abel.

'I won't forget it in a hurry,' replied Hooter. 'We suffered one storm after another, and to make matters more difficult we had to look after the Bog we'd taken prisoner; he wasn't at all well you know.' Sadness fell across Hooter's face. 'I'm afraid the poor Bog passed away despite our efforts to save him.'

Not wishing to lay blame on anyone, Abel reassured Hooter with an air of compassion. 'You were not at fault, Inspector. When we have more time I shall explain the workings of a Bog to you; they are far different to those of a duck, but you were not to know or understand what was happening that night.'

The police ducks were relieved by Abel's account, but they had a feeling there was more to come.

'Do you recall what you did with the Bog after he'd passed away?' Abel asked.

'Oh yes,' Hooter replied. 'I had my constables bury him behind the stable at the inn several miles back.' The inspector was quite sure of his facts and went on, 'Once they'd tidied the grave, we all gathered round it while I said a few words to bid the Bog farewell.'

'Quite right, my dear Inspector. You were not the cause of the problem, but you and your constables unwittingly played your part; therefore, it must fall to you to put matters right.'

The birds had heard everything that had been said but still didn't understand what they were supposed to have done wrong.

Sergeant Uppendown broke the silence. 'I'm sorry, sir, but you will need to explain to us what we did wrong, in order fer us to put it right.'

Abel replied, 'Rather than explain it here, I think it better that I show you.'

'Fer sure, sir,' replied Sergeant Uppendown, his Canadian

accent ever strong.

'Yes, of course,' said Inspector Hooter, emphasizing his English brogue while rubbing his bill in puzzlement.

Abel asked of the inspector, 'How long did it take you to get here from the inn where you buried the Bog?'

'Ooh, erm, not long…about half an hour.'

'In that case, we shall go there right away,' Abel replied.

The group left the hut in an orderly fashion, each with unanswered questions floating around inside their beautiful heads.

'It's a strange to-do and no mistake,' said Hooter, emerging into the sunshine.

'Fer sure, sir,' said Uppendown, 'but I'm sure Mr Nogg will explain everything when we get to the inn. Are you sure you can't think of anything you might have done to have caused him such concern?'

'Yes, quite certain, Sergeant,' replied Hooter, rubbing his bill once again. His constables stood behind him, equally baffled and rubbing theirs in support.

Dick hastily made his way back to Punch who was now enjoying a bowl of food and a large bucket of water. 'How are you doing, mate?' Dick stroked the horse's thick neck of muscle. 'I've got to go with the inspector and the others for a few hours, but I'm sure you'll be well looked after while I'm gone.'

Moira Maywell instantly spoke up. 'Don't you worry, my dear, I'll make sure he has everything he needs.'

Punch continued eating while his eyes gathered the air of kindness about her.

'Time to go, Gentlebirds,' Abel called.

Hooter gathered his constables. 'Squad, fall in.'

The six mallards lined up smartly. Sergeant Bob Uppendown joined them at one end, and Dick, having given Punch a long hug, fell in at the other end; all perfectly straight.

As always, Hooter was pleased with the discipline of his squad, including the two new additions. 'There's not enough room here to take off, so we shall move to the front of the fort.' He puffed up his chest of fine plumage, aware that everyone in the fort was watching him and his charges. 'Squad, left turn, by the front, quick-waddle.' They promptly waddled in perfect time with each other to where the fort wall lay in the dust. 'Squad, halt. Prepare to take off.' They moved a few paces apart, and waited keenly for the order.

Abel Nogg called out, 'Beeroglad and I shall wait in the air for you, Inspector.' The two pterosaurs then sprang their wings and pulled the air down, climbing vertically into the sky as if ascending an invisible ladder. With slow gentle strokes of their massive wings they hung like giant puppets waiting for the birds to join them.

'Take off!' called Hooter. The mallards lifted from the ground within a couple of paces, working their impressive wings vigorously. Sergeant Uppendown, being a Canada goose, needed a little more runway before raising his legs and tucking them up beneath him.

The squad moved quickly into V formation, and not an inch out of place.

Those on the ground looked up in admiration while the Sun returned their stare with streaks of sunlight striking off the helmet badges of the young constables.

With the two pterosaurs leading the way, the entire squadron rapidly shrank into the distant sky, racing the Sun towards the western horizon and the inn where their quest would be revealed.

Printed in Great Britain
by Amazon